That's (Not Exactly) Amore

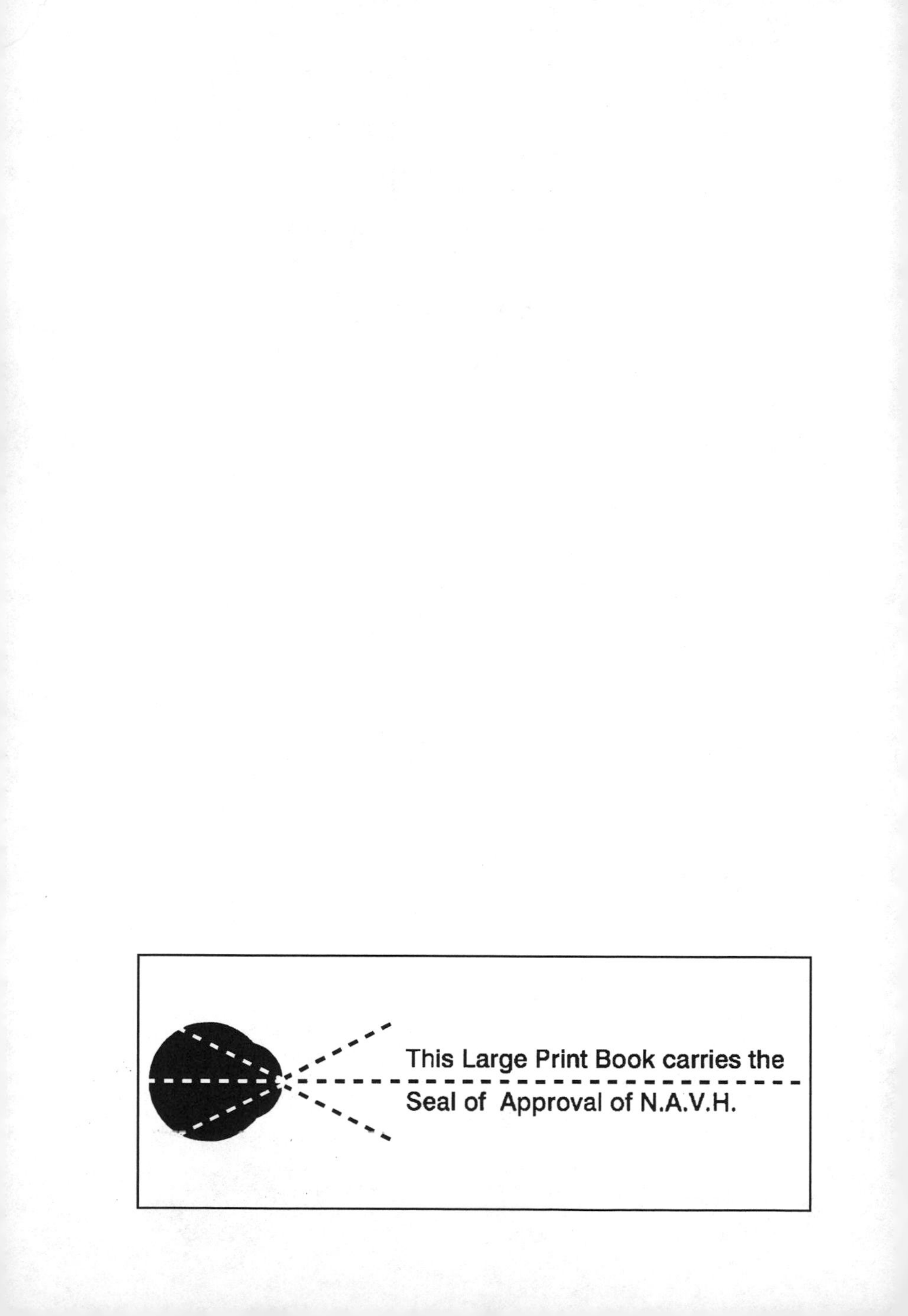
This Large Print Book carries the
Seal of Approval of N.A.V.H.

THAT'S (NOT EXACTLY) AMORE

TRACEY BATEMAN

THORNDIKE PRESS
A part of Gale, Cengage Learning

Detroit • New York • San Francisco • New Haven, Conn • Waterville, Maine • London

Drama Queens Series #3.

Thorndike Press, a part of Gale, Cengage Learning.

Thorndike Press® Large Print Christian Fiction.
The text of this Large Print edition is unabridged.
Other aspects of the book may vary from the original edition.
Set in 16 pt. Plantin.
Printed on permanent paper.

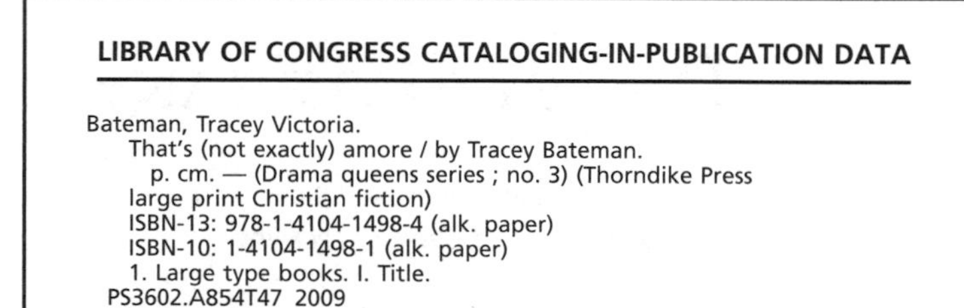
LIBRARY OF CONGRESS CATALOGING-IN-PUBLICATION DATA

Bateman, Tracey Victoria.
That's (not exactly) amore / by Tracey Bateman.
p. cm. — (Drama queens series ; no. 3) (Thorndike Press large print Christian fiction)
ISBN-13: 978-1-4104-1498-4 (alk. paper)
ISBN-10: 1-4104-1498-1 (alk. paper)
1. Large type books. I. Title.
PS3602.A854T47 2009
813'.6—dc22 2008056145

Published in 2009 by arrangement with Faith Words, a division of Hachette Book Group, Inc.

Printed in the United States of America
1 2 3 4 5 6 7 13 12 11 10 09

Dedicated
to Julie Young — a forever friend

ACKNOWLEDGMENTS

Rusty, Cat, Mike, Stevan, Will, my family: I hit the jackpot when God gave me you guys.

Thanks to Mom as always. Everyone needs a biggest fan — I'm yours.

Nancy Toback: Thanks so much for being willing to share your time and friendship.

Thanks to Janelle Mowery for your help with critiques and for your friendship.

1

If this is the chance I've been waiting for, then why does it feel like I'm in over my head? I mean, like I'm five feet tall in seven feet of water and haven't the foggiest idea how to swim. In short, I'm sinking fast.

"So, do we got a deal?"

I stare at Nick Pantalone's beefy hand but hesitate before taking it. At this point, anyone with a smidge of conscience would just admit to being out of her league and walk away before she could do any actual damage to the place. But as I look around Nick Pantalone's newly expanded coffee shop, I know this is my last chance to get anything close to a passing grade in my interior design course.

My final semester is about putting what I've supposedly learned into practice. It's a joint project for my partner, Jazz, and me. Sort of like that show *The Apprentice*? Only there's just Jazz and me. As project manager (and don't ask me why I have to be the head cheese — Jazz gets better grades), it's my job to find our project, assign tasks, and oversee every detail to its completion.

Renovating the coffee shop seems like the perfect idea, really. Nick desperately needs to expand after a newspaper article last summer proclaimed his shop "the best-kept secret in Manhattan." Now the little place is bursting at the seams as hordes of customers breeze right by the Starbucks across the street in favor of Nick's — the new trend. You know how we New Yorkers love to find the "latest thing." Who knows how long the upward swing will last for Nick? But I doubt he'll ever return to the obscurity he enjoyed once upon a time.

I mean, it's been six months and he's had to hire four new employees. Not to mention hiring Joe, his good-looking Italian nephew, to manage the place. And when I say "good-looking," I'm not talking about one step up from passable. I'm talking over the fence, out of the park, to the moon good-looking.

But this isn't about Joe.

I consider ours — Nick's and mine — to be a symbiotic relationship. Nick needs to expand and redecorate, and I need a passing grade. I truly have no lofty goals about any of this. Give me any letter grade higher than a D and I'll be fine. My mother doesn't have to see my grade to know I've passed. I won't lie about it, most likely, but I'm not exactly going to volunteer the information either.

"Well?" Nick growls, casting a pointed glance at his proffered hand, waiting for me to cinch the deal.

My breath is uneven as I slide my clammy hand into his. He nods and the wrinkly folds of his face push together with a grin. "That's better. Now what'll you have, kid? Anything you want is on the house."

"I shouldn't." The truth is, since I started the two-year design program (that I'm finishing in eighteen months by taking summer classes), I've put on about twenty pounds. Call it my frustration with my probable failure — my first ever. I cook and eat. It's cathartic. But I haven't had lunch and, let's face it, nobody makes meatball subs like Nick. I grin. "But I will."

The bell above the door dings and I turn. My insides go hot and cold all at once. Joe Pantalone. He's the man of my dreams — but he's way out of my league. Even if I weren't a redheaded Irish girl from Long Island, he'd be too much for me.

"Good to see you, Laini." He flashes that million-dollar smile, making me feel like the only woman on earth who could possibly win his heart. Guys like that don't play fair. They make you think you have a chance when, really, well . . . you just don't.

Joe's a hugger, so I try not to make anything of it every time he pulls my five-foot frame into arms that I swear could wrap around me twice. Well, maybe once and a half — since the weight gain.

I wish I could convince my heart not to get my hopes up when he greets me with his cozy hug, but who am I trying to kid? If he'd ask, I'd be his. But he won't. A guy like that doesn't have to settle for a thirty-year-old, freckle-faced redhead with way too many extra pounds on her petite frame. He can have anyone he wants.

Still, without a fight, I melt into his embrace, thoroughly enjoying the manly scent of soap and maybe just a hint of some sort of cologne that I'm not hip enough to identify. (Tabby and Dancy would have nailed it at first whiff.)

He lets me go and I stand weakly at the counter as Nick jerks his head toward me. " 'Ey, Joey. You're lookin' at the new interior designer for Nick's. What do you think?"

Wow, I'm not sure what I expected from Joe, but certainly not a frown. Maybe the first one I've ever seen on his face as he looks from Nick to me. "You graduated?"

My cheeks go hot, and I know from experience that I have blotches of embarrassment all over my face and neck. Some people blush prettily (gorgeous, dark-skinned Italian women, for instance). I don't. I get all splotchy. So I know I look hideous. "Not yet. I'm doing this for my final grade."

Joe turns to Nick. "Remodeling and redecorating are pretty big projects, Uncle Nick. No offense to Laini, but don't you think we should hire someone with some real experience?"

Please, floor. I beg you. Open up and swallow me whole. Seriously. Right this second would be good for me.

"Uh — Nick. Maybe Joe's right. I wouldn't want to mess anything up, and you know my grades aren't very good. As a matter of fact" — I hold up my thumb and forefinger and measure an inch — "I'm this close to flunking out. I probably don't have a clue what I'm doing." I don't even give him a chance to speak. "Actually, I withdraw myself from the project. I changed my mind."

With the agility of a man half his age and size, Nick whips through the swinging gate that reminds me of something from an Old

West saloon and heads me off before I can sprint for the door. " 'Ey, now. What is this baloney? Didn't we just shake on it?"

"Well, yes. But that was before the voice of reason walked in the door. I won't hold you to it, Nick."

His head swings from side to side in a vehement shake. "Where I come from, a handshake's as good as a signed contract." His voice is filled with so much indignation, I'm afraid he might have a stroke. "You goin' back on your word, little girl?"

"Come on, Uncle Nick," Joe groans. "Don't talk to Laini like that."

"You stay out of this, Joey. You're the one who started it anyway." He turns back to me, his stern frown making me feel shorter than I already am. "Well?"

"Okay, Nick," I say, carefully avoiding Joe's gaze. "I'll bring Jazz in tomorrow for a look at the place and we'll have some ideas to present by the end of next week." I glance around the room like I really know what I'm looking at. "The project is going to take some time, so we should get started on hiring an architect and a contractor. Then we'll need to figure out what permits we'll need."

Nick shakes his head, cutting me off. "Don't tell it to me. I won't be here."

"What do you mean?"

"I'm headed to L.A. tomorrow."

"You just got home!" I mean, less than two weeks ago.

He gives me a shrug like it's none of my business. "I never meant to come back after Christmas, only I had to take care of some financial paperwork and finish turning things over to Joey, here. I'm sick of being away from my Nelda."

Nelda is Nick's wife and his true lady love. She's been in California for months taking care of their daughter, who has cancer. The outlook is better than originally hoped for, but Nelda won't leave the grandkids and Nick is lovesick without her. So off he goes. I knew it was coming, but somehow I didn't expect it so soon.

"So, I'll be working for Joe on this?" I can't hold back the dread in my voice, even though I know it's impolite. If Joe isn't in favor of my working on the project at all, how on earth am I going to come in every day and do what needs to be done while he stands over me disapproving of every suggestion?

"This place is amazing, Dancy!" I stare at my friend's newly redecorated condo, loving the Victorian decor. This is the first time I've been here since the redo was finished, and I have to say, I'm impressed. And maybe a little jealous. "I'm so glad you didn't try to modernize the place."

"Mother is fit to be tied. She can't believe I had the audacity to go back in time."

I laugh. "Well, I heartily approve."

You can't help but envy Dancy a little. Her parents not only gave her their ridiculously expensive condo, but footed the bill for redecorating. I didn't expect to be consulted, but still . . .

Even Dancy's life in general seems perfect. A swoony new boyfriend with a British accent who just happens to be her favorite author writing under the pseudonym Cate Able. I truly expect her and Jack to be engaged any day now.

Dancy is throwing her first dinner for the girls tonight. And I'm here just a little early to do the cooking even though Dancy offered to have the meal catered. As if! Cooking makes me happy. It's what I do. Tabby and Dancy buy things for us from their ample cash flow. I, on the other hand, contribute to the friendship by supplying us all with ample calories — much to the chagrin of our mothers and Freddie, Tabby's trainer. But they love it. So I'm happy.

I sort of wish my two friends had come back to the apartment we all shared until

Tabby got married last month and Dancy moved into the condo, but I understand Dancy's desire to entertain around her own table. I think we might have to do a rotation or something, though. I miss seeing my chums in the apartment.

"So where's Brandon?" I ask as I step into the gorgeous, dream kitchen.

"Off skiing with some friends."

Brandon is Dancy's little brother. A musical genius, sixteen years old, in high school and accepted for the weekend program at Juilliard. He's lived with Dancy ever since his mom took off and his dad and Dancy's mother retired to Florida recently.

This kitchen takes my breath away. Truly. I've been dying to get my hands on the stainless-steel, digital, do-everything-for-you appliances. The floor and three of the countertops are ceramic tile. The others are a fabulous gray granite. My goodness, if I had a kitchen like this one, I'd just pull in a cot and live here. (Is that odd?)

"So, Chef Laini," Dancy says with a grin, revealing gorgeous white teeth. She's an Italian beauty — someone Joe would be attracted to, most likely, except she's taken. "What's on tonight's menu?"

I lift my shopping bag, which contains the fixings for our favorite meal together.

"Shrimp Alfredo with linguini. Salad with petite shrimp and blue cheese crumbles, and lovely grilled asparagus spears."

"Mmm." She cocks a silky eyebrow. "And for dessert?"

"Raspberry swirl cheesecake with a dollop of whipped cream."

Her eyes roll back and she lets out a breathy sigh. "Sounds divine."

"Don't assign divinity to me," I say with a laugh. "I bought the cheesecake at Nick's."

"Well, you can't beat Nick's anyway. Anything I can do to help?"

I shake my head. "Just keep me company while I work. I miss you guys like crazy."

She gives me a look akin to pity and I wish I hadn't mentioned it. "Your time will come, Laini."

I hate it when people say that to me! Dancy should know better, considering a mere two months ago she was in the same boat. I look at her as evenly as I can, determined not to play into the pity. I find it's always easier to pretend it's not an issue.

"Hey, I'm not complaining. My rent is paid up for another month. I have the money I make baking goodies for Nick's to tide me over, and I have all the peace and quiet I could ever want." Much, much more than I want. But I'd die before admitting that to my dear friend.

I finish unloading the groceries while Dancy chatters on about the man in her life, as though he hung the moon and stars. Jack Quinn this and Jack Quinn that. "He's actually sewn up a deal for me at Lane Publishing. My book comes out in about a year. Isn't that great?"

I stop what I'm doing right then and there and grab her in a hug. "That's fantastic, Dancy! I can't wait to read it."

"That's not all," she says with a wide grin.

I gasp. "Did he propose?"

A frown puckers the skin above her nose. "Not yet."

"Oh." Oops. "What's the great news, then?"

"Jack landed a book deal with his real name."

"You mean he's truly hanging up the Cate Able hat?"

"Completely." She gives a proud smile. "He's good enough to write under Jack Quinn. And they'll be promoting his new book with the full disclosure that Cate Able was nothing more than a pen name for Jack Quinn. He's also going to keep writing thrillers."

"But not the same series?"

"Well, no. I'm still mad at him for killing off my favorite character of all time. But I see why he needed to start over completely with his own name."

Dancy grabs a slice of cucumber from my cutting board and plops down on the barstool as she nibbles, elbows resting on the counter. "So. Your turn. Tell me how it went at Nick's today."

Weird how I'm both happy and hesitant at the same time. Happy for the opportunity, hesitant because I'm experiencing a sense of impending doom about the whole thing. Plus, Joe isn't thrilled.

I share all of this with my friend. Normally, we'd wait for Tabby before diving into heart-to-heart stuff, but our soap-actress friend just got married, so she's probably having trouble tearing herself away from her husband, David, and her step-twins, Jenn and Jeffy.

"Well, you'll just have to prove Joe wrong."

"I guess." I hear the doubt in my own voice and it doesn't sound pretty.

"Who's in charge of the colors?" Dancy's gaze is averted to the gray countertop.

"Jazz."

She seems relieved, which sets off my warning bells.

"Why?"

"Well, you know. I just wondered."

Tabby and Dancy know I have some slight trouble with colors. But it's not *that* bad. I mean, I can do bright colors okay. Besides, I heard an eye doctor say once that women can't actually be color blind — or it's only a percent of a percent chance or something like that. So, while I might have issues distinguishing certain close colors, I'm certainly not afflicted.

"Hey, I could do the colors if I had to!" I say, grabbing a Roma tomato and starting to slice. "For instance, don't you think this shade of gray would be terrific for a base color on the back wall at Nick's?"

"Um, sure." Dancy's hesitation doesn't thrill me at all. I look up from the cutting board.

"What?"

"Well, it's nothing, really." She swallows hard, like she does when she's trying not to hurt somebody's feelings.

"Come on, Dancy. Spit it out. What?"

"The countertop is green."

I stare down at the granite, which is clearly gray. I jerk my chin and stick out my tongue. "Maybe *you're* the one who's color blind."

Her chin dimples as she tries to keep from laughing. Hopping from the stool, she comes around and gives my shoulders a squeeze.

"Don't worry about it. You have great decorating ideas. Just leave the colors to someone else and you'll get a passing grade."

I know she's trying to be encouraging. But my goodness. I'm not going to have Jazz, the color-coordinated genius, stand over my shoulder after graduation — provided I do, in fact, graduate.

No one is going to hire a color-blind interior designer. And that's all there is to it.

I turn back to my preparations for dinner. "At least I can cook," I say flatly.

Dancy grins. "Better than anyone I know!"

Great. So I won't starve. Are tomatoes orange? Please tell me I haven't had that wrong all my life? Apples are red, bananas are yellow. Yes?

And Joe Pantalone's eyes are the color of a mocha latte — without whipped cream.

2

Three hours later, I walk up the steps to my empty apartment. Depressing, really. I think back to six weeks ago, when it was all abuzz day and night. Tabby was preparing for her wedding in the midst of the big Christmas rush, and Dancy was working on her book or editing around the clock. Now there's this silence that makes me want to cry.

I've even had fleeting thoughts of moving back home with my mom. Which is what she's always wanted. But I would never actually do it — I don't think. Not because I don't love my mother. She's awesome in so many ways. But she has this desperate need. Not for anything in particular. Just need. She's never quite content. And that can get exhausting, especially for the person futilely trying to provide contentment.

I can imagine us in twenty years . . . I'm still there (unmarried), attending to her every whim, and she's taking full advantage of the situation.

Poor Mom. Daddy died twelve years ago, and it's been so hard on her. He was her light and truly catered to her every whim. Which is great. I mean, any time a woman finds a man who loves her so completely he wants to cater to her, she should definitely keep him. But now Mom still wants someone to do what he did. And as the only child, guess who that whim-catering falls to?

I can take it in small doses, like every weekend when I'm expected to come home for a "visit," but that's about it. I guess that answers the question of whether or not I should move back permanently.

I reach the top of the steps and something is . . . wrong. Fear lumps in my throat as I realize the door has been jimmied and is cracked open just so.

Oh no, oh no, oh no. My strong sense of self-preservation kicks in full force and whips my body around like a rag doll. I drop the container with the leftover shrimp linguini and rush back down the steps and out the door. At breakneck speed, I sprint full force down the city street, which is filled with passersby. But I can't stop and ask for help from just anyone. Who knows if the thief is still lurking about waiting for me, the unsuspecting victim, to ask for help? Although I never actually looked inside my apartment. (What if it's not a thief but a stalker?) I see a blue-uniformed guy walking out of a little Chinese joint up ahead, and I feel like God has smiled upon me. "Officer!" I holler through the crowd. "Officer, wait! Please."

He doesn't appear to have heard me as he saunters toward a waiting squad car. I'm gasping for air by the time I reach him, but thankfully I make it before he even opens the door.

I make a grab for his arm.

He jerks back. "Whoa. Take it easy, lady." He eyes me in an I-could-Taser-you motion, and I swallow hard, hand on my chest to slow the rapid beating of my heart.

"I need —" (gasp for air) "— help, Officer," I gulp out.

"Calm down, ma'am." He takes my shoulders in his iron grip, and I look up into a dashing face with blue eyes and a bewildered smile. But I don't have time to think about what a great-looking cop he is. My apartment has been violated! The entire world has been violated! I don't have time to be attracted to this guy!

"I need you to come with me!" I try to turn, but he's not letting me go.

"Wait a second." He gives me a wary don't-make-me-cuff-you look. "What seems to be the problem?"

Around us, people stop and stare, most likely taking bets on how long before the police officer arrests the crazy woman accosting him in full view of a crowd of witnesses.

I feel my face crumple as tears spring to my eyes. He frowns, and I'm gratified to see that it's a concerned frown and not one of those oh-good-grief-another-emotional-woman frowns. "Ma'am? Are you all right?"

"No! I am not. I think I might have been robbed."

"Did you report it?"

"What do you call this?" I wave my arms like a maniac. "You're a cop, right? I'm reporting it to you. Aren't you supposed to protect and serve? My apartment is just a block from here, and there might still be someone inside stealing all my things."

"All right, ma'am. I'll call it in while we walk."

"Okay, but . . ."

"But what?" He looks at me through narrowed eyes.

"Don't you need to call for backup or something? On *NYPD Blue* they always make sure there are two of them before going into an uncertain situation." I know because I watch reruns every night. Besides, I'd think the actual NYPD would use that as a textbook or something.

"You're talking about TV?" His lips twitch.

He's mocking me. I can't believe I've come to this man for help. This man whose salary, by the way, my taxes pay. "Okay, fine. It's your decision. Live dangerously, for all I care. I was just trying to help."

"Trust me, ma'am. I'll ask for backup when I call this in."

We take quick steps toward the apartment as he walkie-talkies the robbery in to the station. "Wait here," he says when we reach the building and I open the bottom door.

"You mean by myself?" I practically whimper. Good grief.

He nods and puts his finger to his lips. Up the steps he goes, stealthily (without that backup, I might add), one hand on the pistol at his side. I'm mesmerized.

When he slowly nudges the apartment door open, my heart slips to my throat and I have a disturbing urge to scream. But knowing the officer might be in danger and my scream might be the difference between his living or dying, I keep my trap shut.

I nibble my lower lip and wait. And wait. And wait. After what seems like hours, he pokes his head out. "It's okay, ma'am. All clear."

Relief floods over me as I hurry up the steps. "Thank goodness," I breathe. "I was so worried."

He takes my arm. "You might want to . . ."

"What?"

"Prepare yourself."

The look of compassion in his eyes (did I mention that they're blue?) tips me off and I push past him to find an empty room. Well, not completely empty. Whoever violated my personal space didn't bother with my old *TV Guides* or crossword puzzles. But that's about all . . . my TV, my DVD player, my *couch,* for crying out loud. The new one Dancy's dad bought for us and she left here for me. All gone.

"I'm sorry, ma'am."

"Stop calling me ma'am," I snap as I continue looking for items that should be there but aren't.

"I'm sorry. Just trying to be polite."

"For goodness' sake, you're polite enough." Okay, maybe that's a little prickly coming from someone who desperately needs his help and support right now, but his overuse of that word is making me feel way too old.

He takes a slow, manly breath. The kind I

miss so much since Dad died. "I apologize." The look he gives me is sort of helpless, and my heart goes out to him.

"Just call me Laini, okay?" I mumble.

The living room is pretty much picked clean. "How the heck did they get a couch out of here without anyone noticing?" We desperately need a neighborhood watch or something.

The officer shrugs his broad shoulders. "Maybe they posed as moving people. It's not a new concept."

That actually makes sense. "Probably," I admit. "We've had a lot of moving going on. First my friend Tabby got married and moved out; then Dancy's parents gave her a fantastic condo with a view of Central Park. So maybe my neighbors just thought I was moving out too." Nerves always make me ramble. I'd sit down if there were anywhere to sit. And I probably should find somewhere. My legs are shaking pretty badly.

"Are you going to be okay?" the officer asks.

"I guess. For someone who is probably going to have to move back in with her mother."

He gives me a great smile, and a little sunshine breaks through the cloud of my life for just a second.

"If it's any consolation, they didn't take the kitchen table and chairs."

The kitchen!

Without another word I shoot across the living room and enter my favorite room in the apartment. Relief floods me as I stand in the middle of the outdated, slightly torn gold linoleum that hasn't been changed since the eighties, most likely. I want to weep with joy as I look at my stove and refrigerator. I start flinging open counters and drawers. "It's all here," I say happily and teary-eyed.

A curious frown creases his brow. But I don't see any reason to elaborate on my elation. Can't a girl be happy to find her kitchen intact when the rest of her life is going down the tubes?

"You'll need to go through the rest of the house and make a list of all the stolen items, then take it down to the station to file a report."

I nod automatically. "I will, Officer . . . I didn't catch your name."

"Hall."

"Officer Hall. Thank you for everything." My face is warm and I'm feeling a little breathless being this close to him. He's staring down from a lofty height and by the look on his face, I think he might actually be attracted to me too.

Before he can confirm or deny my suspicion, the buzzer goes off, alerting me to someone downstairs, and I nearly go through the roof.

"You want me to get that?" Officer Hall asks like a gallant knight.

I shake my head. I'm not a total weenie. "Will you walk with me, though?" I walk back through the living room and press the intercom button.

"NYPD. There's been a report of a robbery?"

I buzz him in.

When the other officer reaches my apartment, he takes one look at my cop and scowls. "Mark. You didn't wait for backup?"

Officer Hall tenses at the slap on the wrist. "I ascertained that the situation was safe and moved forward."

"That's not the point. I'm your partner. You should have waited for me. How do you think I felt coming out of Mr. Wang's to find you gone?"

"Okay, McNealy. It won't happen again."

The frowny officer turns to me. "Do you have somewhere to go until you get that lock fixed?"

I shrug, unwilling to be friendly to this

guy. He's not very nice to Mark. "Lots of places."

He nods. "Then I suggest you pack a bag."

"I-I haven't been in the bedroom yet."

The first officer — Mark, as it turns out — gives me a reassuring smile. "I have. Do you want me to go with you?"

The thought of walking down the hallway to that room alone is a little more than I'm prepared to deal with right now. I nod. "I'd appreciate it."

I start walking that way and he follows. I'm almost sure I hear the other officer mumble something about a "nursemaid." Whatever!

Later, curled up in my old bedroom at my mother's house on Long Island, I try to make sense of where my life is going. It's weird. I'm an accountant by degree, but I don't want to live that boring calculator life. I've done it. For eight years I worked with other people's numbers. I truly wanted to do what would finally make me happy. I mean, I'm thirty years old with no marital prospects on the horizon, and I just decided, life is too short to be an accountant if one doesn't love accounting. And darn it, I don't. What I love is design — at least I think I do. Like in college. We all did tent theater, Tabby, Dancy, and me. Tabby was the great lead actress and got all the best roles — and now she's an Emmy-nominated soap-opera star. Dancy wrote scripts — and now she's a writer after a few years as an editor. And me? I designed sets. Where did accounting come from? It only makes sense that I should become an interior designer, right? If my two best friends can follow their passions, why can't I?

My parents were both accountants before Dad passed away and Mom retired. Before Daddy died, I was trying to screw up the nerve to break it to my parents that I didn't want to major in accounting. But then he died from a sudden heart attack and my mom just knew his last request in life would have been for me to follow in his footsteps and be an ace accountant. I got close. Finished school, graduated near the top of my class at NYU, and went to work for Ace Accounting for a number of years. I almost wept with relief when one of the brothers embezzled from the company and I was laid off due to bankruptcy.

You'd think as hard as I'm fighting to become an interior designer, I must have an actual aptitude for the whole thing. More than one instructor has gently mentioned that perhaps I should pursue a different field, but I can't give up on my passion. Right? I can't fail!

Besides, I owe my aunt for the tuition plus some living expenses that she graciously offered to pay — after I buttered her up by dragging Tabby (her favorite soap star) to lunch at her house.

At midnight I'm still pretty wide awake, so it doesn't really bother me when my cell phone rings. I figure it's one of the girls. Who else would be calling this late? And I did leave messages on their voice mails about the break-in. It's a number I don't recognize, so I almost don't answer. But at the last second, I click the button. "Hello?"

"Miss Sullivan?"

Vaguely familiar male voice.

"Yes?"

"I'm sorry to call you so late, but I thought you'd like to know we apprehended the man who broke into your apartment."

My heart does a little loopy loop as I realize I'm speaking to Mark Hall. The hunky cop from earlier. "You did? That was fast."

"I had a hunch and it panned out," he says nonchalantly, and I imagine him shrugging those wide muscley shoulders. "People like you make my job a lot easier."

"People like me?"

"People who hang on to receipts and serial numbers." He hesitates.

"I come from a family of accountants. We never throw away receipts, paid bills, or bank statements."

He chuckles. "Lucky for you. We found your TV and DVD player. Your computer too."

"That's wonderful." A broad smile stretches my lips as I imagine this handsome, blond Norse-god type speaking into the phone.

"The guy was an addict and lived in your building until a month ago. He knew you and still had a key to the downstairs door. Tomorrow, I'll head to a few used-furniture stores in the area, and hopefully we'll find the furniture you lost."

"Thank you, Officer Hall," I say, because it really seems like the only thing left to say.

"Well, I am here to protect and serve, after all."

How cute is that? He's flirting.

Oh, my stars! He's flirting.

"Well I definitely feel protected and . . ." Good grief.

"Served?" His voice is rife with amusement.

I really don't know how to answer this man. Anything I say is going to sound so Magoo. While I try to think of something oh-so-clever, I finger the wedding-ring quilt my grandmother left me when she died. I'll take it when I get married. If that ever happens.

"Listen," he says, maybe picking up on the fact that I have nothing to say. "I was wondering if you'd be interested in having coffee with me sometime?"

Is he kidding?

"Sure. Sounds good." Real smooth.

"Great. How does tomorrow strike you?"

"Tomorrow?" I croak out, definitely no longer smooth.

"Too soon?"

You're blowing this, Laini Sullivan! I think in my mother's voice. *Pull it together before he writes you off as a nutcase.*

I sit up straighter in my seat and pretend I'm dignified even though no one can see me. The action works because I feel better already. More confident.

He clears his throat as though my long silence has made the poor guy uncomfortable. "Well . . . sorry to have bothered you."

Say something. *Quick.*

"No bother at all, Officer. I appreciate the call. And I'd love to have coffee with you."

"You would?" He seems genuinely surprised. I can't say that I blame him. "I just thought . . ."

"Sorry about the delay. I — uh — dropped the phone."

How terrible is that? Starting the relationship off on a fat lie. "Well, I mean, I didn't exactly drop it."

Oh, bummer. I'm making it so much worse. Okay, either pony up completely, lie, or just shut up.

This is a no-brainer. I decide to end the conversation.

"So, Officer Hall," I say, completely ignoring the fact that I have been rambling stupidly and lying to boot. "I know a great coffee shop just around the corner from my apartment. It's called Nick's Coffee Shop. You know the place?"

"Sure I do. Everyone knows Nick's. Tomorrow morning . . . say . . . ten?"

"I was actually thinking maybe Monday? I'm on Long Island at my mom's."

"Oh, okay. I guess that's too far for coffee."

It wouldn't have taken much for me to hop the train and meet the guy. It's not *that* far. And with a little nudge I would have agreed, but he doesn't nudge. As a matter of fact, he sounds a little down, like he thinks I'm not interested. Say something quick! "I'll be back on Monday. I have a class that night, so maybe we could meet at eleven at Nick's. Would that work for you?"

"That'll work out great. Only, I was hoping to see you over the weekend."

My stomach does a somersault. I'm not used to guys being open and honest.

"That would have been fun." Now might be the time to say something about meeting him after all, but a girl can't start changing plans for a guy she just met. And Mom counts on me to spend my time with her when I visit. Every single weekend of my life. Okay, beside the point. "I spend weekends at my mom's anyway, so I'm not usually around for dates."

"That's admirable."

"You think? Most guys are afraid I'm still tied to my mother's apron strings."

"Who isn't?"

"Well, I'm glad you're not worried about it, Officer Hall."

"Not at all. And, Laini?"

"Yeah?"

"If we're going to have a coffee date on Monday, you'd better drop the 'officer' and just call me Mark."

"Okay, Mark." I nod, even though he can't see me.

"Great." I hear the smile in his voice. I wonder if he can hear mine.

3

Saturday mornings are for sleeping in. For everyone but me. I love the early morning. Sunrise pumps my blood like a great workout seems to do for Tabby. On weekends when I'm at my mom's, I love to sit on the deck, look out across the backyard, and just breathe.

Don't get me wrong. I really do love Manhattan. It's a fun, exciting place to live. But it's not where I see myself in ten years, five years if God smiles on me and finally sends that guy I've been waiting for all my life. It's not where I see myself raising a family.

Speaking of guys . . .

I barely slept a wink after hanging up with Mark last night. I kept thinking about his sparkling grin and the way he blushed when his more-experienced partner chewed him out right in front of me.

I liked the way he handled it. Admired

him, in fact, and felt oh-so-safe when he walked me through the apartment to gather up my belongings. Mark's a guy I definitely want to get to know better, although I can't help wondering what he sees in me. But hey, even if this is a mercy date, I'll take it and try to wow him while I have his attention.

I'm feeling absolutely swoony, sitting on my deck chair thinking about those blue, blue eyes and big muscles, when my mother opens the French doors that lead from the kitchen to the deck.

"Morning, Mom."

She gives a weary sigh. A weary sigh less than ten minutes after rising from her bed. Her pink house slippers make a flapping sound as she walks across the planks. Her hands are wrapped around a steaming coffee mug with the New York Mets logo etched into either side. She drops into the cushioned deck chair with a grunt. "Good morning, honey. How did you sleep?"

Now, I know this question is the preface before she launches into the sad story of how she "didn't" sleep, but I give her the "fine" answer anyway and let my mind wander while she begins the inevitable diatribe.

Sometimes you just have to face facts. And the fact at this moment is that my morning solace is over for today. I'm not bitter. It's just the way things are. I know my mom depends on me.

As far as immediate family goes, it's been just the two of us since Daddy died the summer after my high school graduation. Mom fell apart and I had to shoulder a lot of her emotional baggage. I make the best of things where she's concerned. I don't mean to imply it's all about me sacrificing for her. There are plenty of good times when I love her company. And plenty of times when I don't. That's life.

For now, while I'm still a little shaky from last night's robbery, Mom feels like a safe place. So I tune out her complaining and take a good look at the woman who raised me.

My mom has worn the same yellow housecoat every morning for years. A chenille, ankle-length zip-up that is practically threadbare in certain areas. The bottom hem is frayed. I know she wears it because it's the last gift my dad bought for her before he died. For their twentieth anniversary. She can't let go.

Mom used to be a lot of fun. Smiled all the time, never let anything keep her from a goal. I knew she loved and missed my dad. But I never realized just how much until my first Christmas break as a freshman at NYU when I came home for three weeks. Anyone can hide depression for a weekend, but three weeks? Not a chance.

I figured out pretty fast that most days she had trouble getting out of bed. Christmas was a nightmare that year — our first without him. She cried from Christmas Eve through New Year's and was still teary-eyed on January 7 when I left to go back to school. I remember her standing in the doorway, clutching the neckline of her robe and waving good-bye, so forlorn and alone. I should have wanted to run to her. But I didn't. All I wanted to do was get away.

Three years ago, I finally broke down and bought her a new robe. A nice new chenille. Similar to the one she's worn for the past twelve years only without the frayed ends and repaired holes near the zipper. Plus, it was white. I love white robes.

She smiled politely, thanked me with a kiss on the cheek, and never wore it. Not even once that I've ever seen. For all I know, she gave it to Goodwill.

"Aren't you freezing, Ma?" The chiminea throws out enough heat to keep things cozy, but not when a person isn't wearing a coat or at least a warm housecoat. "That housecoat . . ."

She gives me a half-smile and interrupts me without taking the bait. "I don't know about you, but I'm starving. How about some breakfast?"

It looks like we're not going to discuss the robe again. That's okay. Avoidance is how Mom deals with life. I understand and don't push. I suppose I have a little avoidance issue too. "Want me to cook?"

She gives me a look. I should have known better. I might be a cook extraordinaire everywhere else, but not in Mom's kitchen. I give her a quirky grin and a peck on the cheek. "Sorry. I'll just go shower and dress while you fix breakfast."

"Good idea."

I step inside just ahead of her and start down the hall to the stairs when I realize she's following me.

"Something wrong, Ma?"

"No." She hesitates. Clearly something is on her mind.

"Come on, spill it."

"I was just wondering who called so late last night."

"Oh! I forgot to tell you. Mark Hall, the officer who came to my apartment, found some of my things and the guy who took them in the first place, so they think they'll be able to recover almost everything."

"That's wonderful, honey."

But her voice isn't very enthusiastic. Her eyes search my face. "I guess you won't be staying long, then?"

Ahh. That explains it.

"Just the weekend. It's too far from school and Nick's for me to stay here. You understand that, right?"

As long as I can remember, my mother has waved that bony hand of hers whenever she's trying to convince someone that she doesn't care in the least. Now is no exception. "Oh, sure. I just wondered how much meat to buy later when I go shopping."

"No more than usual." I smile. "I guess I'll go shower now."

"Laini. One more thing."

I knew it was coming. I should never have called him "Mark."

"This officer. What's he like?"

Deep breaths. Try really hard to stay cool. This is not so easy when I'm picturing the better-looking-than-Brad-Pitt cop and remembering how his eyes smiled as his lips curved up. Gorgeous lips, full and inviting.

"Laini?"

Snap out of it! "Mark is very nice. About my age, I'd guess."

"Oh?" She fingers the thin material of her robe. "Is he married?"

Shoot. She's on to me. I sigh but can't help grinning at the way she picks up on signals. "No. He isn't married." At least I don't think he is. Oh, good grief. What if he's a slimy two-timing toad? I clear my throat and try to deadpan. "Anyway, we're going for coffee at Nick's Monday." Where I intend to make sure he's not looking for an adulterous affair with the desperate chubby chick.

A frown creases her brow. "Oh, honey. Do you think that's a good idea?" She takes a cautious step toward me.

"Why not?"

"He has such a dangerous job. You'd be worried all the time."

I understand her fears. After Dad died, it was all about self-preservation and safety for everyone she loves.

"Relax, Ma. It's coffee, not marriage."

"Sometimes marriage starts with coffee."

From her lips to God's ears.

I send her an indulgent smile, walk the few steps between us, and kiss her on the cheek. "Let's not jump the gun."

Cringe. Why did I have to mention guns? Her eyebrows lift as though she just thought of Mark's need to carry a weapon.

Before she can voice the thought, I turn and sprint down the hall, calling over my shoulder. "Gotta go shower, Ma. I'll be back in a few minutes."

For all intents and purposes, the weekend is pretty uneventful. Mom and I trudge down the street to the community church she's been attending for the last few months. I've been with her several times and I like it all right. This Sunday, she kept smiling at a nice-looking older man across the church from us. I don't think she knows I saw. But I did. And I noticed him staring at her more than once when she didn't appear to be paying attention to him. If getting past Saint Peter meant I'd have to give a brief summary of the sermon, I'm afraid I wouldn't make it.

But my mother flirting — yes, flirting! It's a little disconcerting.

During the weekend, I received three or four calls, each, from Tabby and Dancy, like I always did when we were roommates. Usually they asked me for culinary advice. And this weekend resulted in plenty of cooking questions too, but that's okay. The normalcy of it all helped me pretend nothing had really changed all that much.

Of course all of that disappears as I walk the three blocks from the subway station to my apartment on Sunday night, amid a

February snowfall. The realization hits me — I mean, really hits me — that I'm alone. All alone. For the first time in years — since our sophomore year of college, Tabby and Dancy are both gone for good and I'm the only one still in our cozy apartment. It used to feel like home. A haven. Now it just feels like a depressing rut.

I let myself in at the bottom of the steps and trudge slowly upward. My legs feel like four-hundred-pound weights, getting heavier with each step. I hesitate when I reach the landing, and stare at my closed door. My friends made sure the locks were all changed, and I find the new key wedged behind a loose baseboard the super keeps promising to have repaired.

The thought of going into that bare apartment has been plaguing me all weekend. I'm seriously thinking of advertising for a new roommate. Well, not advertising exactly. But definitely looking around.

I step over the threshold into darkness, and when I switch on the light, I'm smacked with a scene like something from a movie. Bodies popping up from behind furniture and shouting, "Surprise!"

I'm truly speechless as a thrill washes over me. Well, it's either a thrill or the beginnings of a heart attack.

Dancy and Tabby are the obvious ring leaders. They step forward, grins spread across their beautiful faces. "What's this?" I say. "You guys know it's not my birthday." Please, give me the three months I have left. Let's hold off on thirty-one as long as possible.

Tabby slings her arm around me. "This is a housewarming party!" On cue, her steptwins, seven-year-old Jenn and Jeffy, begin to blow party-favor noisemakers.

And then I notice something really different. Furniture I've never seen. A gorgeous modern red sofa and love seat, a fluffy off-white recliner — these things look vaguely familiar — a desk in the corner with a computer sitting on top, wrapped up in an enormous red bow.

I give a sharp gasp. "What on earth . . . ?"

Dancy grins. "Mother left all of her old furniture behind when she and Dad got back together. It was just sitting in storage collecting dust. Mother doesn't care what I do with it, as long as she doesn't ever have to look at it again. So I felt like this was a good time to get rid of it."

"But Mark said they caught the thief. I can get my old furniture back." I run my hands longingly over the sofa top.

"This suits you better," Tabby says, giving

me the permission I need to let the other stuff go.

I throw my arms around Dancy. "Thank you, thank you, thank you!"

"Hey, I bought the computer." Tabby steps up and wraps her arms around us both.

Not that I'd let her take the wonderful machine away, but I do feel I should be honest. "Mark recovered the old one."

"That old thing?" Tabby waves away the very thought. "It was ancient. Five or six years old. So obsolete it might as well be a typewriter."

I nod. "Thanks, guys."

I include their new men in my gratitude. And the twins. "I can't believe you did all this for me." And oh, darn it, tears start flowing. Dancy grabs tissues from my new coffee table and shoves them into my palm.

Even though they don't think I see it, Dancy and Tabby exchange "the look." It means "girl talk." Tabby turns to David and the twins, her gaze encompassing Jack, Dancy's boyfriend.

"Hey, why don't you guys head over to Nick's and grab us a big chocolate cheesecake?"

"I don't like cheesecake!" Jenn announces with a stomp of her pink snow boot.

David swings her up into his arms. "Then we'll get you something else."

Jeffy hops on the bandwagon. "I don't like cheesecake either."

Jack swoops the boy up for a piggyback ride. "Let's go, then, shall we?"

"Can we walk in the snow?" Jeffy asks.

"That's up to your father, lad," Jack says in his oh-so-British accent.

They bustle out the door and Tabby heaves a sigh. "I love being a mom, but sometimes . . ."

She flops down onto my new swanky sofa and stretches out, legs straight, arms slung over the back of the couch.

I join her on the couch and Dancy takes the recliner.

"Those two are full of energy," I have to admit. "But so much fun. That week they spent with me during your honeymoon was awesome. Any time you two want to go away, just let me know. I'm game."

"Thanks," Tabby says, her eyes looking a little guilty. "We just might take you up on that sometime soon. I'm pooped and need a vacation away from here. Even if it's just a weekend at a bed-and-breakfast somewhere."

"Just let me know." I look around. "It's not like there's anyone for them to bother."

My eyes go wide. "Not that they'd be a bother anyway."

Grabbing my hand, Tabby sits up and faces me. "I know what you mean. Now, let's talk about you."

"Yes," Dancy says, adjusting in the recliner so that she's facing us. "What are we going to do about you being so alone?"

I shrug. "I don't know. Maybe being alone isn't such a bad thing."

Tabby produces an unladylike snort that I'm positive would offend her mother. "Oh, come on, Laini. Without someone to cook for, you're completely lost."

"I just cooked for you two Friday night, didn't I?"

"I mean on a regular basis." Tabby grins. "I don't suppose you'd want to move into my guest room and be our full-time cook?"

Is it pathetic that I almost jump at this completely rhetorical question?

Dancy saves me a response. "Hey, if anyone gets a live-in cook, it's me." She waggles her eyebrows at me as though we're negotiating. "We have a state-of-the art gym in the building with an indoor track and a swimming pool."

"Yes, but in my world, you could work out with Freddie."

Dancy shoots me a mock look of horror.

"That human torture chamber? Don't be swayed by anything that so-called friend has to say."

"What I want to know," I say, keeping my tone and face sober, "is why both of you are trying to sway me with promises of exercise. Do you think I'm fat?"

I swear their gasps suck all the oxygen from the room. They practically trip over each other's words trying to apologize. Until I take pity on them. "Guys, guys! It's okay. I'm teasing."

Dancy shoots a throw pillow at me, and Tabby backhands my leg. "That wasn't very nice!"

"I'm definitely going to be looking for a roommate. So if either of you hear of anyone looking . . ." I stare at Tabby pointedly because as an actress she knows all kinds. "Only normal people need apply."

"Fine. But I can't be held responsible if I'm not sure what normal is anymore." Her eyes twinkle and she moves in closer. "Okay, it's time to talk about something very serious."

I frown and glance from Dancy, whose face holds the same expression, to Tabby. "What's going on with you two?"

"I want to know all about 'Mark.' "

"Mark?" Way too innocent. They'll never

buy it. "Mark who?"

"You know," Tabby says — not to me, to Dancy, "I once played the role of a German interrogator. I learned the dark arts of torture."

She comes at me with menacing fingers. "No tickling!" I say, moving back. "You know I can't stand that."

Dancy suddenly closes in on the other side. "Seems to me, if you don't want to be tortured, you should start talking."

"Okay, okay! Stop it!" I jump up and scurry to the love seat. Dancy and Tabby dissolve into laughter.

"Are you going to talk?" Tabby asks.

"There's nothing to say. He's cute."

"Rugged cute, or pretty-boy cute?" Dancy asks.

David is rugged; Jack is pretty-boy.

"A little of both, I guess. He's tall, blond. Blue eyes. Big muscles."

"Sounds dreamy," Tabby says.

"Down, girl. You're a Mrs. and a mommy."

Tabby sticks out her tongue. "And you're taken."

"You're right about that! I am off the market."

I clear my throat. "Ahem, girls. We're talking about me."

"Oh, *now* she wants to talk about Mc-

Dreamy."

"We're having coffcc tomorrow at Nick's."

They share another look.

"What?" I ask.

"You're just trying to get Joe jealous."

My mouth drops open. I cannot believe Tabby just said that. I mean, that's just the most ridiculous thing I've ever . . .

I stop, stare, and grin. "Well, maybe a little. Not that he'd ever notice me."

Tabby's eyes practically bug out of her head. "Is she kidding?"

Dancy shrugs. "Who knows?"

"What? I've suddenly been sucked into an invisible cloud?"

"Honey," Dancy says with smug determination, "Joe noticed you the first time he saw you. He practically swallowed his tongue."

"You're crazy. He did not!"

Tabby sends her a wink. "How much should we bet this little coffee date with Officer Hottie gets our Laini here a date with the Italian stallion?"

"If I wasn't so broke," I grumble, "I'd take that bet."

Let them joke. Let them make bets. Let them talk over my head. But oh, please, please, let them be right!

4

"But why don't you like the idea?" I'm following Joe Pantalone around like a lovesick teenager. He hates all of my ideas for decor. I'm getting frustrated and, quite frankly — fed up. Jazz and I did a conference call earlier and came up with a few ideas. Old New York — retro, yet very hip. Old is new, you know?

But Joe is having none of that. So as far as the redecorating, we have to go back to the drawing board.

"I like the idea of a sloped awning between the two buildings."

Well, at least he's throwing me a bone.

"That was Nick's idea in the first place," I admit. Which isn't easy considering Nick's on the opposite side of the country and I could really use the credit.

Joe stops for a minute and turns to an employee. "Take over here, will ya?" Then he looks at me. "You want to sit out front and have some coffee? We could discuss what I have in mind."

I glance at my watch: 10:55. "Actually, Joe, I'm meeting someone in about five minutes, so we're going to have to wrap this up."

He glances at the door as the bell dings. "Is that who you're waiting for?"

A blonde wearing a skirt that's way too short for this time of year wiggles her way to the counter. Have I ever given this guy any indication that I would hang out with someone like that? I'm uncomfortable wearing shorts more than two inches above my knees.

"No." The bell above the door dings again, and my heart does a flip as Mark saunters in. I almost don't recognize him in regular clothes. Jeans, a tan T-shirt under a striped button-down shirt. He's wearing a leather bomber jacket. I can't help feeling a bit smug. "That's him."

"Him?" Joe's eyebrows scrunch together. "Are you telling me you brought a date to the coffee shop?"

"Well, it isn't a date, exactly. He arrested the guy that broke into my apartment Friday night and we sort of hit it off." I look at him askance, a lot more casually than I feel inside. "It's just coffee."

Mark is walking toward me, his face split by a great smile.

"Just coffee, huh?" Joe mutters. He stays planted by my side and I'm starting to wonder if Tabby and Dancy are right. Maybe Joe is a little more into me than he lets on.

"Hi, Mark." I know I'm a little more effusive in my greeting than I would be if Joe weren't standing there just begging me to make him jealous, but it's not every day a girl gets a chance like this, so I'm making the best of it for however long the illusion lasts.

Mark gives Joe a once-over, and his smile fades just a bit before he turns his attention to me. "You seem much better than the other night."

"Thanks to you catching the guy."

"Did you recover everything?"

"Just about."

Joe is really frowning now and chomping at the bit a little. I know I'm being rude by not introducing the two men, but, quite frankly, it's women like short-skirt-blondie who get guys like this to practically come to blows over them. So since it's me and not her and she's looking a little jealous too, I decide to enjoy the melodrama. Still, just standing here while they growl is becoming awkward. And I don't want that.

"Joe," he finally says with a jerk of his chin.

Mark nods back. "Mark."

"You want coffee?"

"Yeah."

"I'll take —" I begin.

"I already know what you want." Joe goes back to the kitchen. I stare after him, bewildered by his rudeness. I was going to say I wanted a mocha latte with an extra shot of espresso and extra whipped cream — my usual. But what if I'd wanted something different? What then? Mr. Smug.

I turn to Mark. "Do you want to sit? Joe or one of the other employees will bring our coffees."

"Sure." He steps back and lets me go ahead of him. I stop at a corner table.

"Is this okay?" I know it's a little presumptuous of me to assume he wants to sit in a secluded spot, but it just seems like the place to pick.

"Perfect." He stares down at me with a knowing look that makes my cheeks warm. It's not a mocking sort of knowing look, though. Not the kind you see in romantic comedies or romance novels where the "hero" is Rhett Butler–ish — you know, rakish and sardonic. Mark seems genuinely pleased. How refreshing.

He holds my chair as I sit and slides it in with finesse. We settle in and then stare at each other like you do when you really want to spend time with someone but you know nothing about the other person and don't know where to start. I wait for him to talk and he waits for me, and suddenly I laugh. I do that when I'm nervous. Darn it. Now I feel dumb. Or actually, I would feel dumb, except he laughs too, and just like that the ice is broken.

"So, Mark, tell me about being a cop."

His lips twitch.

"I guess I shouldn't have said 'cop,' huh? Is that politically incorrect?"

He shrugs. "That's what I am. Although I guess some prefer to be called 'police officer.' "

I try to dazzle him with a smile. Who knows if it works or not, because at that moment Joe shows up and practically throws our coffee cups onto the table. "One regular coffee. One mocha latte shot of espresso, extra whipped cream. On the house." He stomps off.

Goodness. Talk about a temper.

"What's his problem?" Mark looks a little bewildered by the entire exchange.

I don't know what to say, so I fake ignorance. "What do you mean?"

"The two of you . . ." His gaze searches mine for answers even though he leaves the question unsaid.

"Good grief. Not in this lifetime." I know that's an answer that would make someone think I have no attraction to Joe Pantalone, and of course I do, but I'm miffed at the way he's acting. Besides, I think my best chance of a love connection might be Mark at this point. And judging from the wide grin that is spreading across his sensuous mouth, I think he's thinking the same thing.

"Good," he says. "Then I suppose I can accept the coffee." He takes a sip. "On the house."

Joe glares at us for one solid hour until Mark finally leans across the table and asks, "Can we get out of here? That guy is starting to get on my nerves."

"Where do you want to go?"

"Anywhere but here. We can walk down the sidewalk and put a dollar in every beggar's cup, for all I care. As long as that guy isn't around." He stands. "What do you say?"

I can't help but toss a glance toward Joe. Sure enough, he's glaring. A split-second decision brings a quick nod to my head. "Sure. Let's go."

When Mark and I reach the front door, I

turn to give Joe a slight wave. Not to rub it in, just to say good-bye, but Joe is suddenly absent. I figure he ducked into the kitchen, or his office. The guy who has been downright hovering for the past hour has suddenly gone invisible. Oh well, let him.

Outside the warmth of the coffee shop, the air on the street is crisp. More than crisp, really; it's the kind of air that can't quite make up its mind if it wants to sting your toes and bite your nose or just nip and nibble a little bit. Perfect if Mark and I knew each other better. I'd snuggle up against him for warmth. Call me old-fashioned, but that sort of closeness is quite a ways off.

"I have an idea," he says just as I'm about to say, "So, what do you want to do?"

"Oh, yeah?" My teeth are chattering a little, so I hope whatever he has in mind takes us somewhere with really good heating.

He grabs my hand and pulls me along toward the subway station. "Wait, where are you taking me?"

A wink, an actual wink from a guy. "Be patient, little one."

Any guy that calls me little one can take me to Timbuktu for all I care.

We hold hands on the subway. Well, we hold hands and the overhead bars. It's awkward trying to keep my footing and hold his hand, but if I wiggle my fingers free he might think I don't like him. So I tough it out. He's still keeping mum about our destination.

We end up at Rockefeller Center. Is it wrong that I'm disappointed? I mean, at Christmastime, there's no place I'd rather be than Rockefeller Center, with the magical tree and lights and decorations. But February is sort of a month without a point unless you're in a relationship and go in for flowers and candy and gifts. But Mark and I are sooo not there. Plus, V Day is a whole ten days away, even if we were.

We step off the subway and walk east toward Fifth Avenue.

"Seriously. Where are we going?"

"Don't be so impatient, woman," he says. "This is an experience to be savored. Enjoyed. Rushing anything just takes the joy out of it."

I lift my eyebrow to let him know I know he's talking about us as much as about waiting for whatever he has up his bomber-jacket sleeve. At Fifth Avenue, we head north and I start to get the picture. A really dark and scary picture. He's taking me to the Top of the Rock. I almost breathe out a sigh as I note the length of the line at the entrance. It'll be a good two hours before we get to the front of the line.

"Maybe we don't have time for this," I offer. "Don't you have to be at work?"

"Day off. Didn't I mention that?"

"No." Butterflies are making babies in my stomach. I have to get a grip. I can't admit to being deathly afraid of heights. Not to a guy who walks in and out of danger for a living.

But here's a true statement: I've lived in New York all of my life, am a huge fan of the movie *An Affair to Remember,* not to mention *Sleepless in Seattle,* and yet I've never even once had a desire to ride to the top of the Empire State Building. I always figured if God wanted me that high up, He would have made me an eagle instead of a big chicken. The thought of standing seventy stories up looking across the city from an observation deck at Rockefeller Center — or the Top of the Rock, as it's called — and being expected to actually keep my eyes open, makes me downright sick to my stomach.

Mark nudges me. I look up into his eyes and am gratified to notice concern there. He's big and strong, good-looking, *and* intuitive. I wonder why he hasn't been snagged by now. Is it him?

"Do you live with your mom?"

His eyebrows scrunch together. "Is that what's bothering you?"

"No. But do you?"

"No. What's wrong?"

"All right." I tip my head and look way up at the building. "I don't do heights, I don't ride roller coasters, and I don't climb mountains."

His expression falls like a little boy who hands his mom what he thinks is a pretty bouquet only to find out she doesn't really want smelly weeds and poison ivy. "So Top of the Rock isn't really a great idea?"

I shake my head. "Not so much. The thought of it makes my head ache."

"Well, maybe if you face your fear . . . ?"

My head is still shaking. "I'd rather live with it."

The smile he gives me is filled with affection and makes me want to kiss him. But of course I don't. First of all, my nose is so frozen I'm not positive it isn't running. And second of all, kissing is at least three dates away. I guess I should admit that I am a schedule, list, and planning person. That's why I like to follow recipes.

"How does lunch sound?"

Aw, he wants to feed me. My kind of guy. "Sounds great."

"There's a great little Italian restaurant a few blocks away. How's that?"

"Terrific." Although the thought of Italian anything makes me think of Joe.

Mark tucks my arm through his and leads me away from the tower of doom. My breathing comes easier now. He gives my arm an affectionate squeeze.

"Okay, so you don't like heights. How do you feel about outdoorsy activities in general?"

"You mean like eating at hot-dog stands? Or camping?"

"I'm guessing you prefer the hot-dog stand?"

Is that a statement about my weight? I'm not going to ask, but isn't that a little insensitive of him?

I shrug. "Camping is okay."

His eyebrows go up. "Really?"

"As long as it isn't freezing out."

He gives me a once-over and frowns. "You're shivering."

"A little," I admit.

"I'm sorry. Let's get you warmed up." He hails a taxi with one arm and slips the other around my shoulders, snuggling me into his warmth.

Technically, snuggling like that shouldn't happen for another couple of dates at least.

But since I'm freezing, I'm willing to compromise my principles. Just this once.

He leads me to a taxi and lets me in first, as any great guy would. I stay close to the other door. I've already held his hand and let him warm me up. Maybe I should put on the brakes a little before he gets the wrong idea about me.

We ride a few blocks until we reach a little Italian restaurant squashed between a wedding boutique and a New Age bookstore. "Maniaci's?"

"Yeah, their son works in my precinct."

Which leads me to ask: "How long have you been an officer?"

"Two years."

Only two years? He seems older than most rookies. Not that I know many rookies. Or any, for that matter. Still, I imagine he's older than most.

He must notice the raised eyebrows or the funny look on my face, because he nods a little as he opens the door to Maniaci's.

"I was in the marines for nine years. Joined up right out of high school."

The marines? I swallow hard. The next obvious question would be whether he'd served in Iraq or Afghanistan, but I don't want to dredge up bad memories, so I don't ask. I figure that can wait for the next date.

I mean, if there is one, that is.

As soon as we step inside, we're greeted by a jovial overweight Italian with graying temples and a big smile. "Officer Mark!" he says, pounding my date on the back. "You bring a beautiful woman to eat at Maniaci's?" He's grinning so big I think maybe he's faking a little. But anyone who calls me beautiful, sincere or not, is okay in my book. Until proven otherwise.

"This is Laini Sullivan," Mark says, and I truly think he looks sort of proud. Which produces this weird sense of hey-maybe-I'm-okay-after-all.

I'm not kidding. My chest actually tightens at the thought. I need to process this new feeling. Usually I'm plagued by the desire to apologize to whatever guy is taking me out — for my extra pounds and questionable wardrobe choices. Today, for instance. I'm wearing a pretty nice pair of slacks. I mean, sure, they were $19.99 on sale at Sears — and they are a size 12, but I like them. I like pink. I like stripes. 'Nough said.

But back to the fat little Italian man who does not remind me of Nick or Joe in the least. Shoot, now I'm thinking about Joe again. Maybe we should have gone out for Chinese instead.

"You come-a with me. I give you best table in whole restaurant."

Seriously, I feel like Lady from the Disney movie *Lady and the Tramp.* But I'll tell you right now I am not sharing a bowl of spaghetti and meatballs with Mark. I don't care how cute he is.

5

Life has been a complete whirlwind of activity over the last week. Classes, study sessions with Jazz and the rest of the group, a birthday party for David and Tabby's twins, and dinner with Dancy and Jack, where all I did was watch them make eyes at each other. My gut is one ball of tightness. It's been over a week and Mark hasn't called. What did I do to scare this one off? I'm not given to delusion, but I honestly thought we had a connection.

But I have to force all distractions from my brain and focus on making myself clear. Today is the day Joe Pantalone will listen to reason. My name is Determination. Determination Refuse-to-Take-No-for-an-Answer Sullivan. He will agree to the revised ideas for the renovations, and he will agree to hire the architect so we can begin applying for all the millions of permits needed for a project this size. It's a lofty goal for one person. But I'll have my team of wannabe designers, the architect, and the contractors. It'll be fine. I'm almost one hundred percent sure of it.

Waiting for Jazz to arrive to provide my much-needed backup, I hesitate just outside Nick's. I'm not in the greatest of moods. Tomorrow is Valentine's Day. Romance is in the air — for everyone but me. And why does all the mooning and sighing have to start the week before? It's Valentine's *Day,* people, not Valentine's *Week.*

The girls and I usually spend it together, except last year Tabby babysat for David's twins while he took another woman to dinner and she ended up so sick with the measles that she picked up from the kids that Dancy stayed with her. This year, of course, the two of them are sewn up in their cozy little romances and I'm out in the freezing cold with no one to call my own. I'd sort of hoped, even though I knew it was unlikely, that Mark might ask me to dinner for the big night. Okay, that was a dumb thing to hope for. I know that. A Valentine's date is for those already in a relationship or at least farther into one than I am with Mark. If a relationship is indeed beginning. I haven't heard from him since lunch at Maniaci's Monday — of last week.

Today is Wednesday so that's — nine whole days. Who am I kidding? I'm never going to see him again.

"Hey!" My friend and project-mate, Jazz Bates, shivers her way up to me. "Why are you standing in front of the door?"

I shrug. "Just waiting for you."

She grins and throws a couple of fake punches into the air just like she's Rocky Balboa. "Gearing up for a fight?"

"Oh, brother. I hope not."

"Don't sweat it," Jazz says, more because she's only twenty-three, I think, than because she has any idea what's going to happen beyond that door with the jingle bell over the top.

I gather a breath for courage and reach for the handle, but it opens and I have to catch myself before I pitch forward onto my face.

Joe is standing there looking like someone out of *The Godfather,* his dark eyebrows scrunched together. I guess he didn't notice that I almost splatted onto the black and white tiles. "Are you going to stand out there all day?"

Sheesh, the longer he runs Nick's, the more he acts just like the guy. On a portly, older man, it sort of works. Gives him that gruff but cuddly persona. With Joe it's just intimidating and I don't care for this side of him at all. What happened to the guy who used to pull me into a big hug every time he saw me?

Jerking my chin to gather as much dignity as possible, I push past him and step inside the yummy-coffee-smelling shop. "I was waiting for Jazz," I say without apology.

"Music?" He gives me a puzzled frown. "You know we play jazz inside."

"Not jazz music. Jazz Bates, my friend from the design group."

Jazz lifts a finger. "That would be me."

His face colors, and he clearly recognizes her now.

"Remember?" I say. "We're supposed to talk about new ideas for the redesign?"

"Oh, yeah." He rakes his fingers through a head of thick dark hair. "Well, let's close the door. No sense heating up the whole outside."

The dining area is predictably full, and two employees are hopping to keep on top of everything. "Where should we sit, Joe?" I ask, slipping my politically incorrect sheepskin coat from my shoulders.

He jerks his thumb behind the counter. "Come to my office. I got an architect in there we can talk to."

My chest tightens. I stare at him, my

depression slipping lower down the emotional black hole I like to call the Valentine's Day blues.

"What do you mean? You have an architect in there already?"

I see his defenses rise. His eyes narrow and his chest pushes out a little. Usually, that would be my sign to back down, but not this time. He's jumping the gun. "I thought we were going to decide on an architect after you okayed a design plan. And unless I misunderstood, we were supposed to choose together."

"Whose place is this? Yours or mine?"

So he wants to play hardball, huh? Tough guy. "Neither! It's Nick's place, and he trusted me to oversee this project. What right do you have to undermine me?"

He gives me a silent glare, and I can't help but wonder if he's about to order me out of "his" shop, or if he's just trying to think of a comeback. Surely his thought processes aren't that slow.

A steadying breath seems to put things in perspective for him. The hostility leaves his face. "The architect is a friend of the family. I think Uncle Nick would approve. She's good. We'll have the meeting and see if the two of you can work together."

"And if we can't?" And did he say "she"?

"Try." His gaze is almost pleading. "Nancy just moved here from Chicago. She could use the job."

The office door opens, and I understand now why he wants her working for him. Nancy, the so-called "friend of the family," is a knockout. Black hair that falls in soft waves over her shoulders, dark eyes (like Joe), olive skin that makes her breathtakingly beautiful. Not to mention her figure. Let's just say she could be a Victoria's Secret model.

My heart sinks at the way she's looking at Joe when he turns around. All familiar and friendly. Almost sisterish, if she weren't so stunning.

"You coming, Joey?" she singsongs in a way that I personally feel is beneath a woman of her exotic beauty.

"Yeah." He swallows. "This is Laini Sullivan." He points to me. "She's in charge of the project for the most part."

She turns her dark gaze on me and one eyebrow goes up the tiniest fraction.

She offers a hand tipped with long blood-red nails.

Even a girl like me — a virtual wallflower compared to this woman, recognizes a challenge when she sees one. Suddenly, my name is no longer Determination. It's Give-

Up-Before-Anyone (Namely Me)-Loses-Any-Blood.

Jazz nudges me and I snap out of it. Thank goodness for Jazz. "Nice to meet you," I lie.

"Likewise," she replies with equal insincerity.

What is it with women like this one? Why on earth would she consider me a threat? Comparing the two of us is worse than comparing Adam Sandler to Brad Pitt. The guy's funny, but come on . . . he's not Brad! Honestly? There's just no comparison. It's worse than comparing a Mercedes with a Volkswagen Beetle. And everyone in the room knows it.

Joe takes a seat in his leather chair. I'm glad to see he's tackled Nick's cluttered desk and has this office sparkling. He motions Jazz and me to the two chairs against the wall, and Nancy (who doesn't wait for an invitation) walks around the desk, where plans are spread out in front of Joe. Apparently these two have been talking awhile. She leans over him, and my claws start to unsheathe as her hair wisps onto his neck. He reaches up absently, as if to swat away a mosquito.

"I like this." He glances up at me and his expression softens. I must have a look of utter helplessness on my face. That look the nerdy girl gets when the cheerleader walks into the room and suddenly no one remembers the nerdy girl's name. But I don't need his pity.

"Do you want to come over and take a look?" he asks. "I'd like your input."

Another nudge from Jazz rouses me from my stupor. I rise slowly to my feet, and even though I'd rather do just about anything else, I walk around the desk and take my place on Joe's other side. I feel like Nancy and I are the angel and the devil on his shoulders.

Guess who gets to wear the halo?

I already took the class on how to read plans, so I can visualize pretty much everything on the blueprint in front of me. As much as I hate to admit it, Nancy's ideas are solid. Stone steps and a cast-iron railing will definitely accent the Italian decor I proposed. We'll have a stone walk leading from one building to the other underneath the awning, and ten small, round tables with cast-iron chairs will add to the old-world feel. Her plans are good. It's like she read my mind.

When I glance up, Nancy has turned and is eyeing me. She's holding her breath — waiting, I suppose, and feeling a bit of the uncertainty that girls like her aren't used to feeling. I smile at her, then at Joe. "It's perfect. I don't think there's any reason to look for another architect."

Nancy's face softens with relief. My skepticism about her fades a little — just a little — as a broad smile stretches across unbelievably flawless skin.

"Great!" Joe says, slapping the plans on the desk in front of him as though giving them a high five. "What next?"

"Permits," Nancy and I say at the same time and smile at each other.

Joe looks from one of us to the other. "All right, then. Let's get some permits."

Five minutes later, we step out of the office, finally armed with a plan. Nancy carries a long cylindrical case that holds the future look of Nick's Coffee Shop.

The place is packed out. Joe gives us a hasty good-bye and jumps in to help. Nancy extends her hand to me and smiles. "Well, I guess I'll get out of here. I'm supposed to go look at an apartment in" — she looks at her watch and scowls — "shoot, thirty minutes."

"You're looking for an apartment?"

She nods. "Something cheap. I'm a poor architect. This is my first job in New York. God bless Joe."

"Yeah."

I'm aware that Jazz is staring at me, but I choose to ignore her. This Nancy friend of Joe's seems nice enough. But when a girl has spent the last eleven years living with best friends and suddenly finds herself all alone, she doesn't just jump at the first candidate that comes along. I mean, sure, I'm looking for a roommate, but I'm not desperate.

"Well," I say cheerily, giving Jazz no chance to stick her nose into something that's none of her business, "good luck with that apartment. It's murder trying to find anything in the city."

She grabs a black leather coat from the coatrack and shrugs it on, pulling her long, shiny hair out of the collar. "You're not kiddin'. See you around."

She spins on the heels of department-store boots.

"I can't believe you didn't offer. Are you nuts?"

"Am *I* nuts?" I scowl at Jazz and slip my coat from the rack. "She could be a serial killer for all I know."

"Sure, a serial-killer Italian architect who just happens to be a childhood friend of your friend."

"Joe isn't exactly a friend. As a matter of fact, I barely know him."

She rolls her eyes.

"What about you, Jazz? You looking for a place?"

"Nope, so don't even think about using me as an excuse for bad manners. You know she's probably going to look at some rat-infested dump while you're sitting over there all alone in a two-bedroom rent-controlled apartment just around the corner."

So my good luck somehow makes Joe's "friend" my responsibility? I don't ask it out loud, but inwardly I'm seething. Why do I always have to be the one to do the right thing?

I huff. Well, darn, that just sealed my fate, didn't it? I admit the right thing to do is to offer Nancy the empty bedroom in my apartment. And it's true I could use help paying the bills.

"Fine," I grumble. "I'll talk to her about it."

"Talk to who about what?" Joe butts in.

"What, are you eavesdropping?"

" 'Ey, don't be shouting in my place if you don't want people to hear what you're saying."

Jazz grins. "She's going to offer Nancy the other room in her apartment."

"You got a room?" His eyebrows are up

practically to his hairline.

"Yeah, both my roommates moved out recently."

He nods, apparently connecting the dots. "Nance will probably jump at it."

Yeah, I'm sure "Nance" will. "She might like the place she's looking at."

"You want I should give her a call before she wastes her time in Brownsville? I never wanted her living over there anyway."

"Hey, Jerry Stiller lived in Brownsville once," I say. "Ben Stiller's dad?"

Joe scowls. "So did Mike Tyson."

Point taken. "Call her."

Eight hours later, a moving truck pulls up to the curb in front of my apartment building. Don't ask me how the driver found a spot. But Nancy must be a real go-getter because she's standing at my door, wide smile, check in hand. "You made it — that's great." I try to be upbeat, but I feel like crying inside. I liked the solitude. But solitude costs more than I can afford.

A wide grin splits her face. "Hi, roomie!" She tosses a box in my arms. "Put that in my room, will you? I'm going to go down and get some more. Oh, and don't worry about the size of the truck. One of Joe's uncles owns a moving company. This one was free." Her throaty laughter fills the hall.

"My stuff has been rattling around in there all the way over."

And just like that, Nancy Costa becomes my roommate.

6

It's Valentine's Day. Whoop-de-do.

I wade through Nancy's boxes as I make my way, not happily, to the kitchen and prepare a pot of very, very strong coffee. Last night the moving guys piled all of her things wherever they could find room, put her bed together, and Nancy crashed around 3:00 a.m.

Which of course means that's when I also crashed. Only I didn't sleep. At all. It's now 6:00 a.m., and I have a day to begin. Coffee at Nick's with Tabby and Dancy at eight — where, incidentally, I have to drop off four dozen cinnamon rolls anyway. All in the shape of hearts — which I made and froze three days ago. Don't even ask me how I pulled that off. I've whipped up pink icing too. They'll look amazing, and I know Joe's going to sell every single one of them. This should be enough to get me out from under my Eeyore cloud, but it isn't. After all, why should I care if some dumb, love (or more likely lust)-sick guy buys a pink, heart-shaped cinnamon roll for his girl? Valentine's Day is such a brutal day.

I pull the frozen rolls out of the freezer and set them on the counter to thaw. My agenda tomorrow will include mixing up a new batch of dough.

I started supplementing my income last fall when Nick fell in love with my baking skills and hired me to provide the coffee shop with continental breakfast items. I have to admit to feeling a bit smug about the whole thing. We started with one dozen cinnamon rolls, and now he easily sells out of four dozen by noon every day. He'd buy more if I had time to make them. But I had to cut him off.

Besides the cinnamon rolls, I also provide the shop with hot stuffed sandwiches made with fresh dough. Some roast beef and cheddar, turkey and swiss, ham and Colby Jack. I'm telling you, no matter what I send, they sell like gangbusters at lunch and dinner.

But I've had to put my foot down and tell them I'll bring the rolls and sandwiches twice a week (Tuesdays and Thursdays) instead of every day like I was trying to do a couple of months ago.

After the coffee finishes brewing, I grab a huge mug and fill it with coffee, half-and-half, and two packets of Sweet'N Low. After a year on Weight Watchers when I was nine, I truly have too many guilt issues to use real sugar. I stir the mixture. It takes less time to mix powder than granules of sugar — that's got to shave hours off my schedule. That's one of the first questions I plan on asking God: "How much time did I save by putting sweetener instead of sugar in my coffee?"

I grab my textbook and open to the chapter I should have read by now considering tomorrow night is class and my professor always gives quizzes on Fridays. This one is about flooring. Ugh. I'd much rather be scouring cookbooks for new recipes.

I glance around and eye the cookbook on the counter. It's a fun little Western cookbook that Dancy brought me back from Oklahoma after she went out there to help her older brother, Kale, and his new bride settle into their house. The cookbook has all kinds of Tex-Mex recipes and how to cook venison and fresh fish — stuff like that.

Wait. No. I can't get sidetracked. Back to the book at hand. I read about tile and actually come up with a good idea for the floor at Nick's. We should do a faux stone floor with fake cracks to give it that old-world Italy feel. I make a note of it. I wonder what Joe will think. . . .

Nancy pops into the kitchen by six thirty. "Early riser, huh?"

I give her a guarded smile. That kind of statement could be construed as a criticism. Night owls always think they're so cool.

She smiles and nods toward the coffee. "May I?"

"Of course!" I'm ashamed of myself for not offering.

"Cups?"

I point to the right cabinet. "Sweetener is in the cabinet above the coffeepot and there's half-and-half in the fridge."

She pours a cup. "Thanks, I drink it black."

Figures.

"You baking at six thirty?" Her sleepy brow goes up. "Should I be worried about you?"

"Those are thawing. Nick sells them." I shrug. "I guess Joe sells them now."

"I've never seen heart-shaped cinnamon rolls before."

I give her a quick glance, scrutinizing her comment. Is she mocking me?

"It was just an idea for Valentine's Day."

"Impressive." She grins. "Can you imagine

all the guys bringing those to girls at the office today?"

I grin back. "That's the general idea. Joe should be happy."

"Speak of the devil. He was a little grouchy yesterday. Not exactly like him." She squints over the lip of her cup, swallows, and cocks her head just a smidge. "You and Joe don't get along so well?"

"Sure we do." If she could hear my heart thunder in my chest every time the guy gets close, she wouldn't say such a thing. "He just . . . doesn't think I should be in charge of this project." I thump my textbook. "Still in school."

"Oh, wow. I see his point. It's a big project."

And I took her into my home. The ingrate.

"Nick agreed to it so that I can get a decent final grade."

"Risky of him to gamble the design on someone not quite a professional." She says this with a smile. But I'm not falling for it.

I square my shoulders and face off with her. Might as well get things straight right up front. "Well, I'm not completely inept at what I do. After all, your plans for the interior came straight out of ideas I proposed to Joe."

She grins. "Well, actually, not really."

"What do you mean?" They were almost identical to mine. Is she stealing my ideas now? My defenses go up and I'm sorely tempted to grab that cup from her hand and tell her to make her own coffee.

"Joe and Nick didn't discuss your ideas with me before I drew up the plans I showed you yesterday."

I stare at her a second without speaking. Because if I say a word, it will be to call her a liar.

"The good thing about that," she continues, "is that we know we're on the same page. Our ideas mesh."

Okay, I'll give her that. Even if I'm not altogether convinced.

"I have another idea." I stand up and slip a pan of rolls into the oven.

"Oh? Let's hear it."

"What do you think about faux stone flooring in the dining rooms?"

Her face smoothes into a reflective expression that I know means she's considering it. Picturing it in her head. "You mean with cracks and that feel of being on the sidewalk in Italy?"

I nod. "Something like that."

"I think it's perfect." She smiles a slow, beautiful smile, and as much as I'd like to hate her, I find myself liking her very much.

"Well, good then. Maybe we're on the same page after all."

An hour later, I leave her to her unpacking, carrying a basket containing four dozen warm, heart-shaped cinnamon rolls — minus one. I gave it to Nancy, who practically swooned after one bite. And three dozen of my stuffed sandwiches, which wouldn't fit in the basket, so I'm forced to pack them in a box.

I hail a cab for the short ride since my hands are full. Plus, I want the cinnamon rolls to stay as warm as possible.

The cabbie, a stocky balding man wearing a cap and a five o'clock shadow even though it's barely seven thirty in the morning, smiles. "Mmm. Whatever's in that big basket smells good. Reminds me of my mother's kitchen when I was a boy."

I smile back. How could I help it after a remark like that? I lift the cloth covering the enormous basket and hand him a cinnamon roll plus the fare and a tip before exiting the cab.

His eyes light up with surprise. "Hey, that's nice of ya, doll." And then he does something cabbies never do. He slams the car into park, even though it's illegal to double-park, and walks with me, opens the door, and tips his hat.

"Thanks," I say, truly meaning it. Four dozen huge cinnamon rolls (minus two) can get awfully heavy. Even on a short walk.

"You're a good girl. You married?"

My senses go on high alert until he continues. "You oughtta meet my boy, Dale. He's a nice one. Goes to church and everything."

Oh, good grief. But what are you going to say to a sweet cabbie when he carries your cinnamon rolls for you? "Sure, um, maybe sometime. Thanks again for the help. You have a wonderful day."

When I step inside, I feel everyone's eyes on me. I even hear a few whispers. "Freshly baked cinnamon rolls."

I swear, it's like being Santa Claus at an orphanage on Christmas Eve.

I'm beginning to feel claustrophobic, like a whale in a fish tank, when Joe strides across the room. My knees nearly buckle when he slips a warm, firm hand around my upper arm and leads me to the counter. He reaches for the basket as soon as I'm safe from the fray. "Let me take those." His smile has returned. I'm so glad. Apparently whatever was making him so grumpy has been resolved. "These smell good."

"Thanks."

"Four dozen?"

"Well, three dozen and ten. I gave one to

Nancy and one to the cabbie on the way over here."

He winks. "You're a good kid."

"Yeah, that's what the cabbie said, just before he asked me to date his son."

Laughter rumbles that beefy chest of his. I swear, Joe's all man. "You told him you have a boyfriend?"

"Of course not."

"That's the easiest way to get rid of unwelcome attention from a guy." He sends me a good-natured wink. "I should know. I get the brush-off like that all the time."

I'll just bet he does. But that's not the point right now. "I don't lie just to get rid of guys."

"Lie? What about you and the cop?"

A short, and might I add *bitter* laugh bursts from me in an unladylike fashion. "I haven't heard from Mark since a week ago last Monday, and that was our first date. Probably our only date."

I didn't mean to spill so much, but I'm feeling a little raw from it, to be honest, especially since it's Valentine's Day and once again I'm out in the cold alone.

"Joe!" one of the employees calls from the register. "The line won't move until those rolls get up here. People want them."

I grin. "Glad I'm good for something."

"You're good for a lot more than baking," Joe says. It's an odd thing to say, but I get his point. And my heart kicks into high gear. "And if Mark doesn't know that, he's more of a dope than I already thought he was in the first place."

You can't help but appreciate a guy like Joe, saying something like that. I mean, sure, I know he's just being Joe. Nice, polite, make-the-fat-girl-feel-better Joe, but still, it feels nice to be on his radar for a few minutes.

"Excuse me!" a testy female voice interrupts our conversation and Joe turns. "Can I please get some service? I'm going to be late for work."

"Sure." Joe sends me an apologetic look. "I have to go," he says warmly, then glances over my shoulder. "Your friends are already sitting in the dining room anyway. They're starting to look impatient."

"Oh?" I hadn't noticed. I turn, and sure enough, there they are. And by those grins, I'd say they apparently saw the exchange between Joe and me. They'll make more of it than it could possibly be, but maybe I'm in the mood for that today. It's better than hearing all about what my friends are doing with their romantic men on the most romantic day of the year.

I hurry over to them. "We ordered for you," Tabby says, smiling.

"Thanks." I drop into the wooden chair next to Dancy, where my latte awaits. My bag, carrying my textbook, notebook, and that Tex-Mex cookbook, thuds to the floor as I slip it from my shoulder.

"So, tell us about Joe." Tabby leans forward with a Cheshire-cat grin, her shoulders stretched in front and her elbows on the table.

"What about him?" I'm going to make them pay for it if they want to hear anything juicy from me.

"Don't play coy with us," Dancy growls. "Spill it before we call him over here and ask him if he likes your eyes."

They wouldn't. But it's enough for me to give in. It's not like there's anything to tell anyway. I relay everything except the last remark about me being good for a lot of things and Mark being a dope.

"Hmm." Tabby strokes her chin, detective-style. "Interesting how he just assumed Mark was your boyfriend."

"Yeah," I say, sarcasm kicking into full gear. "Interesting considering I had one date — and a daytime one at that. And we all know what that means."

They don't even pretend otherwise. A

daytime date is for guys who are just testing the waters before committing to a nighttime date. If Mark had been scheduled to work that night, it would have meant something different. Because daytime would have been the only time he could take me out. But since he was, in fact, off that night, took me on a daytime date anyway, and then never called . . . Well, there's no point in going on, is there?

"Who needs that dope anyway?" Tabby says. "What ever happened between you and Jeremy?"

I shrug. Jeremy is a guy who played an extra on Tabby's soap opera. He hit on me last year at a *Legacy of Life* cast party I attended with Tabby. "He was okay. I don't think I was his type, though."

A frown mars Tabby's face. "What do you mean?"

"He pretty much told me to lose weight." I grin. "And that was before I gained the last ten. Can you imagine spending a lifetime with him?"

Dancy sets her cup down. "What a creep."

"Guys like skinny," I say, shrugging again. "It's not their fault. Society conditions them for it."

"Okay, back to Joe. He doesn't seem to think there's anything wrong with you."

I follow her gaze and suck in a breath. "Tabs! You could have told me he was looking over here."

"And spoil the moment?"

"You've played in too many romantic scenes on that soap opera of yours." I roll my eyes.

"Maybe so, but I know a guy who's interested when I see one."

"You're crazy."

She opens her mouth to continue the fight, but her phone begins to sing "Home" by Chris Daughtry. "Hi, honey." Her eyes are bright, and she's suddenly gone breathless.

Dancy and I roll our eyes. She's obsessed with her new family. Don't get me wrong, we're thrilled for her. But *"Home"*?

But then her expression drops. "Oh, well. It's all right," she says, trying to be brave. "There's nothing we can do this late. We'll just spend the evening at home with the kids."

Dancy and I exchange frowns. "What is it, Tabby?" I whisper.

She holds up a shush finger. "I'll see you at home. Love you too. I know it's not your fault. I'm fine with this. We'll order in."

She hangs up a moment later.

"What happened?"

"Oh, it's nothing, really."

Dancy fishes in her purse and hands Tabby a tissue. "It's something, or you wouldn't be about to cry your eyes out."

"Our babysitter fell through for tonight."

A little gasp works through Dancy's chest and exits her mouth. "For your first Valentine's Day together? What happened?"

"Strep throat. And there's no one else we can call."

"Surely there's someone!"

I hate to state the obvious. "Uh, guys."

They don't seem to hear me. Dancy continues. "What about Freddie?"

A rueful smile tips Tabby's quivering lips. "David would never allow it. Freddie doesn't watch his mouth enough. Last time 'Uncle Freddie' watched the twins, Jeffy had to have his mouth washed out with soap four times in ten days before he stopped swearing, poor kid. So that's that."

"I'd offer . . ." Dancy begins.

"You're going to have a fabulous time with Jack. Maybe he'll propose."

Dancy shakes her head. "Too cliché."

"Guys!"

Finally, some attention. They both stare. "What's wrong, Laini?"

"Well, it might have escaped your notice that I don't happen to have a date for tonight — being that I'm single and all."

"We're sorry, Laini. We didn't mean to be insensitive."

"Oh, for goodness' sake." Sometimes those two . . . "Why didn't it occur to you that I'd be more than happy to stay with Jenn and Jeffy tonight so you and David can go have your romantic evening?"

Tabby's eyes light up for a second, then cloud again. "I can't ask you to do that! What if Mark comes through at the last minute?"

"Yeah, right. It's been ten days since I heard from him. What are the chances?"

Neither responds to the rhetorical question. I appreciate it, actually.

Dancy lifts her chin toward the counter, but there's no way I'm falling for it this time. "The hunky Italian might come through."

"Not a chance. And even if he did, how desperate would I be to go out last-minute on Valentine's Day? I'd much rather eat pizza and watch a kids' movie with the twins." I give Tabby a pleading look. "As a matter of fact, it would answer the question of what I should do tonight. And I'll have an answer if anyone asks what I did on Valentine's Day."

The girls laugh so I keep going.

"I'll just say, 'I couldn't accept a date, I was babysitting for my best friend's steptwins.' " I grin. "See how perfect it is? You would be saving me from humiliation. And you know the kids adore me."

"That's true." Tabby smiles. "You always bring them homemade brownies or cookies or something equally beyond my abilities."

"All right, then my Valentine's Day plans are set in stone."

"You girls need refills?"

I nearly jump out of my skin as Joe sneaks up behind me. "Geez, Joe."

"What?" He frowns. Great. The frown is back. "What'd I do?"

"Nothing, you just scared me to death, that's all."

"Sorry." He looks past me to Tabby and Dancy. "Can I get you anything?"

"No. We're good." Tabby stares at me. "How about you, Laini? Need anything?"

"No. Thanks anyway, Joe. I'm good." I hop up. "As a matter of fact, I have to do some studying."

I say good-bye to my pals, feeling good about my offer to sit with the twins. It'll be fun. I like them.

I can't help wondering if maybe I'll have some just like them one day. Kids of my own. The sound of my ticking biological clock drowns out all of the obnoxious sounds coming from the street as I head back to my apartment.

7

An evening with a couple of energetic seven-year-olds is two things: fun and exhausting. But one good thing about Tabby and David being married now is that they don't stay out late. A nice dinner and they're home by nine thirty. By ten, I'm hopping off the subway (even though David tried to give me cab money). I like the subway. I know it's weird. But it reminds me of Dad taking me to work with him during the summer when I was a kid. It was what we did together.

Shops are closing up, but people still clog the sidewalks. Of course there are a couple of clubs and restaurants open. I peek inside Pierre's, a little French restaurant, as I walk past. Next to the window, a man is on his knee, offering a ring to a stunned woman. I stop and stare. "Say yes," I whisper.

As though she really needs my prodding, she hesitates before reaching forward. Tears spring to my eyes and start to roll. I reach up to wipe them from my cheeks and that's when they notice me — the Peeping Tom. The woman says something to the would-be groom. He turns and scowls.

"I'm sorry," I say, even though there's no way they can hear me.

I move on. And my heart nearly stops. Coming toward me, utterly handsome in his uniform, is Mark Hall. He smiles as though he's genuinely glad to see me. "Laini! How are you?"

Lousy, I want to say. Lousy because you never called me, you jerk. Instead, I swallow my pride and smile. "Good. Just headed home."

"I'm sorry I haven't called."

"Oh. It's okay. Really, don't worry about it."

He falls into step beside me. "I wanted to call. Truly. But they put me on midnight shift for a few days to cover for a guy that broke his arm, and it lasted longer than I expected."

"You couldn't have called after you got home?" Oh, I could just kick myself for bringing that up. Why do I have to say what's on my mind all the time?

A completely apologetic expression stretches across his handsome face. "The schedule threw me for a loop. Working all night. Sleeping when I could and still doing everyday stuff like laundry. I felt half dead. I'm sorry."

"Don't worry about it." I pat his arm because it seems like the thing to do. "I forgive you."

His hand shoots up and covers mine. "I want to see you again." The intensity in his eyes convinces me.

"All right."

"How about Saturday night?" He grimaces. "No. You go to your mom's on weekends. I don't mind coming to Long Island for a date . . . if you don't mind."

Is he kidding?

"I don't mind. But I have to warn you — my mom is pretty against me dating a cop. She's got fear-of-death issues since my dad passed away."

He nods gravely. "I understand. Not everyone can be married to a man in law enforcement. It's a dangerous job. She's right to be concerned for her daughter."

Great. Mom's going to love that. "Call me tomorrow," I say, sliding my hand out of his. "I'll give you the address and we can decide on a time."

I watch his mouth as it spreads into a smile. Wow. He's really cute. Even cuter than I remembered.

"Do you want me to walk you home?"

I shake my head. "I'm sure you have a beat to walk or something."

Amusement covers his face. But not the kind that makes me feel mocked. It's more like delight. "I do have somewhere to be. If you're sure you'll be okay."

"I'll be fine. It's barely ten."

Reaching forward, he squeezes my shoulder. "Okay, I'll see you Saturday night, then. That's the day after tomorrow."

As if he really had to tell me.

When I walk in the door, I'm shocked to find all evidence that someone has just moved in swept away. There are no boxes, no packing bubbles or crates . . . nothing. Just a clean room. I would think I'd imagined the whole thing if not for the sound of someone singing in the shower. Off key, I might add. Which makes me feel better. I sing great.

I slip on a pair of lounge pants and a loose sweatshirt and head to the kitchen. I run water into the teakettle and set it on the stove. My mind is buzzing from the events of the day. I snatch up the phone and start to dial Tabby to thank her for inadvertently getting me a date, but then I realize newlyweds do not want to be interrupted on Valentine's Day after the kids are in bed. So I set the phone back in its cradle and slowly back away.

Nancy shows up wearing a white terry-cloth robe, her hair wrapped in a towel. She smiles. "Did you have a date tonight?"

I shake my head and use the excuse I'd planned (God bless the former babysitter and her strep throat).

Her eyes widen. "Really? I thought Joe was taking you out to dinner."

"Joe?" I laugh. "Why would he?"

A shrug lifts her very slender shoulders. "Just a hunch. Guess I was wrong."

"Slightly. Joe and I have never been like that."

"I see."

"So what did you do tonight?" I practically dare her to make me jealous. "Go out on a date?"

"No way. I've sworn off all guys for as long as I can stand it."

"For as long as you can stand it?"

I never noticed before, but her nose wrinkles when she grins. "Well, I'm not exactly a nun. Right now I'm getting over a pretty bad breakup. But eventually I'll need a man with big arms to sweep me off my feet."

As if to demonstrate, she drops into a chair at the table and props her feet up on the chair across from her.

You have to admire her spirit. And those toenails. Pedicured. *Figures.* "Who did your toenails?"

She wiggles her toes. "Me. I have a kit. Want me to do yours?"

"Really?"

"Sure. What are roomies for?" She stands. "Besides, after that cinnamon roll, I owe you."

Just wait until she gets a taste of my cheesecake.

Saturday morning when I get out of the cab, Mom greets me with a smile on her face. No, not that sad thanks-for-noticing-me smile. I mean, a genuine I'm-truly-not-depressed smile.

The blinds are pulled back and actual sunlight is bursting through the windows. If I had the guts I'd make a vampire crack, but better to leave well enough alone.

Only, another weird thing . . . There are bouquets all over the room. Gardenias on the table. Roses (roses?!) on the coffee table. And daisies, which happen to be my mom's favorite flower but are not in season in February.

"What's up with the flowers?"

Mom blushes. Is this an alien invasion? Mom doesn't blush. Or open blinds, or smile without a darn good reason. What is going on?

"Mom?"

She gives a nonchalant little wave. "Oh, those are knockoffs from the florist down the street."

"Aaron's Flowers?"

The blush deepens as she nods.

"They have flower knockoffs?" I frown. "You mean like Prada?" Tabby and Dancy wear the real Prada. I can't even afford the knockoffs.

But that's beside the point. The actual point is that my mother is buying flowers and turning my Addams family home of depression and darkness into a sunshiny Care Bears house. It can't be menopause. She went through that years ago.

"Ma?"

She turns to me with wide-eyed innocence. "Yes, darling?"

"Come on. Give it up. What's going on?"

The phone rings. She smiles with fake apology. "Excuse me, I need to get this."

"All right. But this isn't over. Be prepared to explain."

She waves me away.

I stare after her for a minute. She snatches up the phone and her face brightens even more — if that's possible.

Something doesn't add up here. Trudging up the steps to my room, I try to put two and two together. Flowers, smiles, light, phone calls. It almost sounds like . . . No, it can't be that.

No way. This woman can't even throw away the holey robe my dad got her twelve years ago. There is not a tiny chance that she's dating someone. Or is there? My mind goes back to the man a couple of weeks ago who couldn't keep his eyes off her. How weird is this? A little flirtation with the florist down the block and all of a sudden Mom's not depressed anymore. I mean, I'm glad and all, but still . . . it is a little weird.

In my bedroom, I pull out the outfit I plan to wear tonight. A long skirt — it's a few years old, but I like it — and a short denim jacket that I happen to think complements the whole thing. No matter what Dancy or Tabby think. They can be slaves to the fashion industry all they want. I'd rather make my own decisions.

Mom taps on my door a second later and walks right in without waiting for me to invite her. But then, she never has, so I wouldn't expect anything different.

"All settled in?" she asks, then notices the skirt. "Is that what you're wearing to church in the morning?"

"Date tonight."

Her eyebrows (which, by the way, are plucked for the first time in as many years as I can remember) shoot up. "You have a date?"

I nod, enjoying this feeling of control as she decides whether or not to go ahead and ask the questions or wait for me to offer the information. Normally, I'd take pity on her and just open up. But first I have some questions of my own.

"So, Ma," I say, sitting next to her on the bed. "What's with all the lights and flowers?"

She sucks in her lower lip and begins to nibble a little.

"Okay, seriously," I say. "Something is going on. Do you have a boyfriend?"

Her eyes go big, and I know I've hit on something. "Do you? Ma!"

"No. Not a boyfriend as in we're going steady or anything."

Aw, she said going steady. That's so cute. Okay, wait. Stop patronizing Mom and get some information.

"Who is he, Ma?"

Her face reddens considerably. "Aaron

Bland — and don't make any cracks about him being bland. Because he's not. He's very interesting. And nice. He goes to church with me. And he knows everything about flowers."

"Even the knockoffs of the brand names?" I snort at my own joke, but judging from her scowl, she's either not amused or she doesn't get it. My money is on the former.

"Anyway, you'll get a chance to meet him tomorrow at the church picnic."

"What do you mean, church picnic?"

"There's a picnic after service tomorrow," she says in a tone that clearly conveys that I should already know this information. And if I don't, well, that's not her fault.

Who is this woman?

"I really don't want to go to a picnic with a bunch of people I don't know, Ma."

She gives me a look, springs up from the bed, and stops at the door. "If I can do it, you can do it. Besides, we've been going there for a while. Maybe it's time to get involved."

And she just leaves! Just like that, before I can remind her that I'm thirty years old, I've been living on my own for years, and I do not have to go to her church picnic if I choose not to. I mean, really!

■ ■ ■ ■

By six o'clock I'm showered, dressed, and sitting at the kitchen table watching the clock.

"For goodness' sake, Elaine. Stop fidgeting."

My mother calls me Elaine from time to time. I don't like it, but what am I going to do? I can't even get out of going to a church picnic once she's made up her mind I'm going.

"I know. I'm just nervous. I haven't been on a real date in a long time." Other than the coffee date that turned into lunch. But this is a real, nighttime date. In a league all its own.

"I'm not sure I like the thought of you dating a police officer."

She says this as though it's the first time it's come up. In fact, we've had more than one discussion today regarding the wisdom — or the lack thereof — of dating a man in such a dangerous profession.

"It's a date, Ma. Not a wedding." My lips twist into a grin. "Unless he asks for a quick elopement."

A deep frown clues me in to the fact that Mom doesn't find my quip amusing. "Is it too much to ask that I not be mocked for caring whether or not your husband dies in his prime?"

Her lower lip trembles. And just like that the mother I know has returned to the premises. I'd better do something quick or the blinds will close, the flowers will fade, and the sun will disappear behind a cloud.

"Ma, believe me, I appreciate your concern." Even if I don't exactly sound sincere. "But it's way too premature to worry about what might happen *if* I marry a police officer and *if* he is harmed or killed in the line of duty. You can't play it safe to the point that you walk away from something good on the off chance you might get hurt."

The doorbell rings before she can respond. I frown. It's only six fifteen. Surely Mark's not the type to be this early.

Mom apparently notes my confusion. "That will be Aaron." She kisses me on the head as she walks past the table. "Good night."

"Wait a minute. You have a date too?"

"Is that so hard to believe?"

Yes, quite frankly. This is the woman who has cried herself to sleep for twelve years. How can she go from prolonged grief to "Hello, Good-Looking" just like that?

I stand and start to follow. "I'll walk you

to the door."

She stops and holds up her hand. "No. If you want to meet him, you may do so at church in the morning. I don't want to put a damper on my evening with Aaron by having him worry about whether he made a good impression or not."

I'm not crazy about sending my mom into the night with a man I've never met. But she's pretty resolute.

"All right," I say, "I won't meet him, then." But that doesn't mean I'm not going to take note of his appearance in case I have to identify him in a lineup.

When I hear the door close behind my mother I speed into the living room and peek behind the curtain, pulling it aside and watching her walk down the sidewalk with a man as tall as Lurch. My heart shoots into my throat and I have to think. I can't let her go off alone with this man. *Think, think,* Laini. I glance about. *Think.* In a flash I snatch up a flower from one of the vases and fling open the door. "Ma!"

The two of them continue down the sidewalk. "Mother!" I call, quickening my steps. Still no response from the pair. Fear rises in me as I imagine him holding a gun to her ribs and saying, "Don't say a word or I'll kill you and then her." I pick up my pace some more until I'm running after them.

"Mom!"

Finally she turns. She waits, her arms folded across her chest. But I don't have time to think about the belligerence in her body language. My mind is still reeling from the mini-nightmare I just endured.

"Didn't you hear me calling?" I can barely breathe. I really need to start working out.

Mom's face is dark, and anger flashes in her eyes. "We heard you, Elaine. I told Aaron to ignore you."

"Ma! I thought he was kidnapping you! The least you could have done was turn around and tell me to buzz off."

"Fine. Buzz off, then." She pauses and then adds, "Dear, I can assure you Aaron was not kidnapping me."

"Well, I can see that now!"

I turn to "Aaron," and his eyes twinkle. "It's okay, Lydia," he says to my mother. "Let's hear her out."

"All right." Mom glares. "What do you need that couldn't wait until later?"

"You . . . um" — I thrust the flower toward her — "you forgot your rose."

"My rose? Good grief." A huff escapes her. "Good-bye, young lady." Without so much as a glance at the flower, she whips around.

Aaron (if that's his real name) sends me a sympathetic smile before turning and offering Mom his arm. "I'll get her home safe and sound by eleven o'clock."

They leave me standing in the middle of the sidewalk, staring after them.

Eleven o'clock? What on earth do a couple of elderly people have to do until eleven o'clock? I can't give up just like that. Risking my mother's anger, I rush after them once more. "Wait."

"Elaine." Mom's tone holds warning. "I'm serious now. You let Aaron and me alone."

"Mom, I'm sorry, but I want to know where the two of you are headed."

"I am not sixteen years old! I don't have to answer to anyone. Least of all to my own child." Her frustration gives me pause, and for just a second I almost back down. Poor Aaron has this bewildered what-have-I-gotten-myself-into expression on his face.

"I know, Ma." I keep my tone even and innocent. "But what if something happens to me while you're out? How will I get in touch, since you don't have a cell phone?"

Her expression softens. "I suppose it would be all right. Just in case you get hurt or something." She turns to Aaron. "Do you mind?"

He shrugs. "Not at all." He reaches into

his pocket and hands me his card. "Here's my cell phone number."

I take the card but give him a dubious frown. "I'd still like to know where you're taking my mother."

"For goodness' sake," my mother huffs. "Fine, we're going to a seminar about insurance after fifty."

"Oh, that sounds . . . informative." I swallow hard. "It — um — lasts until eleven?"

Aaron chuckles. A manly chuckle that sort of reminds me of my dad. "I was planning to take her out for coffee or a bite to eat afterward." One eye drops in a wink. "Would that be okay?"

He's mocking me. "Fine."

Mom stares me down, and I know that as soon as she gets home, I'm in for it. "May we go now?" she says through clenched teeth.

I step back and nod. As I watch them go, a weird sense of nostalgia grips me. Aaron is much like my dad. Tall — six-one at least — twinkly kind eyes, good sense of humor. From behind, I would swear the couple walking away are my parents.

I wonder if Mom is trying to find a substitute. Poor Aaron if she is, because no one could possibly measure up to my dad.

8

Mark is sitting on the porch swing when I get back to the house.

"I knocked," he says. "No answer."

I glance past him to the door, which I didn't bother to close in my urgency to save my mother from kidnapping. In retrospect, the last ten minutes of my life seem ridiculous. But then, the last ten years seem that way too. "Why didn't you go in and stay warm?"

He grins. "It's called breaking and entering. Not a good way to start a relationship."

A sense of unrestrained power surges through me — don't ask me why. "Are we beginning a relationship?"

His hand is on the door and when he looks at me, I see only one side of his face in the shadow. Very Phantom of the Opera. "I hope so, Laini. I'm tired of being alone."

Now, what's a girl supposed to say to raw honesty like that? I fidget with my collar and duck past him, afraid he might grab me. If this were a movie, he'd do just that. Grab me as I brush by him, pull me close, look down into my face with intensity that takes away my voice and my breath. . . . Then he'd plant a John Wayne on me.

What's wrong with that? I could use a great kiss, honestly. I try to think back to the last time I was honest-to-goodness in a man's arms. Too long!

"Let me just get my coat." No sense belaboring the issue. And really, now that I think about it, a kiss can't happen until at least the next date. Because, technically, this is the first one.

I leave him in the living room while I rush to grab my coat from the kitchen chair where I left it earlier. Before joining him, I pause at the mirror in the hallway to check my appearance. Not bad. That jog in the cold gave my cheeks some color. And for once, my nose isn't beet red.

"So what did you have in mind for tonight?" I call, running my fingers through my curls. No matter how much gunk I use, these curls are almost impossible to tame. I'm seriously about to chop off my hair and buy a straightener.

He's looking my way as I reenter the living room. "I want to take you to meet someone."

Meet someone? "Like who?"

"You'll see when we get there."

"You know someone in Freeport? Or are we going somewhere else?"

He grins. "I spent a lot of time here growing up. I thought we'd find a bite to eat on Woodcleft and take a walk if it's not too cold."

"I'll bring my coat."

I love the Nautical Mile on Long Island. It's a tourist attraction in the summer, but in the winter it slows down to a nice easy pace. Less hectic. Far enough away from Manhattan that I can breathe.

I love Manhattan too. But if I could, I'd own a home on Long Island for the weekends and summers. I know it's an unlikely dream, but a person can't help the dreams in her heart, can she?

"So who is this person you want me to meet?" I say, taking Mark's arm like I'm some 1940s movie star.

He covers my hand with his, like he's a 1940s leading man and I pretend we're Humphrey Bogart and Lauren Bacall as we walk along past restaurants and nightspots and little novelty shops. We land in a tiny seafood shop, a little run-down and almost invisible in the midst of all the renovated hot spots.

"Seafood." I smile as he opens the door. "My favorite."

"Of course. You can't grow up here without loving seafood." He leans in close to me. So close I can feel his heat and smell his musky aftershave. My stomach does a flip-flop.

"I guess not."

"But that's not why I brought you here."

The place smells of clam chowder, fried shrimp, and the sea. I gather in a deep breath, a wonderful full breath that fills my senses. I'm not sure why I'm responding this way to a place like this. But I almost feel like I've come home.

The hostess appears, and her face lights up when she sees Mark. I'm almost jealous. Almost.

She's blonde and petite and cute as a button. She's also at least six months pregnant. She reaches around him and gives him a hug. "You did come by! Wait'll Pop sees you."

Pop?

The lovely girl turns to me, her enthusiasm infectious. "You've got to be Laini." Her pudgy little hand reaches for mine and gives it a shake. "Mark's told us all about you."

I turn to Mark. I know I look surprised, but I don't want to embarrass him, so I don't play off her words by stating the obvious, which is that he hasn't said a word about having family on Long Island — especially so close to where I live.

"Put a cork in it, Liz." Clearly Mark is shutting her up before she can reveal any more secrets.

"Sheesh, edgy, ain't he?" Grabbing a couple of menus, she motions for us to follow. "Pop kept number eighteen open just in case you showed up. I told him he should wait and see before saving our best table. But he knew you'd come."

Liz turns back to me over her shoulder as she walks without looking where she's going. "In case you're wondering, I'm his sister. Our pop owns this place. Our mom divorced him and lives in Brooklyn."

I can't help but laugh. "Thanks, Liz. I don't usually learn that much about a guy on a first date — not from his sister anyway."

She stops at a corner table and moves aside for us to sit. "Well, I didn't figure he said anything about us. You're the first date he's brought here in a long time."

I look across at Mark. A boyish grin curves his lips and he gives me a shrug of those incredible shoulders. This is a great guy. I think I actually might have hit the jackpot.

"Anyway, you two decide what you want." She turns to Mark. "I'll tell Pop you're here." *Here* sounds like "He-ah."

"So, this is your dad's place," I say. A statement of the obvious — just trying to break through this tension. It seems to work . . . a little. In the past few minutes, Mark has suddenly become the strong, silent type. But then, Liz didn't exactly give him much of a chance to speak, did she?

"Yeah, like I said, I spent a lot of time here growing up."

"How long have your parents been divorced?"

Absently fingering the checkered tablecloth, he keeps me in his sights. I like that, a guy who makes good eye contact. "At least twenty years. Dad moved to Long Island where his family is from, and Mom stayed in Brooklyn with hers."

"Did either of them remarry?" I know I'm being nosy, but these questions just seem like the natural progression of things today.

He shakes his head. "They're both too stubborn. No one else would put up with either of them."

"Mark! You made it!"

Mark's dad is an average-looking man, barely embarking on his senior years. Hard to tell if he's fifty or seventy, to tell you the truth. I don't detect much in the way of gray hair. One thing is clear: he adores his son.

Mark stands and the two men embrace. "Good to see you, Pop."

"Good to see you too, son. Been too long." Then he turns to me. "But if this is the reason, I don't blame you."

Mark slides back into his side of the booth while his dad ogles me and takes my hand. He steps close and presses my hand against his chest. "You're a vision, honey."

Feeling a little uncomfortable with this man. . . . I can see why Mark doesn't bring dates around to meet him. That's for sure.

Mark looks embarrassed. "This is Laini Sullivan, Pop."

Mark's dad leans forward and kisses my hand. I can't believe this guy!

"Hands off," Mark says. "She's with me." He sends me a wink. "I'm sure you've figured it out, but this is my dad, Carl Hall."

"Nice to meet you, Carl." Inwardly, I'm begging him to give me back my hand and stop creeping me out.

Thankfully, he does so and turns to Mark. I tune out their conversation and watch the two men.

I stare at Mark, whose features are so similar to his dad's that I picture him in thirty years or so, holding a young woman's hand, making her feel uncomfortable. Hmm. How far does this apple fall from the tree?

The food is perfect: shrimp scampi served in garlic butter, an enormous baked potato, crab cakes. I had to forgo the biscuits and dessert, which seemed to disappoint Mark's dad so much that I finally agreed to take home a large slice of chocolate fudge cake. Not that it took much persuading.

Carl and Liz walk us to the door. "You make sure you come back, you hear?" Carl says.

"I'll do my best." I'm not exactly one to promise when who knows if Mark will ever want to see me again? And if he doesn't, I'm not likely to waltz into this restaurant alone and order fish.

The temperature has taken a dive during the past two hours and a strong north wind creeps under my jacket pretty quickly.

Mark raises the collar of his bomber jacket as we step away from the warmth of the restaurant. Then he snatches my hand and pulls me along the sidewalk.

Hand-holding is permitted on a first date. By the time dinner is over, if you're still interested, a little finger-weaving is definitely acceptable. Especially through gloves. Who can feel a thing anyway?

He smiles down at me. "I thought maybe we'd walk a little, if it's okay with you."

What is he, nuts? It's like Antarctica out here! "Um, sure. I love to walk." Okay, it's official: I'm lying for a guy.

He tugs me closer to his side until I'm practically walking on his feet. "Warm enough?" he asks.

I nod. "Sure." But my chattering teeth give me away. I shrug. "I will be as soon as I get used to being outside."

An indulgent smile lifts his lips. "Let me get a cab. I'm not going to take a chance you might get sick all because of me."

I'm so grateful that by the time the cab stops and we slide into the backseat, I'm willing to snuggle close while Mark's arm encircles me — clearly a second- or third-date privilege, but in this case, I'll let it slide. I need the warmth.

By the time we arrive back at Mom's, I've finally thawed out. Mark opens the door but speaks to the cabbie before climbing out. "Wait for a sec, will you? I want to walk her to the door."

The guy points to the meter. "It's your money."

Mark's arm is firm around my shoulders as we walk. "I had a really nice time." His voice is sort of husky all of a sudden. I have a weird feeling he's going to move in for a kiss . . . and I don't care how cold I am, a kiss is not a negotiable option until the third date, and even then only if I really, really like the guy. I'm definitely not ready for Mark to make a move.

I smile as big as I can and stick out my hand. "Thanks for dinner, Mark. I had a great time."

A look of bewilderment, then amusement, flickers to his eyes. "Can I call you again?"

Is he kidding? *Play it cool, Laini.* I give a slight nod. "I'd like that."

"Okay, then." He gives my hand a squeeze. "I'll call. Don't forget your cake."

"Hmm?" My mind is still on the non-kiss when he presses a to-go box into my hand.

"Oh, yeah. Thank your dad again for me."

"Will do."

I watch him walk back down the sidewalk and return his wave as he slips into the cab.

Predictably, Mom is waiting up, sitting in the kitchen with a cup of tea and a *Soap Opera Digest.* She pretends she barely notices me as I float into the kitchen. "Oh, you're home." A nod toward the magazine. "Your friend Tabby is in this one. They're talking about her wedding to David."

"Really?" I take it from her and skim the

article. Tabby looks beautiful, pictured with David at a charity event for cancer patients. "That was a big night," I comment and head to the stove. I switch on the burner under the kettle.

Mom sips her tea. "Did you have a nice time?" Aww. She held out three whole minutes. I'm impressed.

"Wonderful. Joe's a great guy."

A frown squeezes Mom's brow. "Joe?"

I take in a sharp breath. Did I really say Joe?

"I meant Mark." I force a laugh. "I've been spending too much time at Nick's thinking about the renovations."

She gives me a dubious nod. "I see."

Does she? Because I'm not sure I see at all. How come, I finally start dating a great guy with a great family, and all I can think of is Joe Pantalone?

The next day is a quiet sort of day for me. I do indeed tag along with Mom when she goes to Community Family Church with Aaron. This time they sit together instead of flirting across the room.

I have to grin when I see Mom tapping her foot during a particularly upbeat song. Afterward, I suffer through a picnic at the park. A *picnic.* In New York. In the middle of February. I'm not sure who did the planning on that one, but all of us are shivering. But you know, one good thing about it is the picnic doesn't last long. Everyone's too cold. By three we're back home and Mom is relaxing by a cozy fire in the gas fireplace while I pack up and get ready to head back to the train.

I drop my duffel bag onto the living room floor. "My cab is on the way. I'll see you next Saturday."

"Oh, honey," Mom says, "about that."

"About what?"

"Next weekend." Her face has taken on that blush again.

"Ma," I say slowly and if I do say so, a little suspiciously, "what's going on next weekend that you don't want me coming home?"

"Oh, no. You can come if you want. It's just that . . . I won't be here."

"What are you saying?" I fold my arms across my chest and plant my feet. "Ma! Are you going away with Aaron for the weekend?"

Her face blanches and her eyes go wide. "Well, not like that! Pull your mind out of the gutter, young lady. Aaron is a fine Christian man and would never take advantage of a lonely widow."

Lonely widow?

I hold up my hands in surrender. "Okay, already. Sorry I brought it up, but you have to admit it was sort of a logical assumption. I mean, we don't even really know this guy."

"Correction," she says belligerently. "*You* don't even really know this guy. I happen to know him extremely well."

"Come on, Ma. How well can you know Aaron? You just started dating him."

"And how would you know that?" She lifts a narrow eyebrow. "You don't even live here and you never call."

How on earth did she turn this into a conversation about my neglect of her?

"So because I don't call you, I can't possibly know what's going on? Last week, you were depressed. The blinds were drawn and there were no flowers in the house. This week, you've turned into Holly Hobbie."

"You don't think I deserve a little happiness after all of my years alone?" Her lower lip trembles.

Oh, brother.

"Of course you deserve happiness. I just don't want to see you move so fast with a man you just met. Even if he does attend your church."

She pats the sofa beside her. "Let me tell you about Aaron."

Apparently we're going to have a woman-to-woman conversation. "Okay, sure." I sink onto the beige cushions.

"We met at the senior center a few months ago. His wife had just passed of diabetes."

"That's too bad."

She nods. "He's still very sad. He loved her like I loved your father."

"I'm sorry for his loss." I mean, what else can I honestly say? His loss is your gain? I absolutely *hate* this conversation. I should have just kept my mouth shut and imagined my lonely widowed mother spending an illicit weekend with the flower shop guy. Instead, I am once again made to feel like it's all my fault that bad things happen to good people.

She pats my hand and continues. "I was able to share my own grief with him, and together, we began to heal from our pain."

"Does this mean you'll start wearing the robe I bought for you?"

Oh my gosh, I don't believe I just said that. It really just flew out without a thought. I must have latent resentment about that robe.

She frowns. "What do you mean?"

Saved by the honking of a taxi. "Nothing. My cab is here. I have to go. Have fun next weekend."

It doesn't occur to me until I'm back in Manhattan trudging up the steps to my apartment that I never did find out where my mother is going with the widower Aaron Bland. I'll definitely have to call her this week. I wonder if that was her plan in the first place.

9

There are approximately one hundred students in my commercial design class. And I'm almost positive I'm the only one who got a D on my midterm. I swallow back tears of frustration, tears of self-pity as the professor stands in front flashing sparkling white teeth that I just know are in contact with whitening strips on a regular basis. I'll bet he has zero enamel left. He's gushing about how well ninety percent of the class has done on the test. I'd like to sink into my seat, but I'm about as far down as I can go.

Jazz is sitting next to me. I show her my paper and receive the expected look of pity. She tries to hide her solid B, but I looked before she could cover it. Later, we walk out of the class together. "Well," she says, "our final is only one quarter bookwork. And the grade we get from the redesign at Nick's will be spectacular."

I shrug, wishing for all I'm worth that just once I could get a B in this class. I'm tired of Cs and Ds. It's embarrassing.

"Why don't you come to yoga class with me?"

I shake my head. I mean, have I ever once accepted an invitation to yoga class? You'd think she'd give up. "I'm more in the mood to eat than exercise. Besides, I have a rotten headache."

"You sure? Yoga will clear your mind and get rid of stress. It might help the headache."

I grin. "So will cheesecake. Believe me, I know."

She rolls her eyes and slings her bag over her shoulder. "I'll call you later. Don't eat too much cheesecake — the sugar will make you sick."

"You'd be surprised how much sugar my system can take. I've trained it that way."

Her laughter lingers as she descends the steps of the hall.

I walk the few blocks to the subway station and shove my way onto the train with hundreds of others. The smells of New York public transit — urine, unwashed bodies, and perfumes — combine to assault my already churning stomach. My head isn't doing great either, and by the time I reach my stop I'm really hurting.

Home is the only thing on my mind until I realize how badly I really do need that cheesecake. Migraine and all. I turn and walk the block to Nick's. Glancing at my watch, I realize it's dangerously close to time for Joe to lock up, but again, it's worth the risk for that cheesecake. At times like this I desperately miss my friends. Normally, I'd grab a whole cheesecake, bring it home, and we'd sit around the kitchen table talking about my wretched day. Or the last two wretched hours anyway.

Joe is just at the door with the key when I show up. I feel like a puppy pressing my nose to the glass when he spots me.

His eyebrows shoot up in question and he unlocks the door.

"What are you doing out alone after dark?"

"I have class on Monday night. I thought you knew that."

"Nope. Didn't know. You sure it's a good idea for you to be walking alone this time of night?"

"My train stops only a couple of blocks from the apartment."

He ushers me in and locks the door behind us. "Well, I don't think it's a good idea. It's dangerous out there."

I shrug, eyeing the cheesecake he has yet

to take out of the glass case and put away for the night. "A girl's gotta do what a girl's gotta do, Joe. And that's the only time my class is offered."

He grunts. "Sit down and I'll get you some of that."

"Some of what?" There are at least six different desserts in that case.

"Please, you don't think I know what you like?"

I grin. Already my headache is easing up. "Prove it."

He grins back. "Go sit down and I will."

"You sure you don't mind? I know you're probably ready to get out of here."

"It's okay. I can't leave 'til Brandon finishes cleaning up in the back."

I wait, my head aching, while he goes back to the kitchen. He returns soon and slides a cake plate onto the table in front of me. "Cheesecake with raspberry swirl. A dollop of whipped cream on top."

"Bravo!"

"Here. I got you some milk too. And a couple of aspirin. Your eyes look like you got a headache."

His warm hand presses against mine as he hands me the aspirin. Gratefully, I swallow them down with a swig of creamy milk. "Thanks, Joe. You're a lifesaver."

He pulls a chair around and sits. "So, you want to talk about it?"

I slip a bite of cheesecake into my mouth. "I got a D on my test."

"That's not so good." He eyes my cake.

"Tell me about it. I'm a terrible test taker. I think I have about the lowest grade point average you can possibly have and still be considered a student in good standing." I shrug. "I think I really might be color blind." Blinking back tears, I meet his sympathetic gaze. "How can an interior designer be color blind?"

"Maybe you're not. Maybe you just need to do eye exercises."

I stop. Stare. "What, you mean like build up my color sensory muscles?" The thought strikes me as funny and I grin.

"Hey, go ahead and laugh. I was just trying to help." His gaze wanders to my cheesecake.

I shove the plate toward him. "Here, have a bite."

"Thanks. I haven't had time to eat all day."

I make a mental note to add an extra cinnamon roll in the morning and make sure he gets it.

"That's not so good," I say, mimicking his comment about my grade. "Breakfast is the most important meal of the day."

"Now you sound like my nana."

"Smart woman."

He snorts. "If she's so smart, how come she's pushing me to marry Nancy?"

My stomach lurches from the combination of cheesecake, milk, aspirin, and the image of Nancy in a bridal gown. I make a run for the bathroom and lose the entire contents of my stomach.

Ten minutes later, I rinse out my mouth and stare into the mirror. I'm such a pathetic loser. How can I possibly go back to the dining room and face Joe? At least I didn't throw up all over his table. I've been in the bathroom awhile, but my stomach is still queasy and I don't want to risk another sprint to the toilet. But I'm not expecting the knock at the door.

"Yes?" I call, as if I don't know who's standing on the other side.

"You okay?"

"Yeah. Just embarrassed."

"Can I come in?"

"It's open. I didn't have time to lock it."

He doesn't hesitate. As soon as he steps inside, he yanks a handful of paper towels from the dispenser and wets them down. He hands them to me. "Your face is white as my apron."

I press the towels gratefully over my aching eyes. "Thanks."

"You ready for me to walk you home?" he asks softly. "Or should you take a cab? I'll take you either way." He steps back as I toss the paper towels into the garbage can.

I'd love to bravely refuse his gesture of gallantry, as I'm sure Dancy or Tabby would do, but the words won't leave my mouth. Besides, I'm too sick to see myself home. I need someone to take care of me. And why do girls always feel like they have to be so independent? God made us to enjoy a man's strength. I just know He did. Otherwise, why would I enjoy it so much that Joe is concerned about me?

I scan his strong face. Nose that takes up much of his face, but isn't too big. Dark eyes that take in everything, including, apparently, the fact that I love raspberry swirl cheesecake and the look in my eyes when I'm suffering from a sick headache.

"Thanks, Joe. I appreciate it. And I think the walk might do me good."

"Okay. The guys are locking up for me. So whenever you're ready, we can go."

Minutes later, I'm walking side by side with Joe. It's only around nine o'clock, so there are still a lot of people on the street. Even on Monday night. My head is swimming — and my stomach . . . Let's just say

I'm not a hundred percent sure I'm going to make it home without an encore of my performance in Nick's ladies' room.

Joe slips his arm around my shoulders. "You doing okay?"

"Not so good," I say wryly. "I think maybe I should get a cab, Joe."

"Look, you come up to my place and wait this thing out."

"What? I couldn't do that."

"You afraid of anything improper? Because let me tell you, a sick woman isn't that much of a turn-on. Plus, you know I go to church."

Even in my condition, I can see the ridiculousness of his assumption. "I don't think you're going to try to make a move on me. I just don't want to put you out." Oh, but fire darts are shooting into my head and my stomach is getting sicker with each step. I stop midstep. "Okay, Joe. I'm begging you. Get me somewhere I can lie down. I think I'm dying."

"Come on," he says. His tone is soothing, melodic. The streetlights and the lights from the store and restaurants are nearly blinding me. I close my eyes as he holds me close and leads me the few steps back to Nick's place. Joe took over Nick's apartment above the coffee shop when Nick moved to L.A.

By the time we reach the steps, my vision has gone black and spotty and I'm having trouble forming coherent sentences.

Joe shakes his head and sweeps me into his Popeye arms. "Am I too heavy?" I whisper, resting my head on his shoulder.

"You're a feather," he whispers back. I know it's not true, but I let him lie to me. I'm too sick to argue.

My eyes flutter open to the sight of sunlight slipping through the shutters. It doesn't take any time at all to remember where I am. Joe took care of me last night. He tucked me into his bed, and I remember a warm kiss to my forehead. And that's all until this moment.

I push back the covers — a lovely off-white with a pattern of little roses. One pant leg is up around my calf. I push it down and pad barefoot to the door. My insides are churning. Nerves. It's my first time sleeping in a man's bed with or without him. (My moral code says sex comes after marriage, and that's ironclad.)

I open the door to the sound of snoring. Joe's, I presume.

Tiptoeing into the living room, I see Joe curled up on a worn-out blue recliner. His blanket has slipped onto the floor and he's shivering. In a rush of sympathy, I pick up the blanket and spread it over him.

Joe looks — well — he looks really good. His face is gentle, like it was last night. He looks like the kind of guy who would pay his elderly mother's rent and take her to the grocery store. The kind who would bring home Chinese food at the end of a long day and rub his wife's feet after dinner. Who knows if that's really the case, but I find the fantasy too appealing to surrender.

His dark hair falls just over his ears, begging me to reach out — just like in a romance novel or a love story on TV — and brush it away. But of course I resist. Instead, I force my gaze from the sight. I think I'll rummage around the kitchen and find some coffee to brew.

As I start to walk away, Joe's warm hand catches mine. He stares up at me silently, his eyes squinting against the light. "Thank you," he says, fingering the blanket with his other hand. "I was freezing."

"You were snoring." I smile. He's still holding my hand.

"I was freezing in my sleep and you saved me." He tugs me until I'm sitting on the arm of his chair. "I guess that makes you my hero."

"One good turn deserves another." I can't

catch my breath.

"That's an old-fashioned phrase." He smiles and reaches up with his other hand to tuck a curl behind my ear.

My cheeks warm, but I shrug off the embarrassment. "What can I say? I guess I'm just an old-fashioned girl."

"Nothing wrong with that."

A knock at the door pulls us from the conversation.

"I'll get that," he says, untangling his fingers from mine. I take the hint and stand up.

I wait, feeling like maybe I should run back to the bedroom so that whoever is at the door won't see me and assume the worst. But not only isn't there time, the thought of hiding away like I've done something wrong doesn't sit well with me. So I stand there, staring at the door while Joe answers it, barefoot, wearing a pair of men's lounge pajamas and a sleeveless undershirt.

Nancy's standing at the door. "It's about time, Joey. For crying out loud. It's raining out here."

"You should have called." He moves aside and allows her to enter.

"I told you I'd bring my roomie some clothes today, didn't I?" With that, she focuses on me. "You feeling better? Joe was awfully worried about you last night."

My face feels hot and splotchy. "Much better, thanks."

She hands me a gym bag. "I picked out an outfit and hair stuff and makeup. I figured you might not have time to go home before your breakfast with your friends."

My eyes bug out. "I forgot about that. What time is it?"

"Six thirty."

I breathe a little. Breakfast isn't until eight so I have plenty of time. I turn to Joe. "May I use your shower?" He nods and points me in the right direction.

Twenty minutes later, I've showered, towel-dried my hair, pulled it into a ponytail, and dressed in the jeans and hoodie Nancy brought.

There's a fresh cup of coffee sitting on the kitchen table with a note next to it. "Laini, help yourself. I'm using the shower in the coffee shop. See you in a few minutes. Joe."

A cozy feeling washes over me.

I always wanted a guy who leaves notes.

10

Tabby stares at me incredulously as I relay my last few days to my two best friends over a steaming latte.

"So, basically," she says, shaking her head, "in the last four days, you've had dinner with a great-looking cop in his dad's seafood restaurant on Long Island" — she takes a breath — "then had another great guy . . ." She stops a second and her eyes rest on Joe. "Correction, great, and *great-looking,* carry you up to his apartment because you were too sick to walk."

"Yes. That pretty much sums it up."

"And he put you to bed without trying anything."

"Right again. But in his defense, I've looked better." A weak joke that Tabby doesn't bite at.

"Laini! Obviously the best thing that ever happened to you was having Dancy and me move out."

Dancy frowns. She is definitely not a morning person. "I don't see what one has to do with the other. She met Joe before we moved out."

"Yes, but if we'd been home, she would have called as soon as she got that D, and you or I would have trudged down to Nick's, bought a cheesecake, and met her at the subway station."

They have no idea how those words bring an ache to my heart.

"Well, poor Joe probably thought it was either carry me to his apartment or carry me all the way to ours — mine."

"Don't slam yourself, Laini," Dancy growls in her I-haven't-had-enough-coffee-yet tone. "You look just like a redheaded Meg Ryan and you know it."

Joe shows up then and gives us each a warm cinnamon roll. "On the house," he says and sends me a wink that burns my cheeks.

"Don't you think Laini looks like a redheaded Meg Ryan?"

I can*not* believe Dancy just said that.

Joe grins. "Prettier. And has a better walk." And then he's gone.

"A better walk?" Now I'm confused.

Dancy sinks her fork into the warm, gooey frosting. "She walks like a boy trying to look macho. No grace whatsoever."

I shrug and stare at my own roll, trying to decide if I should wait and start my diet tomorrow. If so, I can eat this without guilt. Otherwise, I'll be cheating on my diet, and that will most definitely induce a measure of unease while I devour it. "I've never noticed."

"How about you, Tabs? You're being awfully quiet. You okay?"

The sound of Dancy's concern pulls me away from the breakfast treat. Tabby's face is white.

"Are you sick?" I ask. "Do you have a migraine?"

She shakes her head. "It's not a migraine." And then Tabby looks from one to the other of us, reaches out, and takes each of our hands. "I'm going to be a mother." Her eyes are misty.

I'm around the table in a flash, sliding into the chair next to her and grabbing my pregnant friend in my arms. "Oh, Tabby. How perfect."

Dancy's grinning. "The two of you sure didn't waste any time, did you?"

Laughter mixes with Tabby's tears and gurgles out of her. "We are praying for at least two or three more. And I'm not exactly getting any younger."

"Hey!" Dancy tosses a napkin at her, which Tabby deflects easily. "I'm exactly the same age as you are, and I'm definitely younger today than I was yesterday."

A grin replaces the sickly look on Tabby's face. "Sorry."

Dancy slips around the table and hugs Tabby. "I can't wait to be Auntie Dancy again." She stops and turns a serious gaze on our little mother-to-be. "How do Jenn and Jeffy feel about the new baby?"

"We're telling them tonight. I just found out myself. Yesterday."

"Is David ecstatic?" I ask. I can't help but imagine the day I carry a child inside me.

Tabby's expression softens. She's absolutely glowing. "I've never seen a man so happy. And to think I put that smile on his face." Her eyes are shining as she looks from one of us to the other. "And I have another announcement." She grins. "I'm quitting work."

"What?"

Dancy is a huge fan of *Legacy of Life* and particularly the relationship between Tabby and her on-screen love, Trey. "What's going to happen to Felicia?"

I toss out a rueful smile. "Not to mention her evil twin."

Tabby laughs. "You do know I'm not

really Felicia Fontaine, right? She's just a character I play."

Dancy sticks out her tongue. "I know. But what about the story line? I mean, with the twins' characters just leaving for boarding school." (A necessary plot revision since David decided not to renew Jenn's and Jeffy's contracts.) "Isn't that going to be difficult for the writers?"

"I'll finish up my contract, which is only another three months anyway. We've been in negotiations. And now we won't have to worry about it anymore. They can wrap up my story line while I'm still there and that's that."

I'm in awe. Truly. Tabby gets to be a full-time mommy.

Dancy downs the last of her coffee. "I have to get to work. All this ticking is about to make me go deaf anyway."

Tabby frowns in confusion. But I know exactly what Dancy means. I swig my own coffee down and stand too. "Me too. I have to bake rolls and stuffed sandwiches today. And the sound of all that ticking is definitely distracting me from my goals for the day."

"What ticking are you two talking about?" Then her eyes go wide with understanding. She grins. "Of course. Biological clocks."

I bend and peck her cheek.

"Get some rest," I say. "I'll give you a call tomorrow."

She nods and takes my hand. "I have a feeling you're about to be off the market." Looking past me, she nods toward Joe. "My money is on that guy."

Dancy follows my example and kisses Tabby's cheek too. "At least she has two to choose from."

"Oh, sure. They're just waiting around for me to decide which one to choose. I've never even had a date with Joe. And only one and a half with Mark. Let's not jump the gun."

But I have to admit, I'm feeling a little smug as I head for the door while Dancy and Tabby finish up their good-byes. I glance around to tell Joe good-bye, but he's busy with customers and doesn't notice me. My stomach drops in disappointment, but to go up to the counter would be too obvious, so I turn away and shuffle across the floor, trying to make the trip across the room last as long as possible. The sound of my name on Joe's lips halts my steps just as I reach the door. "Laini, wait!"

My heart rushes as I turn.

Wiping his hands on his apron, Joe seems a little out of breath as he reaches me. His gaze peruses my face. "You — uh — feeling okay now? No headache?"

I smile. "Yeah, it was a quick one this time. Thanks for everything, Joe. I don't know what I'd have done without you last night."

He rubs the back of his neck. "I just . . . I don't want you to think anything of it. I'd have done it for anyone."

Humiliation surges through me. I get it. He's trying to tell me not to make more of the encounter than there was. So much for Joe being on the menu. Tabby is so wrong about his interest in me.

"Trust me, I didn't think you had any ulterior motives. You were just being a nice guy. And I truly do appreciate it." I clear my throat. "Well, I have rolls to make."

"Oh, good. We're about out."

"Okay. I'll deliver them fresh tomorrow." I turn and push the door.

"Laini, wait a second." He looks down at his feet. "I was just wondering if maybe you'd want to go out with me sometime."

I can't tell you the relief I feel. As a matter of fact, I'm too relieved to feel self-conscious. "Sure."

His face brightens. "That's good. Real good. Okay. I'll call you."

My heart is light as I walk the two blocks to my apartment. This has already been a good day. Waking up to Joe, Tabby's news, and the promise of a date with a good-looking Italian man.

And it's only nine o'clock in the morning.

I can't wait to see what the rest of the day brings.

I can't believe it. My stove is on the blink. My first instinct is to call Dancy. But that turns out to be a dead end. "I'm so sorry, Laini. Any other day I'd be happy to have you come to the condo, but the exterminators are there. Roaches. I think they must have come in in a shopping bag or something." I hear her shudder. "I hate those things. Anyway, it wouldn't be safe to cook in the kitchen for a few more hours."

I assure her it's no problem and consider my other options. I don't want to bother Tabby because she's getting ready to tell the twins about the baby.

I'm so desperate, I even consider calling Joe. But that would just be too awkward.

Reluctantly, I pick up the phone and call my mom. Looks like I'm in for a subway ride to Penn Station and a forty-minute train ride, then a cab ride to Mom's.

"I'm glad you came," Mom says when I pull up in the taxi two hours later. "Here, let me help you with that." She takes some of the bags from my hands and leaves me with the rest.

I pay the driver and follow my mom into the kitchen.

"Thanks so much, Ma. The super is supposed to get my stove fixed in a couple of days. So hopefully this will be the last time I have to impose."

"Honey, it's no imposition. It's my pleasure."

"How's Aaron?"

Her face flushes. "He's well. Thank you for asking. As a matter of fact, he's coming for dinner tonight, so you'll have a chance to get to know him better."

"You're cooking for him? Will you need the oven?"

"No. Don't even worry about it. I'll be cooking on the stove." She sends me a wink. Weird. "Aaron has been craving sausage and kraut lately, and I promised to make it for him."

Sausage and kraut. Okay, this is a meal I'm not looking forward to at all.

Mom swats me on the shoulder. "Don't frown. You'll get wrinkles. You don't have to eat it if you don't want to."

"Good."

"I'll leave you to your baking. You know where everything is."

Surprise jolts through me. The thing is, my mom loves her kitchen, and she's not completely comfortable with anyone rummaging around in her cabinets. Any time I cook anything she gets out all my ingredients, spoons, mixing bowls, and pans. My mom is definitely changing into someone I don't recognize. Or maybe I do. Maybe she's becoming the woman she was before Dad died.

And maybe I should be grateful to a certain widower named Aaron who fills my mother's house with flowers and her heart with joy.

There are certain childhood memories that come back to me from time to time in the form of nostalgia. Things like spaghetti night that rolled around once a month from as far back as I can remember. It was the only time Mom left the kitchen and allowed my dad to take over a meal. Mom stayed out and I was allowed to help. I don't remember whether or not the spaghetti was truly any good. But my time with Dad was delicious. During dinner, Dad's rules applied. Laughter, funny stories, and noodle-slurping reigned supreme. Back then, Mom's eyes smiled. Last night I dreamed about them.

My eyelids, the so-called windows to my soul, lift and I glance around the darkened room. Dawn hasn't even broken. It's this time of day when I can never tell if it's midnight or four in the morning. My gaze rests on the nightstand clock: 4:30. Time to haul it out of bed and get ready to deliver my rolls and stuffed sandwiches to Joe.

I push back the covers, shove down the PJ legs that always insist on bunching up around my knees while I sleep, and stand, pulling the quilt up over the mattress.

I gather my things for my shower and as I open the door, another wave of nostalgia hits me. The sound of my mom clanging pans and spoons in the kitchen. The sounds of childhood, but more than that . . . she's humming. No — wait. My mother is *singing.* "Blessed assurance, Jesus is mine . . ."

Her voice is beautiful. I'd forgotten. Mom always sang while she cooked. Dad would sneak into the hall and hide, so he could listen without being caught. Because once she knew anyone was listening, she clammed up.

My throat tightens as I walk quietly down the hall to the bathroom. The water steams over me along with a sense of bewildered optimism. My mother is changing.

Last night, our dinner with Aaron was

pleasant enough. Mom enjoyed his company, I could tell, but I wouldn't say she's anywhere close to being in love. I mean, well, maybe. She did smile (with her eyes), when he complimented her sausage and kraut. And again when he ate two slices of peach pie à la mode.

By the time I finish upstairs and join Mom in the kitchen, she's quietly standing over the stove, dishing up breakfast.

"I heard you singing." I take the plate she offers and head to the table.

"Oh? I didn't realize I was."

She touches the collar of her robe — still the threadbare chenille my dad bought her, so I guess she's not completely ready to let him go. For the first time in years, I'm actually fine with her wearing that robe.

"Breakfast casserole." I slide my fork into the egg, sausage, and cheese dish. My mother never met a low-fat cheese she could abide, so it's all fat, all the time. And oh-so-yummy.

Mom sits across from me and smiles. "I know it's your favorite."

My radar kicks in as I swallow my first bite. Is she buttering me up for something? I catch her gaze. "Everything okay, Mom?"

"Of course. Why would you ask?"

"Making breakfast casserole at five thirty

in the morning, singing hymns . . . What's going on?"

She blushes. "Well, I wasn't planning to tell you like this, but Aaron has asked me to marry him."

I laugh. "I bet you gave him a good piece of your mind."

She doesn't crack a smile. "Actually, I said yes."

I lose my grip on the fork and it clatters against the plate. "You what?"

"I've accepted his proposal."

"Ma! For crying out loud. You hardly know the guy."

Her lips tip slightly. "I only knew your father two weeks before we married. And I think you'll agree that worked out pretty well for over twenty years."

I'm speechless. I mean, I knew about my parents, but for her to throw that back in my face as an excuse to rush into marriage . . . "Are you sure you're not just over-romanticizing this thing with Aaron? I mean, what are the chances of love at first sight happening twice in one lifetime?"

"I don't know how it happened twice, Elaine. But it has and I'm grateful."

Anger shoots through me. How can she sit there, wearing my dad's robe, and talk about falling in love with another man? A man whose bed she'll be sleeping in. Or . . . I gasp. "Mom. He's not moving in here, is he?"

A scowl twists her face. "Of course not. We're selling his house and will buy a small house of our own."

I suppose that means she'll sell this house too. "Sounds like you have it all worked out." I push back my plate. Who can eat?

The right thing to do, of course, is to walk around the table, hug my mom, kiss her cheek, and congratulate her. So I do precisely that, although I admit I'm fighting back tears.

Mom rises to her feet and gathers me close. "You'll see. Aaron is a wonderful man. He's not taking your father's place."

"I know." I mean, goodness gracious. I'm not six. "Well, my cab will be here any time, so I have to grab my stuff."

I'm a popular gal on the train ride back to Manhattan. Even cold, my baked goods smell wonderful. Good thing for me I'm in a sour mood. Otherwise, I'd probably give away half my hard work to the commuters who are staring at me like hungry wolves at a flock of sheep.

But like I said, I've had a lousy morning and I'm not in the mood to share. This is the second day in a row that has started off great and then plunged into disappointment. I might just stay in bed all day tomorrow.

11

I don't understand Italian, but it doesn't take a genius to figure out that the angry voices shaking the walls outside Joe's office are not reciting nursery rhymes.

"I wouldn't go in there if I were you." The counter boy looks at me wide-eyed and positively trembling. "Frankie Pantalone is in there."

"Oh. You mean Nick's brother?"

"Yeah, otherwise known as Joe's dad."

"What are they yelling about?"

Brandon gives a shrug. "I'm not sure. I forgot to learn Italian on the way to work today."

"Wise guy."

"We'll get the permits." Joe's muffled growl slides through the door. Finally some English.

Another man's voice shouts in Italian and the door flies open. I jump back. A tall, thick-chested man wearing an impeccable suit that I know cost at least three grand thunders out. He barely gives me a glance as he sweeps past. "I'll be in the car, Mama. You talk some sense into the boy."

Mama?

I peek inside the office. Joe is frowning after the man. An elderly woman steps up behind Joe and places a hand on his shoulder. His face softens and he turns. He lifts her hand to his lips. "It's okay, Nana. It'll all work out."

"You listen to your papa, Joseph Pantalone. He is good man."

And then it's as if Joe remembers seeing me from the corner of his eye, because he turns to me, slips his arm about his grandmother, and walks her forward.

"Laini, I'd like you to meet my nana. Cecelia Pantalone. Nana, this is the girl I told you about."

He told his grandma about me? Pleasure slides through me like a warm river of rich honey. I reach forward to take her hand. "It's a pleasure to meet you, ma'am."

I wait for her to slide her wrinkly, cold hand into mine, but she snubs me! She gives me a haughty perusal. When her gaze takes in my hair, she actually sneers. Sneers! Like her gray hair is better than my red? And what's that grunt as she takes in my figure?

The woman weighs two hundred pounds if she weighs an ounce.

Slowly, I lower my hand and hide it behind my back. I've never been so insulted.

"I go now," Cecelia says to Joe. "You listen to your papa. It is the right thing to let him help."

She gives me another unflattering once-over and brushes past.

Joe tosses me an apologetic glance and squeezes my elbow as he follows her. "I'll be right back."

"Right back" turns out to be fifteen minutes later. I settle into my booth with a white chocolate latte and pretend interest in the *Times* that was left on the table by the previous customer.

Joe slams into the coffee shop, anger splashed across his face and storming in his brown eyes. He stomps toward the counter, then seems to remember me and detours. "Thank you for bringing in the new rolls and the rest of the stuff."

"My pleasure. I'm just glad they sell so well for you." I probably don't need to state the obvious, but I'm not great at small talk.

"Be sure to stop by my office on your way out and I'll cut you a check."

Deflated, I take a sip of my latte, thus preventing my need to speak. But I do have to swallow, I suppose. And Joe seems to be waiting for an answer. "Actually, I'm ready to go now. I have a class tonight I have to study for."

"You walking home from the subway tonight like the other night?"

I nod. "Same class. Monday, Wednesday, and Friday."

"You didn't mention that you do it three times a week."

"It never occurred to me that I might need to give you my schedule."

He gives me something of a bewildered frown.

"Sorry," I mutter. "It's been a rotten couple of days."

"Tell me about it."

"You want to join me for a latte?" I ask him with uncharacteristic boldness.

He hesitates and I feel ridiculous. Is he actually trying to figure out a way to let me down easy?

Then just like that, he nods. His face seems to relax for the first time since I arrived. "I'll be back."

And this time he is. A couple of minutes later he returns with his own steaming cup of regular coffee.

He takes the seat across from me and inclines his head.

"Your nana seems nice." Why do people lie about the obvious? His brow goes skyward and I grin.

A chuckle rumbles his chest. "What can I say about Nana? She has her days of niceness, but today wasn't one of them. So let me apologize for her not-so-niceness to you. I assure you it wasn't personal."

Oh, yeah? It felt personal.

"It was more about me than you. She's been on me about finding a nice Italian girl and settling down. I told you, she's been trying to get me interested in Nancy since we were kids."

I feel my claws unsheathing. If she wants a fight . . .

Joe shrugs. "Let's not talk about her anymore." He sips his coffee. "So, tell me about your rotten day."

I sigh and launch into the tale of my confusing day. All about my mom. How she's been in a state of grief and depression for twelve years and all of a sudden she's singing hymns and smiling with her eyes and letting light from the sun into the house. I've always wanted my mom to find the silver lining in life. But there was no transition. No time for adjustment. Not for me anyway. Ma knows how I hate change. Couldn't she have sort of eased me into this new romance of hers?

I sit back when I'm done, expecting, oh, I don't know, some sort of validation of my feelings. I mean, he's the one who asked, right? So why is he giving me that idiotic boy-grin? "I'm not sure I understand the problem. Well, except the part about the oven going out. That was inconvenient. Don't you want your mom humming and letting in the light?"

"But what about the flowers and Aaron?"

"Isn't she entitled to a little happiness?"

I stare at him. Have I been talking to myself here? "How can you not understand why I'm upset? My mother is a completely different woman. Church and flowers and picnics in February. I think she might be getting Alzheimer's or something."

A grin spreads across Joe's face. "You sure this isn't about you not being ready to let her go?"

"Well, if you mean I should be happy she's probably having a nervous breakdown, then I guess you just don't get it."

His gaze narrows and he leans forward in his seat. "My mom died when I was ten. My dad was dating again less than a month after he buried her. I still resent him for not loving her enough to be heartbroken over her death." He shrugs. "Your mom grieved for twelve years. Now she's ready to move on. Be happy for her and let her enjoy the rest of her life."

I hate it when other people can be so nonchalant about things they obviously can't identify with. In all fairness, I have to admit he's right. And my mom does have a right to be happy after all these years. But again, let's take it easy with life's big changes, shall we? Some of us don't adjust well to sudden movement. What can I say? I'm the jumpy type.

Anyway, in the spirit of reciprocity, I take a swig of my neglected white chocolate latte and settle my attention on his brown, beautiful eyes. "Okay. Your turn. What was all that about with your dad and Nana?"

Joc's whole demeanor changes in an instant. I can see frustration build at the very thought of one or the other of his elders. I'm guessing his dad is the cause, but after meeting the old woman, I figure it could be either. He scowls. "It's nothing."

"Oh, come on. I told you my problems. You tell me yours. You're messing with a code of honor, here."

"It's not the same. Trust me."

"Why?" I say, my voice flirtatious. "Is your dad trying to make you an offer you can't refuse?"

Tabby, Dancy, and I have always joked about Nick being a mobster. He looks like one and he is Italian. It was always a fun little fantasy. Only I guess Joe doesn't think it's very funny, because his expression remains sober.

"He wants to use some of his influence with city hall to get our permits to go through quicker than normal."

I shrug. "That would be great. We could get started."

He scowls again. Fine, sheesh. I shrug. "Just a thought."

"You don't understand, Laini. It's better to go through proper channels just like anyone else." He stands. "I'll go get your check."

I watch him go, his shoulders drooping a little. I guess I should have left well enough alone.

Meg Ryan stands on the wooden bridge panning the horizon on every side, looking for her NY152. We see a dog and hear an offscreen Tom Hanks call for Brinkley. And then we know. Well, we already knew. But now Meg starts to figure it out too. Tom Hanks comes into view and their eyes meet. It's a magical moment. Made even more magical because of the knowledge that Tom

Hanks won Meg's heart even though he single-handedly forced her Shop Around the Corner out of business. Now that's romance.

Nancy and I are both dateless this Friday night and are truly fine with it. (Well, one of us is fine with it. One of us wonders why Joe bothered to say he'd call and ask me on a date if he wasn't going to do it.) Anyway, what is a Friday night at home without a great chick flick? And that's how I find myself watching Tom Hanks finally take Meg Ryan into his arms and seal the relationship while Brinkley jumps all over the two of them. That's the only part I find annoying, but not enough to ruin my enjoyment of these two finally kissing. (They never actually did kiss in *Sleepless in Seattle* — I felt robbed.)

Nancy gives a heavy sigh just like me. Her head is resting on the back of the sofa. She rolls her neck and turns her head to look at me. "Want to watch it again?"

A friend after my own heart. I grin. "Yeah."

She stops the DVD mid-credits, just as her cell phone blasts out, "We welcome you to Munchkin Land . . ."

Like any considerate roommate, I get up and go into the kitchen to make us a snack.

I'm trying to drop a few pounds, and Nancy's one of those women who naturally calculates every calorie, so I prepare each of us a dish of fresh strawberries, a dollop of light whipped cream, and a few chopped walnuts. Nancy shows up just as I'm loading a tray with cups of herbal tea and the dessert dishes.

"That looks good," she says. "You're a regular artist when it comes to food."

I can't help being pleased by the praise. "Thanks."

I follow as she takes the tray into the living room and sets it on the coffee table. "So," she says. "You won't believe it, but we got the permits."

"What do you mean?"

"For Nick's." She gives me a shrug.

"You mean all the permits went through?" The thing is, we shouldn't be able to start knocking down walls for at least two more months.

Nancy averts her gaze. I know she does it on purpose.

"What do you know that I don't?" I ask.

She shakes her head. "Nothing, really. I guess we get to start demolition as soon as Joe agrees to shut the place down for a few weeks."

"Wow. Lucky for us, huh?" I'm starting to

put two and two together, but I'm not sure how it adds up.

"Um-hmm," she replies around a bite. I don't think she wants to talk about it. And really, I'm a little afraid of waking up to a big horse's head on my pillow, so I'm not going there either. I shudder at the thought of Mr. Pantalone's flashing eyes as he stormed out of Joe's office two days ago. How could he possibly be Nick's brother or Joe's dad? I mean, yeah, Nick's a tough guy and Joe is a little rough around the edges, but they're both good-hearted and gentle when it counts. This guy looked more than rough around the edges; he looked downright mean. And he wasn't even polite when he brushed right by me. It's hard for me to imagine that beneath that surly exterior resides a fluffy teddy bear. I have a feeling he's not a bit like Nick.

Nancy and I look at each other with unspoken agreement and we both shrug. I point the remote toward the TV and we once again enter the innocent world of *You've Got Mail.* It seems easier than speculating on the world of a Tony Soprano wannabe.

12

Something good comes from the permit situation. For the first time since two weeks into the class, when I failed my first pop quiz, I'm able to smile with confidence at my professor as I walk into class. This guy never looks me in the eye. I'm guessing because he's afraid I'm one D away from going postal on him.

I walk with confidence to the small metal music stand he uses for a podium. He glances up nervously. "Miss Sullivan," he says with a nod. I can tell he wishes the podium was bigger so he could hide. But too bad for him. Besides, I have good news for a change.

I slide copies of the permits in front of him. "Just wanted to let you know our project is going forward." As soon as we find the contractor. But that shouldn't be too hard, should it? Especially if Joe's dad railroads him on the contractor like he did on the permits.

Mr. Brooks's eyebrows go up in surprise as I toss him a grin and head to my seat.

Jazz greets me with her twenty-three-year-old smile and scoots her legs out of the way so I can get by. "You should have seen his face when you walked away," she says, laughing.

"He can't believe I did something right for a change." I sit next to her in the theater-style seats and look down on our bewildered professor. "Does he look disappointed?"

"Maybe a little."

Sheesh. Aren't teachers supposed to hope their students succeed? I thought that was a sign of a good teacher.

"Hey, how in the heck did we get those permits so soon anyway?" Jazz opens her design book and flips her spiral notebook open, pen poised to take notes as Mr. Brooks (aka Mr. I-Want-My-Student-to-Fail) stands, clears his throat, and switches on the overhead projector.

I shrug. "Who knows?"

Mr. Brooks pierces us — and when I say "us," I mean me — with a shut-up stare.

Jazz leans in close and whispers, "I'm not going to look a gift horse in the mouth. As long as we don't get in trouble for anything *they* do."

Why does everyone assume there was something sinister involved? I write on my notebook to her: *Maybe we just hit city hall during a slow time for permit requests.*

Jazz laughs and writes: *Oh, sure. End of February? When everyone is gearing up for spring renovating?*

I lean in and whisper, "Fine. Point taken."

After class, we walk out into a rainy late-February night. I, of course, forgot my stupid umbrella. "Lucky for you," Jazz says, popping her umbrella open, "I'm taking the subway tonight. I'll share my umbrella if you carry it."

"Gladly," I say with a laugh. "No yoga?"

"Instructor is having a baby. I've been doing it by myself at home." We dodge in and out of umbrellas as we hurry down the street to the subway station to catch the next train. We just make it.

We both find a seat, which is rare. Jazz looks at me. "Maybe you have a fairy godmother."

"What?"

"You know. The permits." Only Jazz can leave a conversation for two hours and expect me to follow her train of thought when she picks it back up as though we never paused for a lecture on French furniture.

"Oh. Maybe."

She snorts. "A fairy godmother named Vinnie."

I nudge her in the ribs. But part of me worries that she might be right.

I dread stepping off the subway and walking up the steps into the pouring rain. Why didn't I have the forethought to carry my umbrella? If Dancy and Tabby still lived in our apartment, one — or more likely both — of them would have walked down to the station with an umbrella. But that's not going to happen. I'm faced with a decision. Do I cover my head with my $150 textbook, risk pneumonia by letting the rain soak me, or take the undignified approach and yank my coat up over my head? I choose option three. Even if it is a little risky because I can't really pay close enough attention to my surroundings. And it is nighttime. In New York. And I am a woman alone.

Good grief. Now Joe's the voice in my head trying to scare me into hailing a cab to go three blocks. And I'm just about to give in when I hear: " 'Ey, Laini! Wait up!"

I turn in the rain, and there's Joe, carrying an enormous umbrella. He's grinning like he knows he did a good thing. "You want me to walk you home?"

"Only if you don't mind sharing the um brella."

"That's the idea." His voice is a little husky and I'm not sure if he's trying to be flirty or if it's just a matter of staying dry.

He slips his arm around my shoulders and pulls me against his side.

"Hey, there's that cop you've been seeing."

My heart skips a beat as I follow Joe's gaze to the corner right outside a little skate shop ahead. There's a group of kids milling around, and I can tell without knowing his exact words that Mark is telling them to break it up. Which they do just as he turns and sees me in the crook of Joe's arm, headed his way. He scowls. I offer a tentative wave and an innocent smile as we approach each other.

"What are you doing out in the rain?" he asks. He's wearing rain gear and a plastic bag over his cap. It's not very flattering. But I guess that's not the point anyway.

"I'm on my way home."

"From the coffee shop?" He gives Joe a once-over and grudgingly extends his hand. Which Joe accepts, just as grudgingly. I swear. Men.

"Actually, I had class tonight. Lucky for me, Joe was there to meet my train since I didn't bring an umbrella."

Joe looks a little smug about it. "I didn't think she should be walking home all alone on these streets at night."

Mark stares, a little hostility in those blue eyes of his. "I patrol this area in the evenings. She's safe on my streets." He turns his gaze on me and his defenses lower as concern washes across his face. "You weren't scared, were you?"

Well, only for a second.

I open my mouth to speak, but Joe does it for me.

"You didn't even know she'd be walking alone tonight."

"Well, I do now, so I can escort her the rest of the way home, if you need to get back to the shop."

"Thanks anyway." Joe sounds anything but grateful. "The coffee shop is closed. I'm free to take her all the way home."

I feel like a rope. You know, the tug-of-war kind.

"Officer Hall, you ready? There's a call, or did you want me to take this one on my own?" That guy again. He's so mean to Mark! My heart squeezes a little. If this were a movie, Mark would get a heroic jump on the guy — save his life or something and get a little respect. Too bad this is real life.

Irritation spreads across Mark's face as he turns toward the squad car parked alongside the curb. I follow his gaze and recognize his partner from the night of the break-in.

"Yeah, McNealy. I'm coming." He turns to me. "You sure you're okay?"

"Hall!" the other officer hollers, his voice impatient. "Come on. Are you deaf? We got a call." How does Mark work with that jerk?

"I have to go," Mark says. "I'll call you."

Joe bristles.

Mark turns on his heel, waving as he goes.

"Glad I'm not the victim of a crime waiting while the cops try to hit on a woman," Joe mutters.

"Come on." I move forward and he lurches to keep up. "I'm freezing out here."

"That's another thing," he says, once again falling into step beside me. "He just kept you out in this without regard for your well-being."

"Don't be surly. Mark's a nice guy."

All I get in response is a noncommittal grunt. Am I wrong to grin at his jealousy?

When we reach my apartment, Joe holds the umbrella over me while I unlock the door.

"You want to come up for hot chocolate?"

I figure it's the least I can do, considering he came out just to make sure I got home okay. He hesitates. "It's okay, Joe. Don't feel obligated." I admit I'm stinging just a bit. I mean, he went all macho with Mark. I figured he'd jump at the chance to come up to my apartment.

"I'm just not sure it's proper. You know, like it doesn't look right."

"Joe, it's barely after eight o'clock."

"I know. But . . ."

"Oh, come on. You owe me a date anyway." Don't ask me why I'm suddenly feeling bold and beautiful. Maybe the exchange between a great-looking cop and a great-looking shopkeeper has given me confidence. "Remember? You said you'd call and never did?" I keep the tone light so he doesn't think I'm harboring any real feelings about it. That would never do.

" 'Ey, I didn't forget. Just trying to figure it all out, that's all."

I grin, stepping inside. "You coming? Since the break-in I don't go up until I'm sure this downstairs door is closed firmly and locked."

And with that, his hesitation seems to melt like sugar in the rain. He nods. "Hot chocolate sounds good."

When he gives me that grin, it's hard to

think about his family having "connections" with city hall that might not be completely legitimate. But then, he did say sometimes it's better to do things by the book. So . . . Oh, why even try to speculate? Just give the guy his hot chocolate and stop overanalyzing everything.

The next night, I meet Tabby and Dancy for sushi at Inagiku, a Japanese restaurant in the Waldorf-Astoria. Dancy's treat. Otherwise, it would have set my budget back a week.

I do some fast talking and explain my dilemma to my friends — the dilemma about Joe's dad maybe being a little too well connected at city hall. "Do you think I should confront Joe about it?"

"Maybe you should just let it go," Dancy says. "If his father has connections at city hall, there's not a lot you can do now anyway. The project is moving forward, so just stop worrying about it."

"Unless you think Joe is involved."

I stare at Tabby. "What do you mean? Do you think Joe is like Michael Corleone?"

"Have you been watching *You've Got Mail* again?" Dancy asks.

A sheepish grin. "Guilty. Nancy loves watching the two of them together as much as I do."

Tom Hanks, Meg Ryan.

"What does *You've Got Mail* have to do with anything?"

I guess it's not completely fair of us to lead her along. I'm about to fill her in when Dancy shakes her head.

"You know how they talk about *The Godfather*?"

Tabby shrugs. "Oh, yeah. That's true. 'Go to the mattresses' and all that."

"I swear, Tabs," I say. "How can you be an actress and never have seen *The Godfather*?"

"I don't like to fill my head with violence. Besides, I'm a New York actress, not a film star."

"And soon you won't even have that. What will be your claim to fame after Felicia Fontaine is no more?" I ask.

Tabby grins and pats her flat stomach. "Mommy and Wife are all the titles I need."

It seems like I can't spend time with Tabby anymore without feeling that sense of jealousy. Not the kind of jealousy that makes me wish I could have what she has instead of her. But maybe just the kind that wishes we were both married and pregnant at the same time.

"Okay," I say, because I really need to pull

myself out of the impossible dream for now. "What do I do if he really is involved with organized crime? Do you think I might get arrested?"

"How do you mean?" Tabby asks as the waiter sets sushi in the middle of the table. "How could you possibly be arrested because Frank and Joe may or may not be bribing someone to hurry a few permits along? You're the interior designer. Your part of the project doesn't even start until the architects and contractors do their part. You're making too much of this, Laini."

Okay, that felt a little rough to me. Doesn't my life feel insignificant enough as it is without my best friend rubbing salt in the proverbial wound?

"Excuse me." Tabby's chair scrapes hard against the floor and she dashes out of the room, leaving me bewildered and feeling betrayed.

"She didn't mean it like that, Laini."

I grab a sushi roll with my chopsticks and shrug. "Oh, I know." But the thing is, I don't know. I don't know anything anymore. For instance. Why are both of my friends in happy relationships and I'm not? What's wrong with me? Why are they both in the careers they want, and I don't have a clue what I'm doing even in my last semester of design school? I ask again, what is wrong with me?

13

I decide I'm not in the mood for sushi after all and leave before Tabby gets back to the table. I head out and walk the two blocks to Fifty-first, where I catch the number six train. I'm feeling disheartened as I reach my stop. I can't help it that I'm sort of hoping to find Joe waiting for me. But then, why would he be there? He didn't know I was having dinner in upper midtown. I trudge home in the cool evening air. It's a few days away from March. Spring is peeking around the corner and announcing that it's heading to Manhattan. I can't wait! I'm so tired of being cold.

Tabby calls me and it turns out she's battling terrible sickness due to the pregnancy. Which, she tells me, is a good sign that hormone levels are rising as expected. It means the pregnancy is going well — less chance of miscarriage.

She tells me this with such relief that I realize for the first time that maybe Tabby has been worried about losing the baby. Such a horrible thing never occurred to me.

Her tone sounds quivery over the phone. "I'm sorry if it sounded like I thought your contribution to the renovation at Nick's wasn't important. You're the frosting on the cake. I hope you know I only meant that your involvement comes along far after the big dogs settle the permit stuff, so you shouldn't get in trouble."

I actually do understand what she's saying and there are no hard feelings. I tell her as much. "I'm just feeling a little nervous about getting the grade. If anything illegal is involved and the project gets shut down, where will I be? I can't afford to take the last semester over."

Financially or emotionally, to be honest. I can't fail. I don't know what I'd fall back on. I've already been an accountant. For eight years I did a job I hated. And I know I could go back to it if I had to, but oh, the thought feels like a crushing weight.

"It's worth taking this risk to be doing what will make you happy, Laini," Tabby says softly, as though reading my thoughts. "I knew I couldn't do anything besides acting. What is it that you feel like you have to do or else you'll always be unhappy? Oh, shoot, Laini. I'm so sorry. I'm going to be sick."

She hangs up and I imagine her making a run for the bathroom.

I think about what she said, though. Is there a certain career path I must follow to be happy?

Young single women in New York are career-driven. Why else would a woman live in an insanely expensive matchbox apartment in Manhattan and work so hard pursuing that American dream?

I'm not even sure what the dream is anymore. When I was in college, it was about doing what my mother expected of me. What she assumed my dad would have wanted. And that's what I did — I became an accountant.

When I was about to turn thirty, I figured out that accounting stressed me too much, made me tired, and not only that — I dreaded going to work every day.

Forget that I was very good at accounting. I mean, the numbers were there and made perfect sense. . . . I just happened to hate working with them. It was my lucky day when Ace Accounting went bankrupt and they had to let me go.

That bankruptcy set me free to pursue something else. Everyone told me I had an eye for putting rooms together, and I liked it, so I decided to take these classes. Okay, everyone questioned my color schemes, but the furniture, art pieces, those sorts of things, were constantly praised. But — oh, I hate to admit it — I'm not the whiz at design I thought I might be. If I don't succeed at design, I might have to go back to accounting, and there's no way I can do that.

Thank goodness the phone rings and pulls me out of the maudlin, whiney thought process in which I find myself.

"Hello?"

"Hi, it's Mark."

The corners of my mouth lift into a smile. I haven't heard from him since last night. When it rains it pours. Literally.

"What's up, Mark?"

"I was just wondering if you'd be interested in dinner Saturday night."

"Sure. What did you have in mind?"

He hesitates. "Actually, it's my dad's birthday. My sister is closing the restaurant early and we're having a huge bash with about fifty family and friends."

"Sounds like fun."

"You sure? We could wait until Sunday night and have a date just the two of us."

"Hey, are you backing out already?"

He chuckles. "Not likely. You'll be at your mom's?"

"Yeah."

"Okay, I'll pick you up at six."

"Looking forward to it."

And that's that. I'm still basking in the glow of it when the phone rings again. Only it's Joe this time. "So, I'm calling."

"Yeah?" I give a little laugh. "It's about time. Glad I wasn't holding my breath."

"So how about Saturday night?" A curious disappointment shoots through me. How can I live in a male-barren wasteland for years and in the span of one month have not one but *two* fantastic-looking, great guys ask me out? And wouldn't you know it, they both want me to go out on the same night. Darn!

I can't believe that, for a second, I consider accepting Joe's invitation and calling Mark back to cancel. But that's not nice. Besides, there's a lot to be said for sticking to the plan. I swallow past disappointment and try not to sound pathetic. "Actually, Joe, I have plans for Saturday night."

"The cop?"

"Sorta, yeah. He just called a couple minutes before you."

"I see." He clears his throat. "Well, better luck next time, I guess."

I want so much to ask if we can make it another night. But I can't bring myself to be that forward.

Besides, Joe's already moving on to the next thought. "So, did Nancy tell you we hired the contractors?"

"Yep. When are they going to start knocking down walls?"

"A week from this coming Monday. I put signs up to let the customers know."

"That's great. You must be excited about it."

"I never thought Uncle Nick should expand this much, to be honest."

"I thought you were the one who wanted the changes, Mr. I-Have-a-Degree-in-Restaurant-Management."

"We definitely needed changes, but not necessarily expansion. It takes away from the intimate feel." I can't help but laugh as the image of all those people crammed into Nick's comes to mind. "What was he supposed to do with the crowd, Joe?" During most of the morning hours and until around one thirty in the afternoon, the place is standing-room-only as it is.

"What's wrong with people waiting their turn? That's what all the good restaurants do. Instead, everyone thinks they oughtta be bigger and better. In a crunch, we could add outside tables — like we're doing between the two buildings, only we could have done it out front instead."

You know, now that he mentions it, he has a point. Why try to fix what isn't exactly broken? Although Nick has a point too. It's crazy to hobble a business when the opportunity for expansion presents itself — for instance, when a shop goes out of business right next door. I mean, what are the chances? How could he not hop on that?

I sigh. This is why I can't figure out my life. It's too easy to see both sides of the issue. I have to learn to take a stand and stick with that point of view.

"I think it's a good idea. Nick needs the extra business now that he's living in L.A. and hiring a manager and all of that. The extra money will come in handy."

He hesitates for a split second. "I guess that's true."

Yep. Now if only I could figure out my own life.

By Saturday I'm more than ready to leave Manhattan and take the forty-minute train ride from Penn Station to Long Island. It's been a depressing, rainy week. One of those weeks where nothing new happens and life feels mundane. I think I have a little spring fever. It's not time for spring buds, but all the excitement of winter has long since gotten old and worn out and I'm ready to move on.

To make matters worse, I'm shocked to find boxes all over Mom's house. Moving boxes.

"Mom!" I call as I wade through the clutter all over the living room floor. "Mom! What's going on?"

"I'm in the kitchen, honey."

She says it so calmly, like I'm not supposed to notice that my childhood is being simultaneously packed into cardboard, taped up, and made ready to go who knows where. I flounce (yes, I'm ashamed to say, I do, like a five-year-old throwing a tantrum) into the kitchen, following Mom's voice. I find her headfirst in the lower cabinets, her behind the part of her that greets me. "Ma? What's going on?"

She pulls out of the cabinet, puffs out a breath, and rests back on her heels. "I haven't done a good cleaning since your daddy died. You wouldn't believe some of the old things I've found." I can't even imagine the look that must be on my face when she looks at me. But her expression washes from fatigue to compassion. "Surely you knew I'd have to start cleaning everything out."

I hoist myself onto a barstool and grab a banana from the fruit bowl on the counter. "I guess."

She stands and presses her hands into her back for a stretch. "I need a break. Do you want some tea?"

"Thanks."

I hold the unpeeled banana and watch her fill the teakettle. "Are you keeping the teakettle, Ma?"

From the sink, she looks over her shoulder. "What are you talking about? Of course I'm keeping it." A soft smile spreads across her face. "It was the first gift you ever bought with your very own money."

Money I earned babysitting for the horrible neighbor boy, Marty Brunstroms. I wonder what ever happened to him. Probably in jail. Or a millionaire. He was a shifty one, that Marty.

"Dad took me to Macy's, remember?"

"I fussed at Daddy for letting you spend all of your money on it."

"Twenty-three dollars and eight cents." That was a ton of money in 1988. I was ten. Actually, it's still a lot of money when you're as broke as I am. I crack open the banana and break off a piece. "I was so excited about the teakettle I'd seen you look at so many times that I forgot about saving money to buy Dad something for Christmas."

She nods, pulling out two teacups and setting them on saucers. "You shoveled snow for so many weeks leading up to Christmas Eve just to get enough to buy him a gift."

"A new adding machine — which he preferred to calculators." I swallow my banana bite and snicker. "He loved it."

"He sure did." I wonder where that adding machine is. . . . The boxed-up room doesn't even look like the room I remember. Things are happening way too fast to suit my comfort level.

"When are you and Aaron getting married, Mom?"

"May."

Exactly what I'm talking about. Way too fast. "So soon?"

"April and June are very busy months for florists. April is the beginning of spring and everyone is looking for Easter lilies and flowers in general. And you know what June is. Aaron has several weddings in June, plus prom and graduation flowers. May just seems more practical."

"Why not wait until July or August? O-or even fall?" I can't quite look her in the eye as I try to manipulate her future. "That would give you more time to know each other."

The teakettle shrills as if in protest to my finagling. Mom sends me a rueful smile. "We know all we need to."

"So you're getting married in two months to a man you hardly know." I don't mean it to be sarcastic. I'm just trying to wrap my head around the relationship that escalates every time I see my mom. I'm almost afraid to speak to her for fear she might tell me she's on her way back from Vegas after one of those drive-through weddings. Or that she's adopting a baby from China or South Africa.

Mom sets my tea in front of me and takes a seat on the barstool next to mine. "I know this seems very fast to you."

Seems very fast? This woman has been standing still while life goes on around her for the last twelve years. Does she even know who is president right now? Does she know what the Internet is? An iPod? I mean, really — how can she just open her eyes one day, see a man, and decide to marry the dude?

"But when something is right, it's just right. Aaron and I don't have the luxury of youth. And we have no reason to wait."

"What about buying your own place

together? I thought Aaron was selling his house. Surely it didn't sell in two weeks."

"No. But it's been on the market since before his wife passed away. Just this week two very promising prospective buyers entered the picture. So you see, it could happen very soon."

"What about this house, Mom?"

Somehow I know it's not going to be my inheritance the way Dancy's parents' condo was for her, but I'm still not at all prepared for the answer. "I'm sorry, Laini. I have no choice but to sell. The equity I have in the house will pay off all of my debts and give us a down payment for a condo."

My suspicious nature takes over. "And what will Aaron contribute from his house?"

"Honey, I know you're worried. But you need to trust me."

"That doesn't answer my question, Ma."

"Okay, I'll tell you, because you have a right to know. The entire profit from Aaron's house will have to go toward paying his wife's hospital bills. There will be nothing left."

"So you'll be taking care of him." I give a short laugh and sip my tea. "No wonder he finds you so irresistible."

Even before her eyes go stormy, I know I've gone too far. "Young lady . . ." She slaps her palm against the countertop. "I'm not a fool and I happen to love this man." Her eyes fill, but she quickly blinks away the tears. "I have work to do."

"I'm sorry, Ma." I toss my banana peel into the garbage. I know I've hurt her, and I fully intend to go back later and offer a better apology. But right now I have to figure out how to talk her out of this silly marriage before she makes a big, big mistake.

14

All six feet four inches of Mark are looking good when he stands on the porch a few hours later. It's hard not to stare at him. He takes my hand as we walk to the curb, where a taxi waits for us. "You look pretty tonight," he says, opening the door.

I look down at my outfit. Gray crop pants, a white button-down shirt, a gray jacket, and knee-high platform boots. I guess I do look good. I even broke out the Ralph Lauren cologne Dancy gave me for Christmas. Just a touch, in case Mark goes in for a sniff.

Our fingers remain laced during the ten-minute cab ride to the Nautical Mile and while we walk to his dad's restaurant. I like the sound of the boats on the canal, and I'm enjoying the time with Mark, but I can't stop thinking about Mom, so I know I'm an awful bore to be around.

Instead of walking to the door, Mark steers me to a vacant bench just a few steps from his dad's restaurant. "Let's sit a minute and you can tell me what's bothering you."

"I didn't realize I was that obvious," I mumble, allowing myself to be led like I have no mind of my own. But I have to admit, I sort of enjoy the way he takes charge.

After I relay my exchange with my mom from this morning, he nods, his eyes awash with sympathy. "Do you want me to do some investigating? Make sure this Aaron guy is okay?"

I'm sure my eyes must reveal the shock I feel. "Of course not." Can he even do that? "How would you go about it?"

"I'd look him up in the system. Any activity out of the norm would show up. Unpaid parking tickets. Arrests."

"Credit report?"

He smiles. "No. But if he's tried to scam any ladies and got pulled in for questioning, it would show up."

I'm conflicted. I want to know what's what with this Aaron who seems too good to be true. But on the other hand, he seemed pretty genuine at church and he really did lose his wife recently. Maybe he's just lonely and likes my mom. That's not completely out of the question. And I have to admit it's refreshing to me that Mark's reaction is different from Joe's — which was a little disappointing, to say the least.

I'm spared the necessity of an immediate response as a very pregnant Liz waddles up the sidewalk next to an average-looking guy who stands barely five feet eight. He must feel like a dwarf next to Mark.

"What are you two doing out here?" She gives me a grin. I have to wonder if she'll make it through the party without going into labor. Not that I know anything about it. But if I had to place a bet, I'd say that enormous stomach is about to deflate at any moment. She follows my gaze and her cheeks pink up. "Who knew a stomach could stretch that much? You should see the stretch marks. I'll have a road map on my stomach for the rest of my life." She reaches up and pats her husband's cheek. "Poor Rick."

Rick squeezes her and presses a sloppy kiss to her cheek. "I love every single mark."

She grins up at him and then winks at me. "What a guy. He's a liar, but what a guy."

The four of us laugh as we enter the building. I'm struck again by how much fun Mark's family is. Can I see myself as part of this crew? I mean, it's different from the easy, quiet life an only child has growing up with two accountants as parents. As different as night and day.

And then there's Joe. Well, there's not really Joe, is there? Or is there? I'm so confused. I like Mark. He's nice and polite and the kind of guy you want around when you want to be protected.

But Joe . . . Okay, Joe is moody, but he did carry me to his apartment and put me in his bed. Joe makes my heart race. No doubt about that. But his family . . . well . . . his family may or may not be mafia.

Country music blares from a jukebox in the corner. "Isn't that great?" Liz shouts above the noise. "We found it at an auction a month ago. Bought it for Dad's birthday and stocked it with old country stuff. George Jones, Loretta Lynn, stuff like that."

"Uh, yeah," I say. "Great."

I hate country music. Old and new. I think it should be banned above the Mason-Dixon Line. But that's just me. As long as I'm not forced to listen to it. Which apparently I will be for the next couple of hours.

Mark leans down and speaks close to my ear. "Let's go find a place to sit."

I nod as he leads me toward the back of the room. On several tables, tubs of ice hold cans of soda. Mark and I each grab a can

— diet for me, of course — on our way through the dining room.

"Uncle Mark!"

I'm just sitting down when a preschool boy practically assaults my date, flying into his arms. "Where's your gun?" he asks through a space where his two front teeth should be.

Mark lifts the boy to his lap. "I'll never tell. Are you enjoying Grandpa Carl's party?"

The little boy nods and then seems to notice me. He ducks his head. Mark meets my gaze. "This is Kyle." He nudges the little boy. "Hey, sport. Meet Laini."

Kyle is having none of it and refuses to look at me. I usually have a way with kids. But right now I have no cookies, cupcakes, or Popsicles handy to use as bribery, so I resort to my winning personality.

"Hi, Kyle. Nice to meet you."

Again with the ducking.

"Hey, sport, you're going to hurt Miss Laini's feelings if you don't say hello."

A chubby hand gives me a wave and my heart melts into butter.

From the corner of my eye I see a figure heading toward us. Mark turns at the same time. "Busted," he says quietly.

A breathless, slightly overweight (but

probably no more than I) woman stops by us, hands on hips as she stares at Kyle. "There you are. Mommy was scared half to death."

"Look, Mommy. Uncle Mark is here." The simple statement brings a smile to my face. I glance at "Mommy." Is this another of Mark's sisters? She looks nothing like Mark or Liz, or their dad, for that matter.

"So he is." The woman lifts her eyes, and I swear she practically devours Mark with her smoldering gaze. A look that quite frankly makes me feel a little uncomfortable. I'm guessing this woman is not related to the hunky police officer, despite Kyle's use of the word *uncle.*

Setting the boy on his feet, Mark stands. "Kellie, it's nice to see you." He bends and gives her a quick peck on the cheek.

There's nothing wrong with that, but then she sort of leans into him and closes her eyes. Hello! What am I, part of the decor?

Mark pulls back as quickly as he moved in. He reaches for me and I stand up as he takes my hand. He sort of yanks me against him. I know it's a defense against the maternal seductress. "Kellie, this is Laini Sullivan. Laini is my — uh — date." Good heavens. Talk about your unnecessary details. Obviously I'm his date. The fact that he has to spell it out leads me to believe one of two things: these two had a really heavy relationship and he needs her to know he's moved on. Or she's dogging him in a stalker sort of way, and he wants her to know he's really and truly not interested.

Her cheeks go red as she looks to me. "Nice to meet you, Laini."

I offer my hand and she takes it. "Come on, Kyle. Let's leave Uncle Mark and his new girlfriend alone now."

"Oh, I'm not . . ." I would say I'm not his girlfriend, but Mark squeezes my hand a little tightly and I know he wants me to shut up and not spoil the illusion.

She whips around. "Not what?" Good grief, is that the look of a hungry wolf puppy?

"Um. I'm not bothered by the little tyke at all. Kyle's welcome to hang out with us all he wants."

"No thanks. That would be a little awkward."

I smile. "Well, you're his mother."

"Yes." She gives me a tight smile in return. "I am." Grabbing Kyle's hand, she practically yanks the kid away.

I pull my hand, which by the way has no feeling left in it, away from Mark and take my seat. "So, Uncle Mark," I say, lifting an eyebrow in his direction, "what's up with that?"

Heavy sigh. "She's a waitress here. Divorced while she was pregnant with Kyle and never saw the father again. He wasn't interested."

My heart is starting to go out to her. "I take it the two of you dated?"

He nods. "Right after Kyle was born until about six months ago."

I know darn well my jaw just opened like a wooden-soldier nutcracker on Christmas Eve. "You dated her that long and didn't marry her?"

He scowls. "I think that was her point too."

Light is beginning to glimmer just a little. "So it was her decision."

Leaning forward a little, Mark looks me in the eye with frankness that commands my attention. "Listen. Call me a jerk if you want, but the main reason I stayed with Kellie for so long was because of Kyle. I wasn't in love with her or I would have married her a long time ago. I love Kyle. But he's not mine either and it isn't fair to Kellie, Kyle, or me to marry her for the wrong reason."

My eyes travel the room until I spot Kellie. Her gaze is on us. Compassion sears my heart. I look back to Mark and nod. "I understand." I try to push away my concern, but something about a relationship that lasted so many years, has a child involved — even if the boy isn't Mark's — just nags at me.

Reaching across the table, Mark squeezes my hand as relief washes over his features. "Do you? I should have told you about Kellie before we got here. I wasn't positive she'd show up, though, and I didn't want to go into it just yet if I didn't have to."

"Mark!" Even across the room I recognize Mr. Hall's booming baritone.

Mark stands again, and I follow suit. Carl beams when he sees me. "I see you brought the good-looking girl back." He holds out both hands and I have no choice but to slip mine into his. He pulls me slightly forward and kisses each cheek — lingering a little too long, if you want to know the truth.

"Happy birthday, sir," I say, timid in the face of this man's show of affection.

"Thank you, sweetheart. And thank you for coming."

"It was my pleasure."

"I hear you're an interior designer."

I feel a blush coming on. I can't bring myself to admit to that. I mean, I haven't even graduated yet. I say as much to Mr. Hall.

"But she's about to graduate." Mark grins at me proudly. "She's designing the new look at Nick's, that coffee shop I was telling you about."

Mr. Hall nods. "Oh, yeah, yeah, I remember."

He looks around and then back to me. "What would you recommend we do here?"

Oh, no. No. Do not put me on the spot. I can't think on my feet.

"Come on, Dad." Mark steps in, my knight in a leather bomber jacket and a great-looking pair of Levi's. "Talk shop another time. Let Laini relax."

Mr. Hall sends me a wink. "Listen to my son, already looking out for you. What do you think of that?"

"I've been looking out for myself for a long time." I lean in a little conspiratorially. "I don't think I'm ready to relinquish the job just yet."

A chortle leaves him. "Listen to her — Miss Independence. She's a feisty one, son. You'll have your hands full."

Mark looks like he wants to die right there on the spot.

"Come on, Dad. You been dipping into the wine?"

He winks at me, then Mark. "Only a little. But it's my birthday, for crying out loud."

"Dad! Come on. Time to cut the cake."
Thank goodness for Liz.

The next morning I wake up early, as usual. As I mull over the night before, a couple of things still nag at me. Kellie, for one. And her son, for two. I think Mark might have gone in for a kiss, except that Kellie happened to be outside looking for a cab when we were leaving and we had no choice but to offer to share. And it just so happened that I was on the way, so we dropped me off first.

Mark held my hand and then walked me to the door. "I'll call you," he said just before leaning in and kissing my cheek much the same way I'd seen him do to the psychotic ex-girlfriend waiting in the cab. I had a feeling she'd do everything in her power to get him to stay late. Or at the very least to kiss her good night.

I try not to let the thought of either scenario ruin my morning coffee on the deck with the chiminea lit and smelling hickoryish from the pieces of bark Mom buys for that purpose. But it's no use, and the images just won't go away. So much so that I'm relieved when Mom gets up a mere fifteen minutes after me even though I normally prefer my privacy this time of morning.

I look up as she steps onto the deck, and shock zaps through me like a hundred volts of sheer power. My mother is not wearing the frayed, worn yellow chenille robe. Instead, she's wrapped cozily in the white robe I bought for her three years ago.

I'm so happy I can't even play it cool. Jumping up, I throw my arms around her. "Look at you!"

She smiles. "I thought it was time to let it go."

And I know, in that simple statement, she's also letting Daddy go.

My throat aches at the thought. Actually, all of me aches at the thought. Clear through to my bones. Daddy is really and truly gone.

"Honey, I didn't have the chance to mention this yesterday, but . . ." She picks at an imaginary thread on her robe. I know it's imaginary because she hasn't worn it enough to have any loose threads. "Aaron's son, Chad, and his daughter-in-law are coming to church today."

"That's nice." Nice like the stomach flu.

"Do you really think so?" Her eyes are so filled with hope, I can't bring myself to tell her I was being facetious. Besides, what will it hurt to tell a little white lie? "Sure, Mom. Real nice."

"Oh, I'm so glad you're coming around about Aaron and this wedding, honey. We're all going out to eat at Valmont's after church. Aaron has already made lunch reservations to include you and his children so we can all meet and discuss things over a nice meal. What do you think?"

Honestly? I think I'm never telling another little white lie again as long as I live.

15

The after-church crowd at Valmont's is packed in like sardines and so loud you might as well be in a nightclub for all the conversation that's possible. Which is fine with me. I'm not all that keen on chatting anyway. I stare across the table and try to look as intimidating as the Jerk (aka Chad Bland) — the guy who, for better or worse, is going to become my stepbrother in two months. But let me just say it's not that easy. For one thing, the guy is the size of a Mack truck. He's at least three hundred pounds and nine or ten feet tall. Well, no, but he'd hold his own in a look-me-in-the-eye contest with Mark, who, as I've mentioned, is six-four.

"Surely you can't think this is a good idea," Chad says in a tone that I hate. To clarify: I hate it when anyone says to me, "Surely you this," or "Surely you that." Like only a fool would think anything else.

And I might be a fool. But I would never betray my mother to the likes of this arrogant creep. I look him dead in the eye and shrug. "Personally, I happen to think our parents make a lovely couple. Whatever they choose to do is perfectly fine with me." Let him put that in his pipe and smoke it.

My mother's face brightens. Aaron's eyes twinkle, and he sends me a wink. A fatherly wink, sort of. Which makes me uncomfortable. I mean, true, I'm not going to sit by while Chad attempts to undermine his own dad, but that doesn't mean I'm ready to sit on my new stepdaddy's knee and tell him what I want for Christmas either.

Chad lifts his eyebrows and leans forward, his considerable stomach pressing against the edge of the table. "Oh, I see. You figure if your mother" — (am I going to have to beat the daylights out of this guy for saying *mother* in that tone of voice?) — "marries my dad, you'll get your inheritance right away. And maybe a little something from him too?"

Mom gasps, and I'm about to come out of my chair when Aaron glares at his son and practically growls, "Chad, I think it's time you shut up and eat your lunch. You're bordering on rudeness and bad taste. And I'm not going to allow you to subject Lydia to one more second of this disrespect."

Chad slams his fist on the table in a dramatic motion that sends the silverware clanging onto the plates. We all jump — even Chad, who by now is pointing his fat, sausage finger at his dad's face. "And if you think I'm going to stand idly by while some gold digger sinks her claws into my mother's things, you're sadly mistaken, Dad."

"How dare you!" I say too loud. Patrons at several nearby tables turn to watch the show. "If anyone's the gold digger . . ."

"Laini Sullivan. Don't you finish that line of thought or I'll — I'll . . ." Mom's at a loss for words, but I catch her drift and decide to revise what I would have said, which would have been that his dad is the gold digger. Even if he is, he's not a very good one. "Chad, the truth is that my mother intends to sell my childhood home and use however much she receives above the mortgage to put a down payment on their new home. So the only inheritance I'm going to receive is a robe that's so old it won't even cover any of my important parts. So there!"

Mom touches my arm. "Honey, you can't possibly want that old robe."

I turn to her. "Daddy bought it for you. I want it, okay?"

Her brow goes up. "Okay."

Chad grunts and sends me a mean, mean glare. "Give me a break here. A robe? What are we talking about? There's no way my dad is going to live in a place paid for by your mother."

I think I hate this man. Brother or no, he will not be getting a Christmas card from me unless he mends his ways considerably.

Aaron clears his throat. "Laini is correct. As much as I hate to bring this up at a time like this, you've left me no choice. Your mother's hospital bills were high. Extremely so. We went through the small amount of insurance she had very quickly. I'm still deeply in debt from the surgeries, hospital stays, medications, and home health care in the end. Everything will have to be auctioned off and the house sold in order to settle all accounts due."

Chad looks like he just got socked in the gut. I want to be smug about it, but I can't. I know how he feels. I felt sort of the same way when Mom told me there would be nothing left for me after she sells our house.

Chad doesn't say one word. I mean, not even a whisper. Instead, he pushes back his chair, tosses his napkin on the table, and nods to his wife, Brenda (who, by the way, looks like she weighs about ninety-four pounds soaking wet — you have to wonder if he's letting her eat). She mouths, "I'm sorry," and follows her husband from the restaurant.

I stare after them, bewildered and getting madder and madder. And then I do something really out of character. I hop up and run after him. "Hey!" I yell when I get to the door. Lucky for me, big boy can't move very fast. So they haven't even reached the curb, let alone hailed a cab. I rush after them. "What's the idea, walking out on your dad?"

"It's none of your business."

"Oh, yeah it is, buster. You insulted my mom."

He rolls his eyes and looks down his nose as though I'm a flying bug that won't leave him alone but maybe isn't quite worth the effort of swatting away. "I'm sure your mother is lovely," he says with a sarcastic scowl that just begs to be smacked right off.

"If you had any common sense at all, you'd *know* she's lovely, not just think it. And you still haven't answered my question. How could you walk out on your own dad? Don't you know how grief-stricken he's been since your mother died and now here he is forced to sell everything that speaks of their life together just so he can pay the bills? Are you truly that much of a horse's" — in honor of the Lord's Day, I stop that line of thought, but it's not easy — "behind?"

"It's all well and good for you to talk — Laini, was it?" Oh, he knows very well it's Laini. He's just all cliché and nothing original. "This is all news to me. I thought I'd live in that home someday. Raise my own children there. Instead, I find out that I'm going to be stuck in an apartment in the city to raise my baby there."

Okay, I'm not seeing a baby. Did they lose it?

Brenda apparently notes my confusion. She smiles. "We just found out we'll be having our first."

You just can't help but like her. I grin at her rapturous expression. "Congratulations! My friend just found out she's going to have a baby too," I say. I'm not sure why I volunteer that information. But there it is.

"I'm sick all the time."

I give her a sympathetic nod. "So is she."

"Is this really the point right now?" I jump at the sharpness of Chad's tone. "I need a few days to sort this out in my head and then I'll be fine. I just can't sit in there anymore while he discusses the end of my mother's life in front of strangers." His voice breaks, and I'm able to work up a little bit of sympathy.

I place my hand on his arm. "I'm sure your dad will understand if you take a few days. Just don't take any longer than necessary. He's going to move on with or without you. But you might not be able to live with yourself if you stay gone too long and force him to go through all this stuff alone."

His lip curls. "He's not alone, remember? He has the bride-to-be."

I step forward and stand as close to him as I possibly can without actually making physical contact. "You know, I'm getting pretty sick of the way you keep referring to my mom like she's some seductive spider and your widower dad is a poor fly lured into her web by her irresistible sex appeal." I can't hold back the tiny laugh that comes up as the image hits me full in the brain.

Judging by the venom in his eyes, he's not catching the funny.

I roll my eyes at him. "Fine. I couldn't care less. Pout because you won't be getting a house. Ruin your relationship with your dad over it. It's not my business whether you do or not." I shrug a nonchalant I'm-a-better-person-than-you shrug. "Personally, I intend to do everything possible to help our parents get everything done and settle their bills, and I will stand up right next to my mother when she marries your dad. I suspect you would be the first choice for a best man."

A snort rips through him — reminds me of a hippo blowing a bug out of his nose. "That'll never happen."

I'm really sick of this conversation. Besides, it's starting to sprinkle out here. I'm not taking a chance on the cashmere jacket I discovered during my last thrift store expedition getting ruined over the likes of this guy. "That's your choice, Chad. But it'll also be your loss."

A cab finally screecches to a stop, and Chad ushers his wife into the car. He doesn't even give me a second glance as the cabbie speeds away into traffic.

I would go back inside, but Mom and Aaron slip out the door. I suspect they've been watching from the glass door and waiting for Chad to leave.

"Sorry, Aaron." I feel sorry for the man. First he loses his wife, and now his only son is behaving badly.

His slim shoulders shrug. "He'll come around."

But the look in his eyes is wistful. I wonder if, by the time Chad comes around, it will be too late for a good relationship between him and Aaron and my mom.

Mom wraps her hand along the inside of his elbow. "Let's go, dear. We'll just have to pray for Chad. After all, look what happened when we prayed that Laini would come around."

Her words jolt me. What's that supposed to mean? Is there a conspiracy going on here?

Nancy laughs at me later when I tell her about my mom's comment. We're sitting on the couch watching *Sleepless in Seattle* and recapping our respective weekends. "What's wrong with a little divine intervention?" she asks. "Mothers' prayers are always the most powerful."

"My mother hadn't stepped foot inside a church since I was a little girl. Now all of a sudden she's going to church again and praying for me to 'come around'?" Maybe I ought to ask her to pray for a good job and a knight on a white horse.

"Oh, Laini. Don't be offended. Just be glad she's happy."

"I *am* glad she's happy." Time to shift. "Tell me about your weekend."

Her face clouds. "Tyson came to visit. He won't give up."

"Tyson, your ex-boyfriend?"

We really haven't discussed too much about her life before she moved in with me. But I know some of the bare essentials. She nods now. "Yeah, he won't give up."

"Are you sure you want him to?" I mean, a guy who loves her that much . . . Maybe it was a misunderstanding.

She rolls her eyes. "He's married."

Gulp.

"And I didn't know it for two years." Her dark eyes flash with indignation. "How did I not know that?"

I shrug. "He was sneaky, I guess?"

"You got that right." She turns to me with a sudden, jerky move. "Do you know he had the nerve to tell me he left her? He just expected me to go running back into his arms." Her voice breaks a little as tears well in her eyes.

I truly don't know what to say. "I'm sorry, Nancy. Is there anything I can do?"

She shakes her head. "No. I sent him back to Chicago. I think he's pretty clear now where we stand." A rueful smile tips the corner of her mouth. "I suggested we call his wife and ask her if he'd left. He wouldn't do it."

So of course that means he didn't really leave his wife. What a creep. If a woman with Nancy's looks can't find a decent guy, what hope do I have? Now I'm as depressed as she is.

"Did he really think I would go back to him anyway? I'm a Christian. I just don't understand how I could be so fooled."

My heart goes out to her and I slip my arm around her shoulders. "Love is blind." I can't believe I just said that.

"You know who I should go out with?"

I shake my head.

"Joe Pantalone. His nana has been pushing us at each other since we were kids. What do I have to lose?"

My arm drops like a load of concrete. *Uh, your pretty little neck, girlfriend.* Doesn't she know that Joe and I — well, I don't know what there is, but there's something. And she should know that.

"You're going with him to Nana and Papa's anniversary dinner next Saturday night, aren't you?"

"No."

She frowns. "Joe said he was going to ask if you wanted to go. He wants to introduce you to a couple of the cousins. I think he's feeling guilty that you won't have anywhere to sell rolls and sandwiches for the next few weeks."

"He doesn't need to worry about that."

"You know Joe. He's a protector-type."

Meaning what? He's the kind of guy who might meet a girl at a subway station in the rain and walk her home out of chivalry instead of affection? Suddenly my confidence that Joe is interested in me as a woman is starting to dwindle. I feel downright deflated. Time to play the we're-just-friends card. "So — um — why haven't you ever gone out with him?"

"I don't know. We grew up together. His father and mine are business associates. Joe and my brother were best friends. It just seemed incestuous." She wrinkles her nose. A smile settles over her lips. "On the other hand, storybook romance is all about childhood friends falling in love as adults. Maybe this is my storybook ending. Why not?"

I swallow hard. "Yeah. Why not?"

"I'm kidding!" She gives a laugh. "Joe's not my type. Besides, he's like a brother." A shudder works through her shoulders. "Can you imagine?"

Can I imagine *her* with him, or *me* with him?

She frowns. "Hey. You're not interested in Joe, are you?"

My proceed-with-caution light flashes behind my eyes. "Why do you ask?"

"I don't know. I thought you and Mark . . ."

"We're dating. No kissing or anything."

Shoot. Why did I have to go and tell her that?

"Oh. You guys aren't exclusive?" She still has that frown.

"I'm not really in a position to have an exclusive relationship right now." Hopefully I'm convincing.

"Why not?"

I heave a sigh. "School, for one thing. Things are pretty uncertain there."

"How so?"

Okay, I haven't exactly confessed to my hotshot architect friend that I'm failing interior design school. I'm not so sure I really want to tell her about it now. But something in her eyes shows real concern. So I open up. "Let's just say I'm not very good. I think I might be at the bottom of my class. If not, I'm pretty close. To tell you the truth, I have about the lowest grade point average a person can have and still be considered a passing student. So I guess Joe was right to have reservations about me in the first place."

Her dark brows lift in surprise. "Your ideas were so good."

I shrug. "Maybe I have a knack for Italian decor."

She nods slowly. "What about the other

decors?"

I sling myself back on the couch and let out a groan. "Nancy! Can I tell you a secret?"

"Sure. What are roomies for?"

"I hate interior design." Tears pool quickly and become two streams running down my face. "I thought I loved it. Truly. I love putting rooms together at home, but once I went to school for it, it just became work. There's too much to think about. I never used to worry about color schemes. If I loved something and thought it worked, I put it together. Period. Now I have to think about sage green vs. forest and burnt orange vs. rust. It's just ridiculous. And I can't see a difference. What if I really am color blind?"

"Not too many people truly are." She hesitates a second, then levels her gaze at me. "But, Laini, design is all about color schemes and putting the right fabric with the right room style." Her eyes sparkle. "From the bottom up. From the architecture to the fabric for the furniture." The passion in her eyes makes me jealous. She takes my hand. "It's like taking all the ingredients for a pan of those amazing cinnamon rolls and putting them together, shaping them, and adding the icing."

I nod. That's language that makes sense

to me. I can almost smell the dough.

"That's what we're doing to Nick's. Taking a blank space and making it beautiful. The entire process is so exciting I can't wait to get started."

See? And I'm not looking forward to the process — I just can't wait until it's done. I admit as much to Nancy and she gives me a look filled with pity.

Standing, she stretches. "I'll be right back."

I stare after her as she walks down the hall to her room. I'm finally starting to get used to Dancy's old room being "Nancy's room."

When she comes back a minute later, she's carrying a Bible. "Ecclesiastes. It talks about the futility of working yourself to death and not living a good, happy life." We read a couple of verses that support her viewpoint. "The bottom line, Laini, is that you have lots of dreams, but you have to filter those dreams and figure out which ones are from God and which ones come from other people's expectations or your own notion that a certain career path is something you 'should' want. Retirement is a long way away. Don't get snaked into a job you don't love."

"But the money my aunt loaned me to go to school . . ."

"Find your true dream and pay her back."

It sounds so easy coming from Nancy. She's doing well in her field. Since she got Nick's job, she's bid on three others and landed two of them. She's booked up for months. And thrilled with each new day.

Me? I just want to get this project over with and hopefully get a decent grade for my efforts.

The phone rings and Nancy answers. "Sure, Joe." She hands it to me and I feel myself blush.

"Hey, Joe."

"Look, I know you were busy last Saturday. But if you don't have plans this Saturday, my family is having a dinner for my grandparents. Sort of a party for their sixtieth anniversary."

"Wow."

"Yeah, so anyway, what do you think?"

"Nancy mentioned you might be asking me."

"Nancy did?"

"Yeah, she said you want to introduce me to some guys who might want me to bake for them."

"Oh! Oh, yeah. If you come with me, I'll get you fixed right up. Deal?"

I feel just like I did when Nick shook my hand and promised me the interior design job. All jumpy inside. Nervous and excited at the same time.

"Yeah, deal."

"Great. I'll pick you up around six. Wait. Should I pick you up on Long Island?"

"No. I'll go after the party. My mom has a lot going on these days anyway."

"You sure?" He sounds unconvinced. "I don't mind picking you up there."

"Don't worry about it. I'll just tell my mom I'm about to land some new business." Please, please correct me. Tell me this is a date with the side benefit of making a connection or two. Come on, Joe — pony up. Call this a date.

"Right. It's not like it's a date or anything."

And after a minute of awkward silence, we say good-bye, and that's that. Suddenly I see my houseful of Italian-Irish children fading away and transforming into some Italian girl's (like Nancy) houseful of full-blooded Italian children.

Not one freckle or strand of curly red hair.

Some girls have all the luck.

16

The next night when I get off the train, Joe isn't there to meet me, but oddly enough, Mark is. Plain clothes and all. I'm genuinely pleased to see him, but I sort of wonder if he and Joe flipped a coin. "You're not working?"

"New shift." He gives me a look of real regret. "I'll have to work Saturdays for a while."

I can tell he's truly sorry. "Don't worry," I blurt before I think. "I have plans with Joe this Saturday anyway."

He pulls back like I stuck a hot match to his skin. "You're dating Joe Pantalone too?"

Sheesh. He makes it sound like I'm cheating. "We're not dating, Mark. He invited me to his grandparents' anniversary party."

"How is that not a date?"

Oh, man. He's actually jealous. I like it. But there's no reason for it and I don't play games.

"Mark," I say calmly. "Joe's about to close down for renovations. He just wants to introduce me to some family members who might need some cinnamon rolls or stuffed sandwiches or whatever. He's just looking out for me. Making sure I don't lose anything financially during this time." Now that I think about it, that's kind of . . . heroic of Joe. But what was I saying? "See? It's really innocent. No need for jealousy."

We stop walking and he takes my hand. Pulling me against the side of the building, he looks deep into my eyes. "I think there is a need for jealousy. Maybe you don't see the way he looks at you, Laini. But I do. Actually, anyone with eyes can see."

Maybe not. Nancy has eyes, after all, and she apparently can't see anything but Joe's sense of honor. I keep the bitter thought to myself. Besides, how can I even think about Joe with a good-looking, Polo cologne–smelling, blue-eyed muscley cop looking at me like I'm the best thing he's ever seen? My heart thunders in my ears. He's moving in.

"Don't go, Laini," he whispers just before landing a kiss. His brawny arms encircle me and draw me softly against him, and I relax in the moment. I don't even want to think about how long it's been since I've been kissed. Let alone kissed like this. His lips are warm and soft, and the man definitely knows how to make a girl go weak in the knees. No wonder Kellie doesn't want to let him go. Ick, why did she have to come up? Go away, old girlfriend — and your son. I close my eyes tighter and shove the images aside.

I'm getting a little carried away (okay, this isn't exactly a third date, but let's call it that anyway. This kiss is just too good to stop on a technicality) and inching my arms around his neck when a loud wolf whistle and a lurid comment from a passerby pull me right out of the moment. Mark's gaze scans my face for a second before he pulls away too, takes my hand, and leads me away from the audience.

"I'm sorry," he says. "I should have waited until we got to your apartment. I just . . ." He looks at me and I think he might do it again. Instead, he shakes his head. "The thought of you with another guy drives me crazy."

"But I told you it's not a date."

"It's you and that guy and his family of criminals, Laini." He pushes out a heavy sigh. "You can't get mixed up with the Pantalones."

The ridiculousness of his hyperconcern

makes me laugh a little. "I admit I wondered how Joe managed to pull off getting those permits in such a short time. But a lot of people have connections with city hall that aren't illegal. Besides, Joe himself said he wanted to do things by the book. And I've known Nick for ages. He's a good Christian man. Definitely not a crook."

"You don't understand." He turns me to him, holding my upper arms. "There are things I can't tell you, but the Pantalone family has a criminal record a mile long."

Alarm seizes me. "Joe?"

He scowls and drops my arms. "No. But he's about the only one in the group."

When we get to my apartment, he hesitates at the bottom step. "Are you still going?"

"Yes," I say quietly. "I told you, it's not a date, but even if it was, what's wrong with that?"

"What about us?"

What about us? It's a valid question. I mean, I did kiss the guy. I curse myself for my weakness. "I like you a lot, Mark. I'd like to keep seeing you."

"But you want to see Joe too?"

I put my hand on his shoulder and laugh. "How many times do I have to tell you I'm not dating Joe?"

He snatches me around the waist with one arm and pulls me close. "What if I asked you to only date me?" His voice is husky as he stares down at me.

Be still my heart. It's on the tip of my tongue to say yes. I'd love that. Only something holds me back. Common sense, I imagine. "I'd say I think it's too soon for us to be exclusive."

Rejection washes over his face. "That's what I thought you'd say."

"I'm sorry. But we haven't been going out that long."

"How long do we have to be going out before you'll consider seeing only me?"

This feels like pressure. And pressure usually makes me run. I fight against rushing inside and leaving him standing alone and bewildered. "Can't we just play it by ear? Take it one step at a time and all that?"

A look of affection passes over him and he leans down, pressing a quick kiss to my forehead. "All right. I won't pressure you. But Joe Pantalone . . . I hope you won't date him. He's bad news. Please trust me."

I reach up and touch his face. I mean, it's nice to have a man so interested. Jealous. Concerned. I've been in a wasteland of male absence for so long . . . and now I've suddenly entered an oasis. How can I not enjoy this? How can I even think of running away from such a great guy? His hand, large and warm, covers mine as he turns his face into my other hand and kisses my palm, once, twice. And then my wrist. He laces his fingers with mine, leans forward, and kisses me again — on the lips this time. "Can we go somewhere and have some coffee? Or maybe I could come up and have coffee here."

I may not be very experienced when it comes to men, but I recognize passion when I see it. I think Mark is hoping for more than coffee. "Actually, I've been dying for some shrimp fried rice from Mr. Wang's. How's that sound?"

He laughs. "It sounds like I just got shot down."

Saturday night Nancy and I get ready together. Apparently Nana invited my roommate to her anniversary party. It wouldn't take much for me to give in to jealousy. But I have to step back and put things into perspective. Just last night I shared quite a few kisses with a very nice, available, good-looking police officer who just happens to want to date me exclusively (although I've yet to confide in him my plan to "wait until marriage," so his desire to have me all to himself might just change if it gets that far).

Anyway, there is no reason for me to be jealous of Nancy's invitation to the party. I mean, Joe didn't exactly invite her, did he? Even though it's understood that she'll share a taxi over there with us.

"Now, don't be upset tonight," Nancy says, standing in front of the mirror by the living room door. "Nana has a bad habit of throwing Joe and me together for little tasks that have to be done by the two of us alone. Going out for ice, for instance, or walking down into the basement for more wine. She's not even close to subtle. Don't let it bother you. Joe and I will do our best to deflect her. Plus, this year we're having the party at a restaurant, so that should help."

"Why would I be jealous?" I stand behind her, nonchalantly crunching my curls. "Remember, this isn't a date. I'll be there long enough to get my introductions to some of Joe's family, and that's all."

"Sure it is, honey. You just keep telling yourself that." Nancy sends me a grin through the mirror where she's applying a thin coating of plum-colored lipstick. Perfect with her dark skin and hair.

When Joe shows up at our door ten minutes later dressed in a black sport coat and a pair of dress slacks, my heart goes into a tailspin.

"Not interested, huh?" Nancy murmurs, and I can only pray Joe didn't hear.

"You girls look amazing." Joe gives Nancy a cursory glance then his eyes swoop over me a couple of times. When he meets my gaze, the appreciation I see in those chocolate brown eyes of his boosts my confidence, and I suddenly don't feel so chubby and awkward.

The party is at Murals in the theater district at the Warwick Hotel. A restaurant with, predictably, murals all over the walls. Joe escorts me in, his hand warm on my back. We're one of the last to arrive, and it's so packed out, there aren't many seats left. As is proper, Joe ushers me to his grandparents' side. "Happy anniversary, Papa and Nana. Papa, this is Laini."

The old man could be Anthony Quinn. Even with age spots and a slight tremor in the hand he extends, he's dashing. I imagine he might have been devastating in his prime. His eyes twinkle as I take his hand. "Very beautiful," he says with a fantastic Italian accent.

I smile. "Thank you, sir. It's nice to meet you."

"It is very nice to meet you as well, young lady."

Nana frowns about as deeply as I've ever seen anyone do. She clears her throat so loudly I'm afraid she might be choking on a bite of bread or something.

Apparently unconcerned, Joe chuckles, bends, and places a gentle kiss on Nana's papery cheek. "You remember Laini, don't you, Nana?"

Her beady black eyes zero in on me like a witch about to cast a spell. I try to hang on, but my gaze falters beneath her perusal. She gives only the faintest nod; then her eyes slide past me and brighten insultingly fast as she recognizes Nancy.

"My Nancy." Extending both arms, she dismisses me and embraces Nancy.

Nancy smiles and stoops. "Happy anniversary."

"You look beautiful," Nana says in her barely discernible English. "Does she not, Joseph?"

"Yeah, Nana." He rolls his eyes. "She's a real looker."

Nancy tosses out a throaty laugh and nudges him.

I feel my claws unsheathe.

The old lady points her crooked index finger across the table where there are two empty seats side by side. "You, Nancy. Sit there."

I can't believe it!

"Nana," Nancy says, "Joe brought a friend. I'll sit by Uncle Frank."

"Your friend will not mind."

Wanna bet? But the look of challenge in the wicked eyes prompts me to say, "I don't mind at all. After all, this isn't a date. Right, Joe?"

His eyes cloud, but only for a minute. "Yeah, right." His shoulders shrug beneath the wonderfully-filled-out jacket. He turns to Nancy. "I guess you're my dinner date."

Somehow I feel like I just got shafted. "Come on, Laini." Joe places his palm at the small of my back and leads me to the seat next to his dad. My legs shake as he pulls the chair out for me. "Dad, do you remember Laini? You met her at the coffee shop."

He gives me a once-over and I know he has no idea who I am. "Sure, sure. Have a seat, doll."

Joe leans in close to me. I fight the urge to close my eyes and take in the scent of soap and aftershave. It's not Polo, but Joe doesn't need expensive cologne to make my knees rubbery. The thought makes me feel a little disloyal to Mark. Anyway, Joe leans in close to my ear and whispers, "You sure about this? Nancy can handle my dad. You should come back to my side of the table and sit with me."

He doesn't think I can handle his dad? A sixty-something guy with gold chains around his neck? Come on. I raise my chin and give him a cocky half-grin. I whisper back, "If she can handle him, so can I."

His gaze slides over my face. He grins and nods. "If you need me, give me a wave." He gives Frank a raised-brow stare. "Dad, behave yourself."

"Huh?" Mr. Pantalone looks up from his conversation with a busty blonde. I fight against rolling my eyes at the cliché.

Joe sends me a wink.

"Joseph!" Nana hollers. "Come and sit."

"Just remember," he says softly, for my ears only. "It was your choice."

"I think I'll live."

I slip into the seat to the right of Frank Pantalone. There's something very Tony Soprano–ish about him, and my bravado vanishes as quickly as it came. I absolutely can*not* hold my own in a conversation with this thug. I look around for someone else to talk to. Anything's got to be better than getting off on the wrong foot with a guy who could very likely order a hit on me for any reason. You never know.

On my right, a slightly-older-than-middle-aged woman is sipping what is too obviously a glass or two past her first of vino. "Hiya," she slurs. "I'm Bev."

Oh, boy. These are my choices? A Marlon Brando wannabe on one side and Bev the Lush on the other? *God, get me out of this nightmare. Please.* "Hi, I'm Laini."

"You came with Joey?"

"Yes, ma'am." I look toward him, hoping he'll be staring back, but he's listening closely to Nancy.

The wine must not be affecting Bev's vision too much, because she notices the direction of my gaze and gives a scowl and a "fuhgetaboutit" wave. "Those two. Why don't they just give in and marry each other? It'd make the old lady happy, and I mean, it ain't like either one of 'em's gettin' any younga, you know what I mean?"

She gasps so loud I'm afraid she might have sucked all the oxygen from the room. I think maybe she's having a heart attack or something, because her palm is flat against her considerable chest as she shakes her head.

"Are you okay?" I ask, about to grab my phone and ready myself for the possibility of calling 911.

"I just can't believe I said that when no more than two minutes ago you said you came here tonight with Joe." She practically growls as she turns her glassy-eyed glare on Joe. "What a bum. Abandoning you for that floozy."

"It's all right, ma'am." How is it that she practically has my date married off to another girl and I'm the one consoling her? My life is not charmed, I tell you. "Actually, Nancy is my roommate and a friend. I don't consider her a floozy. And Joe only brought me to meet some prospective clients. So you see, there's not a problem." I don't think I'd sound too convincing to anyone with less than three glasses of chardonnay in her. But lucky for me, this woman doesn't seem to be able to hold her liquor.

"Clients?" she says in a voice almost as nasal as Fran Drescher's. "What sort of clients, honey?"

Embarrassment catches my throat a little. It's not that I think there's anything wrong with baking, but in view of Nancy's position as a hotshot stinking architect, the thought of 'fessing up sort of fills me with a case of "not on your life." It's pride. Yes, pride. Most likely the kind that goes before a fall. But I'm powerless to stop myself from blurting out, "I'm a designer."

She scrutinizes me and a funny look slips across her pudgy face. "Since when did designers start wearing JC Penney?"

Okay, this woman doesn't need even one more sip of that wine. How the heck did she know I'm wearing department store clothes? "Let's get something straight right off the bat," I say with a sniff. "These are from Sears, not Penney's. And I'm not that kind of designer anyway. I'm an interior designer."

Interest springs to her Tammy Faye eyes. "Well, that's a different story, isn't it?"

"What do you mean?"

"I mean, maybe I have a job for you."

At this moment I am keenly aware of two things. One: the Laini angel sitting on my right shoulder all dressed in white and wings. And two, the Laini devil wearing a skintight red bodysuit and carrying a pitchfork.

The angel tells me I should definitely confess to this woman — explain that even if I graduate, I'm pretty sure I'm not going to be any good at this job and I'm seriously rethinking this career path.

"Do not," Angel Me says, "allow her to hire you for a job you're not only ill-equipped to take on, but for which you also do not have a degree."

Devil Me, on the other hand (or shoulder, to be precise), tells me, "Don't be a chump. Take every bit of advantage of this drunken woman who so callously made you see how perfect Nancy and Joe look with their heads close together talking about something that obviously needs close-to-the-ear communication."

I stare at Nancy and Joe again. Joe doesn't seem to remember he brought a different girl. Doesn't he even wonder how I'm doing over here all by myself, sitting with people I don't know? I mean, even if it is a non-date, I deserve the occasional glance from him. I think I do anyway. And so does Devil Me.

"Wh-what sort of job?" Oh, boy. Dread infuses me. This can only end badly. Unless, that is, I turn to the light side and start listening to my inner angel.

"I got a couple of rooms need changed. My husband, Ernie" — (sign of the cross) — "may he rest in peace, had the same nasty wood paneling in his office from the day we bought that house until he died two ye-ahs ago." Another sign of the cross. "I been plannin' to change it ever since. You want the job?"

"B-but I don't . . ."

She takes a sip of her wine. "If you're good

enough for Joey, you're good enough for me, honey."

Speaking of Joe, he just touched Nancy's hand and then laughed at something she said. Even the feathers on my angel's wings ruffle at that. Is it any wonder I suddenly turn to this woman and say, "I'd love to take a look. We'll fix up your husband's (may he rest in peace) space before you know it. Can I get your number?"

All I can say is, the devil made me do it.

Twenty minutes of discussing Bev's dead husband's office and I'm wishing I was a drinking girl myself. I almost cry real tears of relief when someone taps my shoulder. "You Miss Sullivan?" I turn to find two men, decked out in expensive suits and gold rings on their fingers.

"That's right."

"I'm Tony." He jerks his thumb at the identical man next to him. I'm guessing identical twins. "This is Sam. Joey says you're looking for some business."

From the looks of these two characters, I'm not sure what kind of "business" we're talking about, but since Joe sent them my way, I'll listen . . . cautiously.

"Hold on, you two," Bev slurs. "This girl is going to design Ernie's office for me. So I get her first."

"Design?" Tony frowns. "I thought you was a baker." Oh, yeah. That was the purpose of tonight, wasn't it?

"I'm baking my way through design school," I say, trying to suppress the sudden rise of laughter at the whole ridiculous situation.

"Hey." Frank pulls himself away from the blonde on his other side and joins our conversation. "What are you two guys trying to do? Nick ain't going to let this girl go. She's a gold mine."

Tony sends him a scowl. "Mind your own business, Frankie. Joey asked us if we wanted to try out some of her stuff."

"Look," I say, swallowing hard, "you don't have to. . . ."

"Don't be silly," Sam says, placing a meaty hand on my shoulder. "We know what a profit your stuff is bringing to Nicky's place." He sends me a wink. "He can't keep you all to hisself, can he?"

I can't help but smile.

Tony grins back. "Shall we step out for a minute and talk business?"

I glance over at Joe. He smiles and nods. My heart soars at the pride shining in those eyes. For the life of me I can't look away, and neither does he. Is something happening here? Self-consciously, I touch my fingers to the base of my throat. His eyes flicker down to my fingers and back to my eyes. His lips part as he takes a long, slow breath. I can almost feel his arms around me.

This moment is going on too long. I know that, but I'm powerless to stop it.

Nana, on the other hand, has all the power in the world. She smacks him on the arm and that's that. He drags his gaze away and I get a glare from Nana. Clearly, she's determined that he's going to marry "her" Nancy.

I turn to the uncles. "Men," I say, "let's go talk business."

17

Joe insists on riding the train with me all the way to Long Island after the party. We drop Nancy at the apartment, where I grab my bag, and off we go to Penn Station.

"I mean it, Joe," I say for the umpteenth time after we disembark from the train and hail a cab. "This really wasn't necessary. I feel terrible that you came all this way." And I do. Feel terrible, that is. Sort of. Mostly I'm thrilled he wanted to make sure I made it to Mom's without being mugged.

"Don't feel bad. I couldn't let you come over here alone at night."

He reaches across me in the backseat of the cab and I draw back, a little startled that he's making a move. If I want to fudge the numbers, I can call this a first date, even though we've both made it clear it isn't. Still, I can't exactly go to a kiss yet. I could hold his hand, maybe let him put an arm around me.

His face is close. So close that if he wanted to, he could move in for a kiss and there'd be absolutely nothing I could do about it. Really, he could. Like, right now. If he wanted to, that is. Is it really fair to hold him to a set of rules that I haven't shared with him?

My stomach lurches as he turns his head to look at me, smiles, then pushes the lock. "Don't want you falling out."

Be still my heart.

He settles back onto his side of the car, leaving me breathless and let down. And I'm pretty sure there's a tiny smile lurking at the corners of his lips. As though he might have done it on purpose, knowing how amazing he looks and smells tonight. But hidden in the shadows, I can't be positive. And why would he toy with me that way? I dismiss the thought as unlikely and relax as the cab whirs through the wet streets.

Joe breaks the silence. "Nana is relentless about Nancy and me," he says. "I want to apologize again for forcing you on Aunt Bev and my dad."

I shrug, still smarting a little over the image of Nancy and Joe with their gorgeous Italian heads together. Why did he have to go and bring that up anyway? "Actually," I say, turning away from the window (which I'm starting to fog up, incidentally), "I had a nice chat with Bev. She might be interested in hiring me to redo her late husband's office."

His eyebrows go up. "You agreed to that?"

What is his problem?

"I agreed to take a look." I narrow my gaze at him and muster as much attitude as the situation warrants. "Why? Do you have a problem with it?"

He shakes his head. "Not at all. I just thought you'd have your hands full with the other stuff."

"What other stuff? I don't plan to pursue the contract until I get my degree."

"The catering business. How did it go with my uncles?"

I smile at him and have to resist the urge to pat his cheek as though he's a sweet ten-year-old boy. "I don't have a catering business, Joe. Just an outside source for making supplemental money while I'm in school."

"You plan to stop baking when you get your degree?"

I open my mouth to say, "Of course." But I can't quite bring myself to do it. Because I hadn't really put two and two together and calculated the cost of getting that degree. If I work for another designer, which is the plan, I won't have time for baking. And if I'm going to contract my own work — well — I won't have time for baking then either. Not the amounts Joe and his uncles are asking for.

"Well?" Joe's one-word question pulls me from my reverie.

"I guess we'll have to wait and see what sort of job I line up after I get my degree." It's the easiest answer I can think of. And thank goodness the cabbie pulls up to the curb in front of my mom's house, sparing me the necessity of elaborating. I pull on the handle, but the door doesn't budge.

Oh, the lock. Joe and I reach for it at the same time. His hand covers mine and we lift the button together.

"Thanks," I say, trying to be cool.

"No prob."

I take a deep breath of cool March air as I step out of the cab. Then I realize that I didn't pay and open the door just as Joe stuffs some bills into the cabbie's hand.

"Close the door, lady," the cabdriver grumps.

Sheesh.

He speeds off, leaving me to stare at Joe. "Hey, I was going to pay for that. I would have had to take a cab whether you came with me or not."

"Don't worry about it."

"Thanks. I owe you one."

Joe walks me to the door and, of course, I ask him in. I can't expect the guy to take a train and then a cab (for which he paid) and not at least offer him a cup of tea. Even if he did leave me at the mercy of his drunken aunt.

He wrinkles up his nose at the mention of tea.

"I could put on coffee."

"You mind?"

"Not at all." I'll be up all night, but he's worth it.

The kitchen light is on when we step inside, but there's no sign of my mother. "She must have already gone to bed." I glance at the clock. After all, it is eleven o'clock.

Joe shifts his position from one foot to the other. "Should I leave?"

"No. We'll just have to be quiet."

Suddenly a rakish grin appears. "We could make out. That doesn't require talking."

My face goes hot, and I can just imagine the splotches on my neck. I know he's kidding. Joe can't help himself. He's probably never gone to a girl's house and not made out. Is that what he expects? Oh, good heavens, I think I feel a migraine coming on. Hyperventilating. That's it. I'm going to die right here and now.

"You okay?" He reaches for me, a frown creasing his brow. "Hey, I was kiddin'."

Escape! "I — um — I have to use the bathroom."

I hear his chuckle as I run away to the safety of the second room on the right, down the hall.

I take breaths. Deep trembly breaths that should steady me, but instead are sort of making me dizzy. I guess I really am hyperventilating. Where's a paper bag when I need one? Fighting for control over my breathing, I stare into the mirror. Yep. I'm splotchy. It's no wonder a guy like Joe will never be truly interested. But how could he just callously throw out the image of me making out with him like it's nothing? I guess in all honesty, to him it *is* nothing. To me, well, it's not, you know, nothing. It's something.

I stare into my own eyes in the mirror. Why do you care, Laini? Seriously. Mark is just as — well, practically as good-looking. He's just as nice. Actually, I think Mark is nicer than Joe. And Mark has one more thing going for him. He really does want to kiss me. And I like kissing him too. Okay, his mouth is a little big for me. But it's not bad. And his arms hold me just right. Joe hasn't ever actually made a romantic move. Not even the night I spent in his bed. Not that anything would have happened. Even if I were that kind of girl, there was that whole migraine–throwing-up thing going on. Still, though. It's a little humiliating.

Okay, my breathing has returned to normal. Practically. My face is no longer red. For the most part. I think I can return to the kitchen with some semblance of dignity.

I'm about to reach for the door when a scream resonates through the house.

"Who are you? Y-you better get out of here if you know what's good for you. I have mace!"

Oh, good grief. Mom's up. How could I forget her four bathroom breaks a night? I fling the door open and beeline down the hall into the kitchen. Mom is holding Joe off with a broom. She sees me from the corner of her eye. "Get back, Laini! Call 911."

Joe's eyes are fixed on the broom, which is pointed a little low for his comfort, I'm sure. "For crying out loud, Laini. Tell her who I am, will you?"

A giggle rises from my belly, and I can't help but let it out. Actually, more than a giggle. "Ma, put down the broom," I say through a constricted throat. "This is Joe."

"Joe? Joe who?" She frowns. "And why are you laughing? This isn't funny. I nearly had a heart attack. And only two months before my wedding. That would have been tragic."

Truly. For more reasons than one. I sober up on the spot.

"Sorry, Ma." Stepping forward, I take the broom from her and watch Joe relax. "Joe is Nick Pantalone's nephew. From the coffee shop? He's my friend."

"Oh." She nods and makes her way to the sink, where she fills the teapot I abandoned a few minutes earlier. "The coffee shop."

"We went to a dinner party tonight. He escorted me home."

She turns to me with a frown. "What about Mark? Don't you usually see him on Saturday?"

Oh, please. Tell me she didn't.

Joe bristles, which just might make the entire incident worthwhile.

Is it wrong that I enjoy his getting bent out of shape at the sound of Mark's name?

"Mark's working tonight."

"So you went out with another man? That doesn't look good, even if he is only a friend." She gives him a once-over and then stares back at me with a look that indicates she doesn't believe I could ever be just friends with a guy like Joe. And of course she's right. But I'm not going to own up to that. Ever.

Joe clears his throat and steps forward, holding out his hand. "It's nice to meet you, Mrs. Sullivan." Mom sets the teakettle on the burner and eyes him. I know that look. She's determined not to believe anything he says. "I'm not trying to come between Laini and Mark. I asked Laini to come to a family function so she can drum up business for her cinnamon rolls and other baking while the coffee shop is being renovated."

Reluctantly, Mom takes his hand. "So this wasn't a date?"

"No, ma'am."

Her eyes narrow, and I know she's thinking, *Why? My daughter isn't good enough for you?*

I can't help but laugh. "Sit down, Ma. I'll get the tea. What kind do you want?"

"Anything, just as long as it doesn't have caffeine. I don't need to be awake all night." She's right about that. Because if she's awake all night, I'm awake all night.

"I'll make you chamomile." I turn to Joe. "It'll just take a minute for the coffee to brew."

Joe glances at his watch. "Actually, I think

I'm going to take off. It's getting late."

A curious disappointment clutches at me. This is why I don't live with my mother.

"Do you need to call a cab?"

He shakes his head. "I told the cabbie to come back in twenty minutes."

So he had no intention of dropping me at the door and leaving without a few minutes of conversation anyway. That makes me feel good.

"I'll walk you out."

"Sounds good." He turns to my mom and inclines his head ever-so-slightly. "It was nice to meet you, Mrs. Sullivan. I apologize for scaring you."

My mom's expression softens. "I'm sorry I mistook you for a thief."

Joe grins. "It's okay. It's not the first time I've been accused of being a crook."

I fight hard not to cringe at his statement as my mind races back to the rushed-through city hall permits.

The word *crook* won't let go as we walk through the living room on the way to the door. I'd like to ask him about those dog-gone permits, but I don't have the nerve.

Joe glances at the boxes littering the floor. "Going somewhere?"

"Mom's getting remarried in a couple of months. She's selling the house." I give a wave to include all the clutter. "Thus the packing."

"This is a great house." His eyebrows go up. "You don't want it?"

"Of course I do." I try not to sound pathetic. "It's just that she has to sell it, and I don't have a real job, so who's going to give me a loan?"

"You graduate soon, though."

"Hopefully . . ."

I open the door and we step into the cloudy night. Shoving his hands into his pants pockets, he rocks back on his heels. "Don't sell yourself short. Your ideas for the coffee shop are pretty solid. Even Nancy said so. Plus, Nancy's getting acquainted with quite a few people in the business. Architects, designers, contractors. Those guys all know each other."

I nod. "Yeah." If I had more confidence in my own abilities, I'd be a lot more comfortable with the concept of asking for Nancy's recommendation. But I'd hate to put her on the spot if she doesn't feel she can honestly put in a good word for me. It's not fair, and I don't like to be put in that position myself, so I won't do it to my new friend.

Headlights loom and my heart sinks as instinctively I know it's the cab returning for Joe. Only, I'm not ready to let him leave. I mean, after all, we didn't really have much time together since he spent the evening with Nancy while I had the misfortune of listening to Bev rattle on about Ernie (may he rest in peace) and his rotten taste in decorating.

"Looks like it's time for me to go."

Joe unstuffs his hands and places them on my arms. "Listen, I'm sorry you didn't have a great time tonight. But did you at least get some business?"

I nod. "Your uncles ordered a ridiculous amount of baked goods. I had to rein them in."

"Have you ever thought about getting some menus made up? You could probably open your own shop or catering service or something. Then you wouldn't even need to work for someone else."

Is he serious? I can't hold in the laugh that bubbles to my lips. "Joe, cooking is a hobby. If I make it a business, I might stop loving it."

He frowns. "How could that happen? Look at Uncle Nick. Only Aunt Nelda could pull him away from that coffee shop."

"True."

His shoulders lift in a shrug. "So what's wrong with you baking for a living? You're good at it. Better than anyone I've ever known."

My heart soars, and I can't stop my cheesy grin. "Thanks, Joe."

The cabbie blares the horn. "Yo! You want a cab or not?"

"Hey, lay off that thing," Joe calls. "People are sleeping."

"You'd better go before he leaves you."

"Yeah." But he doesn't look like he's even close to leaving. He reaches out and fingers a springy strand of my hair. "Your curls are pretty."

I avert my gaze. Embarrassed. I don't like my hair. Too red and too curly, especially on nights like this when the humidity is pretty much a hundred percent. And compliments make me feel uncomfortable. Like the person on the giving end is telling a whopper. But sincerity flows from Joe. "Thanks."

"Hey, buddy!" That dumb cabbie. "Kiss your girl good night and let's go."

"Keep your shirt on," Joe responds, but he grins down at me. "You heard the man."

My lips tingle with anticipation as he bends forward. Only, at the last second, he presses a soft, warm mouth to my cheek instead of my lips. "Good night, Laini. Thanks for being such a good sport tonight.

I know Aunt Bev is a pain."

"Especially after her third glass of wine." And that was after she introduced herself. No telling how many she had before I even got there. I try not to make too much of the fact that he doesn't seem to want to leave. Could be for any number of reasons. The cabbie has BO, for instance. Or maybe Joe doesn't have enough money for a cab ride home. No, that's silly.

The cab slowly begins to inch away as the driver obviously decides to make his point. Joe heaves a sigh. "Good night."

"Good night, Joe. Thanks for inviting me."

He hesitates, leans forward, and kisses my other cheek. "You're welcome."

I can't begin to describe the extent of my disappointment as I watch him saunter down the steps and along the sidewalk to the cab.

He turns and gives a little wave before ducking into the car.

I'm still smiling as I enter the kitchen. Mom is still up, sitting with her legs crossed, two cups of tea on the table. She gives me a stern frown. "All of a sudden you're seeing two men and you don't bother telling your mother?"

"Sorry, Ma. I'm not actually seeing Joe."

She gives a humph. "Could have fooled

me. He couldn't take his eyes off of you."

If only. Mom isn't finished. "Come sit down and tell me about Joe. Then we can decide."

"Decide what?"

"In my day, there was a word for a girl that dated too many men at once."

My lips twitch. "What was it?"

"Loose, that's what. And wipe that smirk off your face."

I wipe it. I sip my tea, and for the next few minutes, I tell Mom all about Joe. Except for the part about me spending the night in his bed. I'm pretty sure she doesn't have a shotgun, but if I told her about that, she'd probably go buy one and shove it into Joe's back all the way to the altar.

On second thought, maybe I ought to tell her after all.

18

The next morning at church, my eyes feel like they've been through a sandstorm. They're all gritty from lack of sleep, and I keep yawning. I know the preacher is staring at me. He's probably seen more of my tonsils today than my doctor has in a year. I'm actually afraid to close my eyes during the prayer for fear I'll nod off and start snoring.

In order to keep from dozing, I do mind exercises, such as replaying my conversation with Joe last night. What keeps coming back to me is the part where he asked me if I'd ever thought about opening my own business. I mean, hasn't everyone? Only, I sort of thought I would do interior design. Start out working for an established designer, then after I'd learned the ropes, do some jobs on the side as a contractor (but nothing that would take away from my employer), and then eventually open my own shop. I wasn't all that excited about the idea, but it would sure beat working for someone else for the rest of my life.

Only now, I can't get the thought of baking for a living out of my head. Baking? Is it even possible that I could do enough business to make an honest-to-goodness living?

"The Lord says, 'For I know the plans I have for you.' "

Huh? The words pull me from my thoughts and bring me back to the present.

" 'They are plans for good and not for disaster, to give you a future and a hope.' " Pastor Moore pans the crowd and seems to settle on my intense gaze. "Most people stop here," says the balding middle-aged man with kind eyes and a white smile. "But the next verse is just as important: 'In those days when you pray, I will listen. If you look for me wholeheartedly, you will find me. I will be found by you.' "

For some crazy reason, I can't shake the urge to weep. And indeed, tears form in my eyes. I don't even bother to blink them away. I need to hear this. I need to know if I have a divine destiny. That's what the title of the sermon today happens to be: "Fulfilling Your Divine Destiny."

I'm suddenly wide awake, and I listen intently for the next few minutes as Pastor

Moore talks about the fullness of a person's future being directly related to seeking God.

"In the book of Matthew, Jesus tells us to seek the kingdom of God 'above all else' and live righteously," the pastor says. "*Then and only then* will He give us everything we need." His eyes seem to bore into mine. I know that's probably my imagination. Maybe he's like one of those pictures where the eyes follow you wherever you go. Regardless, he keeps staring. Intentional or not, it's freaking me out a bit. But not to the point that I want to leave. Rather, I can't take my eyes from him either. If there's a secret to gaining God's purpose for my life, I want to find it.

As the service concludes, Pastor Moore looks me in the eye and speaks. "God's eyes are on you. He knows where you're going. His greatest desire is for you to walk out the life He's prepared for you. All you have to do is seek and you will find."

The closing prayer follows and then Mom leans in. "I always feel like he's preaching right to me."

"Yeah," I mumble. "Me too."

I leave the church that day pondering: Do I turn my life over to God and start reading my Bible (thus, seeking Him) just so I can have my needs met? I don't know. . . . Seems a little like I'd be using God for personal gain. On the other hand, it is in there, isn't it? But maybe I could think about it for a while. Then if I can honestly seek Him, I will. Otherwise, I guess it's just my loss. I suppose if I'm honest with myself, I have to admit I've turned a corner. I became a Christian when I was a little girl. Officially. But something about Dad dying and Mom changing so drastically made me a little bitter. Lately, though, somewhere between regular church attendance and off-the-cuff prayers, I've come to this place where I'm more aware of God. His presence, His power to direct my life, even conviction when I do things that don't feel right. It feels like I've recently slid back into the Christian life. I'm still not positive what it all means. All I know is that I'm different. In a good way. And I'm not willing to go back to where I was before.

The phone starts ringing at eight o'clock the next morning as I'm sitting at the table with Nancy, eating the first breakfast I've had time to actually cook in two weeks. Spanish omelets and English muffins. Not exactly gourmet, but a nice effort. It makes me feel like I'm doing something worthwhile. I'm especially gratified watching

Nancy gobble up every single bite. Seeing skinny girls eat like truckers always gives me a sense of glee.

By eight thirty, I've gotten orders from two more coffee shops around the city and one sandwich shop that claims my sandwiches are the stuff legends are made of. Those Pantalones are serious about keeping me working. Orders for a total of twelve dozen cinnamon rolls and six dozen stuffed sandwiches. All due by Wednesday.

Nancy's face clouds a little when I deliver the news. "Does that mean you'll need the oven all day tomorrow?"

"All day today, tonight, tomorrow, and tomorrow night." I'm disappointed in her lack of enthusiasm, to be honest. My former roommates would have been happy with this great order. It'll help me out a *lot* financially. "Is that a problem?"

She shrugs. "I was going to cook for a couple of friends tomorrow night. But it's okay. We can make it another time."

My eyes go wide. "Oh, Nancy. I didn't know. I'm so sorry." My mind calculates the possibilities. "How about if I cook here today and then go to my mom's tomorrow?"

Her eyes widen. "Are you sure?"

"It's your apartment too, Nancy. I sort of monopolize things. I'll call my mom and just make sure she doesn't mind." Sheesh, I might as well move in with Mom for all the time I'm spending there lately. Except . . . well, she's not going to be living there much longer, is she? In just a couple of months, she'll be marrying Aaron. They're moving into a rented apartment until the house sells. Heaviness presses against my chest.

I pick up the phone and okay my plans with my mom, who is, of course, thrilled to have me come to Long Island twice in one week. I nod at Nancy's questioning glance when I end the call. "I'll cook here today and then go to my mom's after my class tonight."

"Are you sure? I hate to throw you out of your own apartment."

"It's no problem. Actually, my mom said she has something she wants to talk to me about anyway. So I guess it's timely."

"Excellent. Then I'll tell Joe we're on for tomorrow night."

"Joe?" I can't believe it. I got myself out of the way so that she could reel Joe in?

I'm such a dope. For all of Nancy's chatter about just being friends with him, she's as taken with the guy as I am.

I barely have time to get the flour out of my

fingernails before it's time to go to school. My mind keeps going over the dozens and dozens of cinnamon rolls I've gotten done, and the stuffed sandwiches I'll make tomorrow. I keep calculating how much money I'll make with all of this. I know it's probably tacky to think about money so much, but with my half of the rent due in a few days, it's all I can think about.

I truly try to look interested during the lecture. But who can get excited about brocade when I have dough rising at home? It'll probably be as high as the ceiling. Nancy promised to punch it down and knead it for me, but she was knee-deep in paperwork and sort of waved me away when I asked and she agreed, so I seriously doubt she'll remember. My professor keeps staring at me — I'm sure he's not too happy about my lack of attention.

As he dismisses us, he says into the mic, "Miss Sullivan, will you please see me before leaving this evening?"

Jazz tosses me a sympathetic look as she grabs her books and heads to yoga.

I huff my way down the bleacher-type steps. Why does Mr. Brooks constantly try to discourage me? Personally, I think if a teacher can't be supportive, he has no business sitting behind that desk. Or standing behind the small, metal podium, as the case may be.

I make my way to the front, hanging back while he hands out missed assignments and answers quick questions as my fellow students file out of the room after a long and boring lecture.

I see and hear his sigh as I approach. "Thank you for staying after, Miss Sullivan."

"No problem," I say as nonchalantly as possible considering my hands are sweating and my knees are quaking. "You wanted to speak to me?"

He hands me a paper I recognize as the revised proposal that Joe, Nancy, and the contractor signed off on.

"Is this your work?"

"Mine and Jazz's. We're partners." I give him what I know must be a confused frown. "Did we miss a step?"

He shakes his head. "Not at all. I'm just wondering how much of this is you and how much is Miss Bates."

"We pooled our ideas. I thought of Italian decor, and she started pulling ideas together with me."

"And the floors? Whose idea were those?"

"The faux stone with cracks to mimic old Italy?" I swallow hard. "That was an afterthought. I just thought it would work." And so did the architect. "I hope Jazz doesn't get points taken off for my mistakes."

"Mistakes?" He smiles the first real smile I've ever seen from this guy. "This is truly a wonderful design. How are the renovations coming along?"

"The contractors start knocking down walls this week. They say they'll be done in three or four weeks and then we get to start painting and adding the new tables and stuff."

"Three or four weeks?" His eyebrows go up.

"They're willing to work around the clock. Two crews."

I know, I know. It's unprecedented. Contractors are notoriously slow and unreliable. But how can I tell this professor who is giving me the first genuine smile I've ever received from him that Joe's dad most likely made the contractor an offer he couldn't refuse? That I'm getting preferential treatment by association with the mob?

I refuse to do it. Seriously. I can't.

He takes the papers back and stuffs them into a file that I can see is marked "Sullivan/ Bates."

"All right. I'll look forward to the unveiling."

"Yes, sir. So will I."

The cool evening wind teases my hair, tickling my face as I walk toward the train station. Stars dot the sky, and I breathe in relief. I'm ready for a night without rain.

My cell phone chirps just as I reach the steps. I know better than to try to answer belowground, so I decide to take it before I descend. Oh, it's Mark. I haven't heard from him all weekend. "Hey, stranger," I say, smiling to myself. "I thought you'd fallen off the face of the earth."

He chuckles. "Liz had her baby."

"She did? Boy or girl?"

"Girl."

"That's great. I bet she and Rick are thrilled."

"Yeah. Anyway, I had to fill in for Pop while he passed cigars to everyone at the hospital."

"You cook?" This information surprises and delights me for some reason. It gives us that much more in common.

"Of course. I grew up in a restaurant, remember? Pop had me running the grill and handling the deep fryer by the time I was twelve."

"Isn't that illegal?"

"Yeah. But Pop figured I was his kid and

nobody had a right to tell him what to do with his own flesh and blood. Liz has been working there forever too."

"It was nice of you to help out." I wait a sec to see if he's going to add anything. I glance at my watch. Trains leave every few minutes, and I don't want to miss the next one. "My train's about to leave, Mark. I'd better let you go."

"Okay . . . I'll see you . . ." and the rest of his message is garbled as I hurry down the steps and through the turnstile and slide onto the crowded train just as the doors close.

I push my way out of the subway, through a sea of bodies, and up the steps to find Mark waiting for me, a bouquet of roses in his hands. His face beams.

My eyes widen. "Are those for me?" The words come out in a gasp. I've never gotten roses from a guy. From anyone. Ever. Well, from Dad, on my sweet sixteen, but that doesn't count.

"Of course they're for you." He bends and brushes a kiss against my lips.

I catch movement from the corner of my eye and lo and behold, there's Joe. Watching and scowling. Mark turns. "Oh, the coffee shop guy." He slips an arm around my waist. I recognize the action as territorial.

Joe's eyes narrow and I know he heard Mark's comment. He steps forward.

"Hi, Joe," I say, my voice a little shaky because I realize Joe witnessed Mark's kiss. "You remember Mark."

His gaze sweeps the flowers in my arms, then goes to Mark. "Oh, yeah. The cop."

I feel Mark tense up next to me. It's tragic, really, and shows the true state of my character, that I'm so glad he's jealous. What I can't figure out is why Joe is here.

"Excuse me," Joe says before I can humiliate myself by thanking him for meeting me. "I need to catch the next train. I'm meeting some friends in Jersey."

I could kiss the ground, I'm so grateful I didn't voice my assumption that he was there to walk me home.

Mark gives a short humorless laugh as we walk away from the subway station. "I just bet he's going to visit friends in Jersey."

"What would be the point of lying?"

"I'm not saying he's not going there, only that . . ." His eyes scan my face. He smiles and squeezes me closer. "Never mind. I'm sure you'll find out soon enough."

"What are you talking about?" I don't like surprises, and I definitely don't like being out of the loop. But by the smug look on his face, I start to get the picture. He's talking about taking Joe down. Legally. "Is this about the mafia rumors?"

"Maybe. But I can't talk about it right now. I shouldn't have said anything at all. But the way that guy looks at you . . ." He hugs me tighter to his side. "It drives me crazy, the thought of you seeing him."

"I'm not. Actually, I think he's sort of seeing my roommate, Nancy. She even invited him over for dinner tomorrow night."

"Pantalone's coming to your apartment?"

I nod. "Yeah, but I won't be there. I have orders out the wazoo and Nancy needs the oven, so I'm going to my mom's tonight."

"Oh." I hear the disappointment in his voice and turn to look up at him as we walk.

"Did you have something in mind?"

"Just being with you. I should have called earlier. Or yesterday. I'm not so good at making arrangements ahead of time. With Kellie I never had to."

I just bet. "Well, with me you do."

We reach the stairs of my apartment and he pulls me close. He smells lightly of Polo and I have to admit my stomach does a little bit of a flip. But not like before. As a matter of fact, the mention of *Kellie* has ruined any chance this guy has of being kissed by me tonight.

"Something wrong?" he asks.

"Not really. I just have to pack up and get to my mom's before it's too late. She goes to bed by ten."

"Can I go to the train station with you? I could help you carry stuff."

All I have is a small duffel bag to take. Mom went out and bought all my food ingredients so I don't have to cart any on the train. I didn't ask her to do that, mind you, but it was awfully sweet of her.

Still, Mark looks a little lost, so I suppose I can let him redeem himself for the Kellie comment. "Yeah, you can tell me all about Liz's baby."

Relief floods his face. "I can do that."

It's not what he *can* tell me that I'm most interested in, though. What in the world does he have on Joe?

19

The greasy, smoky aroma of bacon frying awakens me the next morning. I stretch and turn onto my back. I usually wake up and bound out of bed, but today my body refuses to move. I think my crazy, hectic life of late is catching up to me. School, baking, the stress of what will happen after I graduate — provided I do graduate. And last but not least, juggling two guys, even if one of them is more interested in friendship than anything else.

The faint sound of "I Surrender All" carries up the steps. Mom's singing again. I snuggle deeper under the covers and smile. Feels like old times. The only thing missing is my dad's wonderful, all-consuming presence.

It occurs to me that I've been spending an awful lot of weeknights here lately. I'm beginning to get used to waking up in my old house more often than just weekends. I have to say, I'm enjoying it. As more items disappear into boxes, however, I also have to admit to a sense of grief. Maybe it's more nostalgia — no, it's definitely grief. Gut-tightening, reduced-to-tears-at-times grief. I wonder what it would have been like to watch my parents grow old together in this house. To bring my kids to see the grands on the weekends. Family barbecues, Christmas, Thanksgiving and Easter dinners. Of course I might have to give up the occasional holiday for my husband's family. I suppose I could allow for Easter at the in-laws'.

I'm so caught up in my nostalgic look at what might have been that I don't realize Mom has stopped singing until she taps on my door.

"I'm up, Ma. Come in."

I love seeing her wearing the white robe. Although it seems a little looser than just a couple of weeks ago.

"Have you dropped some weight?" I ask, pulling myself up and hugging my knees to my chest as she sits at the foot of my bed.

A pleased smile spreads across her face. "I've been eating better. It means a lot to Aaron for us to take care of ourselves. I signed up for that Silver Sneakers program at the YMCA. We've been working out."

"Well, you look great."

"Thank you, honey. I have some turkey bacon and egg-white omelets staying warm in the oven. I'm just about to make some whole wheat toast. Come on and eat before you get started on your baking."

"Whole wheat toast and egg-white omelets, huh? You really are eating better."

She nods. "Aaron's first wife died of diabetes. Even though she didn't do anything to cause it, he just wants us to do everything we can to stay healthy and not rush our deaths by irresponsible lifestyle choices."

"Wow. It sounds like he wants to keep you around for some time."

Her cheeks blush a pretty rose. "That's the idea. As a matter of fact, that's what I wanted to discuss with you."

"What?"

"We've decided not to have a large wedding after all."

My jaw goes slack at the unexpected announcement. "Why would you do that, Ma? I was just starting to warm to the idea of being your maid of honor."

"You can still stand up with us." She draws a deep sigh. "We're just not waiting and having a big wedding. Chad has been making terrible threats about getting a judge to declare Aaron incompetent and naming Chad his guardian."

Outrage yanks me out of bed. I plop my hands on my hips. "He can't do that, can he?"

She shrugs. "I doubt it. But we both feel it would be wise to nip it in the bud before he can even try. If I'm Aaron's wife, Chad won't have a leg to stand on."

I see her point. But I hate the idea of my mother having to sneak around and have a tiny ceremony instead of standing up in front of her friends at church like she and Aaron had planned. "I'm sorry, Ma. I know the wedding meant a lot to you."

"Well, the marriage is the important thing."

"So when were you thinking of taking the plunge?"

"We're going to Pastor Moore this Saturday. That's what I wanted to talk to you about. We're going to take a few days away for a honeymoon." Her gaze falters as her face blushes a deep red.

I feel my own cheeks burn. I definitely don't need to think about my senior citizen mother on her honeymoon. Ick!

"Anyway, I'd like you to stay and housesit if you don't mind."

I push back the covers and scoot to the

end of the bed. I wrap my arms around her, and hold on for dear life. "Of course I'll stay here while you're gone. You have nothing to worry about."

Mom pulls away and gives me a pat on the back. "Thank you, honey. I'll let you get dressed. Come down soon so you can eat while it's fresh."

I watch her leave and something squeezes my heart. I feel like I'm losing my mom. Not that I wish she was still in deep mourning over Dad. She's definitely in a better place emotionally, at least from what I can see. But it seems like everyone is moving on. Why am I the only one standing still?

By the time I arrive home that night, I'm exhausted and ready to take a shower and fall into bed. Thank goodness Mom has a double oven, which allowed me to bake twice as fast as I could have at home. It'll take me most of the morning tomorrow to make my deliveries. I'm tired just thinking about it.

Laughter from the kitchen greets me when I step inside. I glance at my watch with a frown. It's eleven thirty. My apartment rules state no men past midnight, so no rules are being violated. But staying up this late on a weekday means not nearly enough sleep.

What is Nancy thinking?

I have no choice but to go into the kitchen so I can refrigerate the stuffed sandwiches. Otherwise the meat will go bad.

I know I'm a mess. A haggard, thirty-year-old mess. I'm not looking forward to walking into the kitchen and giving Joe the opportunity to compare me to Nancy.

"Hi, Laini!" Nancy's smile seems genuine. "Have you eaten? There's some spaghetti left over. It's Ragu. Don't tell Nana."

"I'm sure I'll never see Nana again," I say, then realize I missed the point. It was a joke. "Hi, Joe."

He stands and takes the load out of my hands. "You look beat."

I roll my eyes as Nancy shakes her head at him. "Joe!" she says. "You're about as sensitive as an ape."

"What?"

"It's okay. Thanks for taking the basket. Just set it on the counter there. I need to put the sandwiches in the fridge."

"Want some help?" he asks.

I shake my head. "Nah. I'll need to maneuver some things around in there to make it all fit."

Joe reaches forward and touches my hair.

He must see my confusion because he grins. "You have dough stuck in your curls."

He pulls his hand back and shows me a clump of dried dough.

My eyes go wide. "Darn it. I guess I rode the train back like that. No wonder everyone was staring at me."

Nancy laughs. "They were staring because you were carrying that basket. I'm surprised you made it home without being accosted."

Joe frowns. "I never thought of that." His brown eyes pierce me. "Why didn't you call me?"

Nancy lifts the bowl of leftovers from the table and walks toward the sink. She gives Joe a light backhand on the arm. "Relax. I was kidding."

"No. I think you might have a point."

I'm starting to revel in his protectiveness a little too much, I guess, when a husky female voice infiltrates the room. "Is the party breaking up already?"

I turn toward the voice. A beautiful brunette (she must be Italian) stands at the doorway of the kitchen looking sexy in a tight sweater and equally tight jeans. Her feet are encased in a pair of leather high-heeled boots. Black. Just like my mood all of a sudden.

I turn my gaze to Joe. He averts his eyes and reaches up to knead the back of his neck. An action I've noticed he seems to do when he's struggling with nerves.

Nancy looks from Joe to me and her eyes widen. I'm not sure what that's all about, but I give her a look as the awkward silence stretches out like a Slinky. And speaking of slinky, the woman — whoever she is — is showing a glimpse of lacy push-up bra around the edge of her sweater. Inwardly, I curse Victoria's Secret.

Finally, I step forward since no one else seems inclined to break the wall of silence. "Hi, I'm Laini, Nancy's roommate."

She smiles broadly, a smile that reaches her eyes. "Nancy has told me so much about you."

"She has?"

"Of course. She says you bake the best cinnamon rolls she's ever tasted."

I wish Nancy would regale her with my knack for interior design, but at least she's praising me for one of my accomplishments.

The woman is smiling broadly. I suppose it doesn't occur to anyone that I still don't know her name.

Joe finally clears his throat and steps forward. He presses his hand to the small of my back. "Laini, this is Cindy. Cindy is a friend of Nancy's."

I gathered that, I want to snap, but I don't. There's no point in making myself look like a jealous idiot. And let's be clear about something. I am *not* jealous. I just feel really duped. It's obvious Nancy's fixing these two up. And she didn't even bother to tell me she was doing it. What does that say about our friendship?

Joe's hand is still on my back. He gives a little squeeze and my heart picks up a beat. "I guess it's getting late. I — uh — better be going."

Cindy pops up. "I'll share a cab with you." She reminds me of a bobble-head doll, all smiles and constant movement. In a beat, she pumps my hand. "So good to meet you, Landy! I swear I'll have to try one of those cinnamon rolls sometime."

She did not call me Landy, did she? In a way, it makes me feel better. Methinks Cindy isn't the nice girl she pretends to be. It won't take Joe long to see through her. If he can keep his gaze from her cleavage and focus on her fake smile and catty personality. But what do I care? It would serve Nana right to have someone like this girl in the family.

I just wouldn't wish it on Joe.

Joe slides into his jacket. "Actually, Cindy, her name is Laini, not Landy."

Nancy springs into action and grabs Cindy's jacket from the back of a chair. Cindy gives a fake gasp. "Oh, I'm so sorry. I just have a terrible memory for names."

"Don't worry about it." I want to say "Cammie" so badly, but I don't. "It was an honest mistake." *Liar!*

I hang back at the kitchen door and watch as Nancy walks Joe and Cindy through the living room to the door. I don't even want to think about what will happen once Cindy gets Joe alone in the cab. Right now she has a look of anticipation that reminds me of a cat hovering over a mouse hole.

Just before leaving, Joe turns and gives me a little wave. "See you, Laini."

I nod and wave back. "Sure. Have a nice evening." With *her.*

Nancy seems nervous as she returns to the kitchen. I start removing plates from the table. Plates for a meal I wasn't invited to.

"So, Cindy seems nice," I say hesitantly.

I don't miss Nancy's rueful smile. "Not as nice as I thought."

"Oh?" How does one convincingly feign surprise when she's not an actress?

"Don't tell me you didn't notice her claws. As soon as she got back from the bathroom and saw you standing there with Joe, she turned from a kitty cat into a big, mean jaguar."

I shrug, scraping dishes into the sink. "I

didn't really notice."

I miss her reply as I switch on the disposal.

When I switch it off, Nancy is still on the subject. "Believe me, if I had known what a . . . well, whatever she is, I would never have invited her and Joe over here at the same time. You don't think he's dumb enough to be taken in by her looks and boobs, do you?" She seems as worried as I do. But probably not for the same reason.

I hope not, I hope not, I hope not. The images of those two floating through my mind are making me sick to my stomach. All I can think about is how much I don't want Joe to kiss her.

We make small talk about Mom and the wedding and my spending next week at the house on Long Island. "You'll be there all week?" Nancy seems relieved — excited, in fact. I'm a little insulted. After all, who invited whom to move in?

I nod. "Starting Saturday."

She jerks her thumb in the direction of the door. "Cindy is Bill Cantanelli's sister."

"Who's that?"

The expression sliding across her face can only be described as one of bewilderment. "The contractor?"

Oh, shoot. I should have known that. "Oh, yeah."

"Cindy is an interior designer too. They work together on most projects. Of course, this one is different."

"Because of me."

She nods, wiping the table with gusto. What am I supposed to do — apologize?

"I actually thought maybe she could use you after you graduate."

My eyebrows go up. "You did?"

"You're going to need a job, aren't you?"

"Well, yeah. I haven't really figured that part out yet."

"Laini. You're set to graduate in two months. How can you not already be lining up a job?"

"I don't know. I thought I'd make sure I do in fact get a diploma before I humiliate myself unnecessarily."

"You have to have some confidence, girl." She plants her hands on her slender, jeans-clad hips. "How do you expect to convince an employer to take a chance on you if you don't believe in yourself?"

See? That's the point. "How can I believe in myself when I've forgotten half of the lessons I've learned over the last year and a half? Jazz knows everything instinctively. She's wonderful and blazes into a room with ideas coming out of her ears." I plop down in one of the kitchen chairs. "I stand there and all I can see is the existing decor. Most of the time I wonder why it needs to be changed."

Nancy goes to the refrigerator and pulls out a cheesecake. "Joe brought it. Said it was your favorite and we should save you some."

Pleasure shoots through me, but I try to hide my delight. "That was thoughtful."

"Mm-hmm." I can feel her eyeing me as she cuts the cake and dishes out two slices. She sets them down on the table. "Are you sure there's nothing between you two? He seemed pretty hacked off that I'd brought him here to set him up with Cindy. I guess he thought when I said, 'There's someone you need to be dating,' that I meant you."

I keep my gaze firmly fixed on the cheesecake with raspberry swirls. "I can't imagine why he would have assumed that. He's made it clear there's nothing but friendship between us."

"He's pretty jealous of Mark." She slips a bite into her mouth and waits for me to comment. So I oblige.

"Mark's jealous of him too. But I've told him there's no reason to be."

"Are things getting serious with you two?"

I have to stop and think about that for a second. I mean, we kiss. But last night's kisses were less than exciting for me. I attributed it to simple fatigue, but I just don't know. I don't have anything to compare it to as far as Joe is concerned. Kisses on the cheek don't count.

"Hello?" Nancy gives the table a little pat. "Did you hear the question? Or are you avoiding it?"

I shrug. "I'm not sure. Mark and I haven't dated that long."

"You've already met his family."

"Only his dad and sister. He's been pretty quiet about his mom."

"She's probably a hag."

"Or a nag."

She grins. "Or a bag."

I giggle. "I can't think of anything else."

"Me neither."

"Besides, she might be a lovely woman."

"Could be."

"Too bad Joe doesn't have a mom."

"I only remember her a little. She was really nice. Quiet. She doted on Joe. I think it bothered Frank how much Joe loved his mom."

"Why would it?"

She shrugs and hesitates.

"Nancy, is Frank in the mob?"

Her face flames. "Don't start thinking along those lines, Laini. It doesn't pay to get too nosy."

I think she just answered my question.

"What about Joe?"

"Joe's a good guy. What he does in private is none of my business."

And once again, I think she just answered the question.

My heart sinks. Joe, the godfather. The very thought makes my stomach hurt.

20

Mom's wedding day is, predictably, rainy, gray, and cold. So cold that if the temperature drops any more, the roads will be a real mess with sleet. I've always hated the weather fluctuations in March and April.

I'm frazzled enough as it is, trying to juggle packing, getting to my hair appointment, and making it to the church by noon. Noon! Who gets married before two o'clock?

The hair appointment turns out to be futile. Even arranged (painfully, I might add) in a French knot, there is no taming my hair by the time I load into the train, get a cab to the church, leave the cab, and walk inside. Humidity and the few sprinkles that got past the umbrella have caused springy curls to sprout all over my head. At least I didn't wear my dress to the church. I lug my suitcase, filled with enough clothes for a week, into the building. I'm leaning against the wall to catch my breath when

Pastor Moore's wife walks down the hall and greets me with a shy smile.

"Your mom is in my office getting dressed. She asked me to show you the way."

Relief floods through me. Just for someone else to wheel my bag while I hold my dress and shoes is huge. My cosmetics bag is slung over my shoulder and feels like a hundred-pound weight.

Mom is standing before an oval full-length mirror when I walk into the office. She is patting her hair. I'm not sure what patting does for short bobbed hair, but if it makes her feel better . . .

And she looks lovely. A cream-colored, tea-length dress of silk and lace hugs her newly-slimmed-down figure. I have the uneasy feeling that my mother looks better than I do.

Okay, Laini. This is her day, she deserves to be the most beautiful woman in the room when she says "I do."

And she absolutely is. The ceremony is short and sweet with Aaron's brother, Ben, standing up next to the groom as best man. He seems to have genuine affection for my mother as he takes her hands and welcomes her to the family with a kiss on the cheek.

He pulls me aside just before we leave the church. "Be careful."

"What do you mean?" Instinctively I know it has something to do with Chad.

"Chad found out about the wedding. The good news is that he and his wife are out of town visiting her folks and just found out this morning. An hour ago, as a matter of fact. My daughter told him." He scowls.

Okay, focus, mister. "Why should I be careful, Mr. Bland?"

"You'll be alone in that house all week, and I wouldn't put it past him to come by and try to find out where your mom and Aaron are going on their honeymoon."

"He wouldn't hurt me, would he?"

"Who knows? I never thought he'd act this asinine over the whole thing. But you just never can tell about people." He gives me a steady, uncle-ish look. "You be sure that you tell that police officer boyfriend of yours so he can keep an eye on things."

Good grief, what has Mother been telling people?

"Mark's not my boyfriend. Besides, he's a Manhattan cop. This isn't exactly his jurisdiction."

A smile tips his lips, making Ben's face even more pleasant. "Trust me, darling. Anywhere you are is bound to be his jurisdiction." He winks. "Just ask him."

I think the old guy completely missed the

part where I said Mark isn't my boyfriend. But it's kind of nice that he's concerned.

I hug my mother and Aaron and watch as they head off for the airport. I hail a cab of my own and go back to Mom's. The place seems strange and empty without many of my mom's things. She hasn't removed everything. But most of the furniture is gone, slowly moved out during the past few days. Her clothes are gone. That's the saddest feeling of all. Home doesn't feel like home without my mom's presence.

During the afternoon I pack some boxes, immersed in my memories. I order take-out Chinese after dark and eat alone. I wonder if this is what I have to look forward to forever. Mark, maybe? If not, is there anyone for me? You'd think in a city the size of New York, I could find *someone* to spend my life with.

I go out on the deck to listen to the sounds of crickets and the city. The rain has stopped, but it's still damp. Dancy calls just after ten o'clock and we catch up on the week. Including my mom's wedding.

"I swear, Dancy. How on earth did she get so lucky twice in one lifetime?"

"Who knows?"

"How are your folks doing?" Mr. and Mrs. Ames have been separated more than they've been together during the last fifteen years, but recently they made a new commitment to each other. They even stood up and renewed their vows.

"They seem to be doing pretty well. Of course I never see them, and rarely talk to Mother. But reading between the lines, I'd say they're having a great time retired in Florida. Hopefully Dad won't ruin it."

I chuckle and sip my tea. "Give him the benefit of the doubt, Dan."

"This *is* me giving him the benefit of the doubt. I said hopefully, didn't I?" I can hear the laughter in her voice so I don't take her too seriously. "So how are your guys? And what are you doing alone on a Saturday night?"

"Ha. First of all, they're not my guys. Mark is working Saturday nights for a while. And Joe doesn't really see me that way. At least not all the time."

"What do you mean, not all the time?"

"Sometimes he seems like he really likes me and would like to date me. Other times it's just different. Like I'm a good friend. Besides . . ." And I tell her about Nancy's comments.

"Wow, well, she would know if they were mob, wouldn't she?" Dancy asks. "Didn't you tell me they were childhood friends?"

"Yep. She seemed freaked out when I brought it up."

"Well, maybe you'd better not bring it up again."

"You've got that right." I pause and so does she. Finally I break the silence. "But I sure would like to know. I mean, he doesn't seem like the type to bash in any heads. And he's never tried to swindle me out of my money."

Laughter explodes across the phone line. "Who still says swindle?"

"Whatever. Mock me if you will. But I have a real situation on my hands. I don't want mobsters giving Nick's place a bad name. Know what I mean?"

Dancy's closer to Nick than any of us after helping out behind the counter and spending so much time in the coffee shop editing and writing during the fall and up until Christmastime.

"Nick knows what he's doing, Laini. If he thought there was anything fishy going on, he wouldn't have turned the place over to Joe. The coffee shop was his life, second only to Nelda and their daughter and grandkids."

"I guess you're right." I take a deep breath. Time to change the subject. "So where are we on proposal watch?"

"Still watching. I think he's doing it on purpose."

"Well, you've only been dating officially for three months."

"True."

We've effectively exhausted our conversation in fifteen minutes flat. After a few attempts to find something to discuss, we both agree that we need to hang up. So that's what we do. I have a sinking feeling that I'm losing touch with my friends.

Is that the way it has to be when you go off in different directions?

I survive a melancholy Sunday and actually look forward to Monday night's class, but at ten o'clock Monday morning, I receive a blanket e-mail from my professor. He's sick. No class tonight. Shoot.

I'm going to be alone with no plans on St. Patrick's Day. We've always enjoyed St. Paddy's Day in my Irish family. I don't even like the taste of corned beef and cabbage all that much, but it's tradition and tradition means a lot to me, even if my mom had to go and be on her honeymoon during the holiday. But I'm not cooking it just for myself. I make myself let it go.

By six I'm bored to distraction, so I call a cab, grab my jacket and purse, and give the cabbie instructions to take me to the Nautical Mile. I'll eat in Mark's dad's restaurant. As I walk down the sidewalk, I wonder if Liz is back to work yet. Surely not. It's only been a couple of weeks.

But I'm wrong. I step inside and there she is, sitting alone, her baby in an infant seat on top of the table. Liz is wearing an apron and rolling silverware. She grins and waves me over. "You alone?"

I nod. "I'm housesitting for my mom." I nod toward the baby. "Can I have a peek?"

"You sure can."

My heart nearly melts at the sight of the tiny creature. She sticks her fist into her mouth and sucks. Liz laughs. "That's not going to hold her for long."

"What are you doing back at work so soon?"

She shrugs. "I'm not, really. Just came in to eat and got roped into rolling silverware since I'm just sitting here."

"Where's Rick?"

"Home. Watching basketball. I couldn't stand it anymore and had to get out of the house. I'm so stir-crazy it's not even funny." She looks around. "I wonder where Kellie is. She should be coming to get your drink order."

I know exactly where she is. I saw her

beeline it for the back as soon as I walked in. But I don't say that.

Liz catches the hostess's eye and waves her over. "Get Kellie, will you? What do you want to drink?"

"Tea is fine."

"Iced or hot?" the hostess asks without bothering to look at me.

"Iced." She huffs off to get it.

"Did I do something to her?"

"Oh, don't worry about Gina. She and Kellie are like that." She crosses her fingers. "I'm sure Mark told you about Kellie."

I nod. So I was right about Kellie still being in love with Mark.

She sighs. "We all really thought he'd marry her." I feel a little uncomfortable sitting here listening to her talk about the sister-in-law that might have been. "You know Kellie named Kyle after Mark."

"I didn't. How did she get Kyle from Mark?"

"Mark's first name. Kyle Mark Hall."

"Mark was thrilled that she named her son after him, even though he wasn't Kyle's father. He moved in with Kellie when Kyle was born and pretty much raised him as a son. But they never let Kyle call him Daddy." She looks at me with a rueful smile. "Good thing, I guess, huh?"

"Sounds like it." Poor kid. I'm feeling a little dizzy from all the information. Why didn't Mark ever tell me about living with Kellie? Something about the situation pushes all my moral buttons. I'm not a prude and I'm not one to judge, but can I really date a guy who pretty much lived as husband and wife with someone and now acts like it never happened?

This is just too awkward. I hop up without giving my next course of action any thought. All I know is that I have to escape. "You know what? I just remembered something I have to do. I can't stay and eat."

"Are you sure?" She frowns. "It's on the house. We'd love for you to stay. Pop hasn't even come out to say hi yet."

"I know, but I really can't stay. Your baby is just beautiful, Liz." I toss money down for the tea and make a quick trip to the door. I know I'm taking the coward's way out. But golly. That was just weird.

I walk along the sidewalk in bewildered silence, reflecting on my life of late. I lived in a barren wasteland where men were concerned. Then I had one interested for sure (Mark) and one maybe interested (Joe). Now it's looking like one has way too much baggage (Mark), and the other is probably involved in the mafia (Joe).

I'm thinking about going back to the desert.

21

The doorbell wakes me up from a sound sleep. I glance at the clock on the night-stand. Good grief. Who rings a person's doorbell at three thirty in the morning? I yank my robe around myself and tie the belt as the doorbell rings again. "I'm coming, already," I mutter. "Hold your dumb horses."

I know better than to answer the door without looking out the peephole first, but for some reason (sleepy fog, most likely), I fling it open without checking.

Chad is standing there. "For creep's sake, Chad. What do you want?"

"Where are they?" he snarls. I'm glad I didn't open the screen door. I check to make sure it's locked. He staggers a few steps as he tries to stay on his feet.

"Good grief, you're drunk as a skunk."

"No kiddin'."

"Get out of here before I call the

cops, Chad."

He sneers. "Go ahead. I'll tell 'em how you and that . . . mmmother of yours snookered my dad."

"Good night, Chad." I close the door, because if I have to listen to him insult my mother again, I might hurt him.

Immediately, the doorbell starts ringing again and he pounds on the door. "I want to talk to you, Laini!" he calls. "I want to know where my dad is."

Suddenly there's a crash and the sound of breaking glass fills the room.

Okay, that's it. I'm officially freaked out. I remember Ben's warning about being careful of Chad, and I'm taking no chances with my life or my mom's house. Snatching up the phone, I run upstairs and lock myself in the bathroom, then dial 911. I hear a few more bangs and know he's doing damage out there.

"Please, God," I beg, curled up on the bathroom floor, phone to my ear, "don't let me die like this."

The police arrive a few minutes later, but there's no trace of Chad. There is, however, quite a bit of damage. He's whacked holes in the siding in more than one place and dented in the gutter. He broke two of the living room windows. I'm sick at the thought of what this will cost. I don't know if Mom's insurance will cover this kind of damage. And if it does, what will that do to her ability to get insurance at an affordable rate for the condo she plans to buy with Aaron?

The police take my statement and my assurance that I'll get in touch with the house's owner, and leave. Just like that, with glass all over the place and the perpetrator still on the loose. Chad might be waiting in the bushes next door for all they know.

Fear seizes me. Real fear. The kind that gnaws at me and makes me seriously feel like I might throw up.

I'm all alone and staring at broken glass. I have no idea what I'm going to do about those windows. *Okay, Laini. Focus.* First thing I am going to do is call someone. Mark seems the logical choice — police officer and all.

I dial his cell phone, but it goes directly to his voice mail. I can't really blame him. After all, it's the middle of the night. But I need to feel safe, and in my world, Mark's the guy who carries the gun. I dial his home phone and cross my fingers. "Pick up, pick up, pick up," I whisper.

"Hello?"

Wait, that's not Mark. As a matter of fact, it's a woman's voice on the other end of the line. "I'm sorry, I must have the wrong number."

"Is that you, Laini?"

Okay, wait. . . . Who is that? *Who* is this woman answering Mark's phone at four o'clock in the morning? *And* she knows me?

Gasp. "Kellie?"

"Yes, but it's not what you think."

I take a really deep breath. I mean, really deep. She doesn't have any idea what I'm thinking. Zero. This woman doesn't have the capacity to look into a brain like mine and figure out —

"I'm not spending the night with Mark."

Okay, maybe she does know what I'm thinking, but it's not rocket science, is it?

"Hello? Laini? Are you there?"

At this moment, I don't even know how I can speak to this woman. I blame my next action on the crazy hour I've just had. I mean, do I need to stand here and talk to the *other* woman?

"I know you're there. . . ." Her tone is becoming rife with irritation.

I hear a mumbled male voice in the background. Guess who?

"It's your girlfriend. And she won't talk. I swear I'm going to hang up if you don't start speaking, Laini."

So I beat her to the punch. I hang up.

My phone immediately rings and of course I know it's Mark. But I'm not answering.

The swine.

I do what I should have done in the first place: I call Dancy.

"Are you kidding me, Laini? That scumbag. I hope they lock him up and throw away the key."

Part of me agrees with her. But I think about his wife, pregnant with their first baby, and my heart goes out to her.

"Listen, is there anyone you can call? Your pastor or someone to come over and stay with you until I get there?"

"I don't know. He's really more my mom's pastor than mine."

"Don't be silly. You've been there every Sunday for how many months now?"

"A few."

"You're probably more faithful than half the congregation. Call him, already."

I make the call, and a sleepy-sounding Pastor Moore promises to be over in a few minutes. "It'll take me at least half an hour to get there. The youth pastor lives just a few blocks from you. Do you mind if I call him to come stay with you until I get there?"

Even in my fearful state, I can't help but find the humor in this situation. "Sure, he can come stay with me until you get here to stay with me until Dancy can make it from Manhattan."

His warm laugh washes over me in a wave of peace. "Okay, now, Laini, I'm going to hang up and call him. Do you know what he looks like?"

"Tom Michaels?"

"Yes."

"I know who he is."

"Good. Listen, Laini. I'm going to put Patty on the phone while I call him. Don't hang up until he gets there, okay?"

I've spoken to the somewhat elusive pastor's wife only once before, at Mom's wedding. But I find her pleasant and compassionate as she keeps me talking. A few minutes later, the youth pastor shows up wearing a loose pair of lounge pants, a T-shirt, and a pair of flip-flops.

"Oh, Tom, come in." I hold the door so he can get in out of the cold. "You could have put real shoes on at least. I bet the ground is really wet from the rain earlier."

"You got that right. My toes are frozen off."

"I'm sorry."

"You have nothing to be sorry about." His voice trails off as he looks at the glass all over the place. He gives a slow whistle under his breath. "He did a number on your place, didn't he?"

I swallow. "It's actually my mom's house. She's on her honeymoon."

"Pastor Moore mentioned that. Have you called her yet?"

"Oh my goodness. I didn't."

"I'll just start bringing things in to cover that window if you want to go into another room and call her."

"What do you mean, cover the window?"

A smile curves his mouth. "You didn't think we were going to come over here, pat you on the back, and then leave, did you?"

Uh, yeah.

He breaks into a pleasant laugh as he obviously reads my mind. "Well, we're not going to do that."

My phone rings. Tom jerks his thumb toward the door. "I'll be back."

The phone rings again and I answer. It's Dancy. "You okay?"

"Yeah, the youth pastor is here."

"Good." Relief is evident in her tone. "Okay, we're about to get on the train, but I wanted to touch base with you before we board."

"We?"

"Me, Tabby, and Jack, of course. David has to stay with the twins."

"Oh, Dancy. You guys don't all have to

come. Especially Tabby. She needs her rest."

"Don't be silly." She's breathing heavily, so I imagine she's rushing to catch the train. "Tabby wouldn't let me come without her. And David wouldn't let Tabby go until Jack assured him he was coming too. Gotta go, Laini. I'll be there soon."

She hangs up and the phone rings again practically simultaneously. I glance and scowl. Mark. I know I'll have to deal with him and Kellie soon, but not now. I have too much on my mind. I hear Tom in the living room. I pick up the house phone and dial the number written on the whiteboard hanging next to the refrigerator.

"Hello? Laini, what's wrong?"

Good grief. I haven't gotten a word in edgewise and darn whoever invented caller ID.

"Ma, calm down, for crying out loud."

"How can I calm down when you're calling me at three in the morning while I'm on my honeymoon?"

Three in the morning? Oh, New Orleans. Central time.

"Let me talk to Aaron, Mom."

"Why do you want to do that? Something is wrong, isn't it?"

I'm not about to fill her in when she's already keyed up just from the phone ringing. "Mom. Seriously."

"Oh. Fine."

"Laini?" Aaron's voice sounds concerned. "What's wrong, honey?"

Honey? Well, I guess that's okay. I fill him in, including what his son did to the house.

"I just can't believe it."

Poor Aaron. I know he's got to be mortified. "The police are looking for him. I'm not sure what they will do. But I imagine Mom's going to have to press charges."

"Yes, yes, of course. We'll come home right away."

I know there's no point in trying to persuade them to stay in New Orleans, so I don't even try.

Aaron hangs up with the promise of calling the airlines and seeing about tickets home.

I walk back into the living room to find Pastor Moore and Patty. They've already started diving into the glass, and they've tossed the majority of the larger shards into heavy-duty lawn-and-garden bags that they must have brought along.

"I can't tell you how grateful I am for your kindness," I murmur. I suddenly feel so shy and unworthy in the presence of these three. People who live out their faith in flip-flops and lounge pants, with plastic bags.

Tom is pulling pieces of glass from the window itself. I see wood planks lining the wall, and I frown. "What's that?"

"To cover the windows. We can't leave them without something on them — for one thing, it's still too cold, and for another, it's dangerous."

Heat fills my face. "You're right. I didn't think about it."

Patty slips an arm around my shoulders. "You've been through a traumatic experience tonight. Why don't we go out to the kitchen and make you some tea?"

"I should help clean up!" I don't need to be treated like a fragile crystal vase, but I have to admit it does sort of feel good.

"Oh, the guys have all that covered. There's not much. Mostly glass. They'll get it cleaned up in no time and then they'll cover the windows."

My phone rings again and I heave a sigh as, sure enough, I see Mark's name.

"Do you need to get that?" Patty asks, eyeing my phone.

"I'd rather not." But he's not going to stop calling until I do, apparently. I decide the very next time he calls, I'll answer.

What a night. Seriously. What. A. Night.

22

Chad sits across from me, his tearful face making my heart squeeze with sympathy even as I want to sock him for damaging my mother's home.

"I know what I did was wrong. I have been coping with my problems lately by drinking. Not that I'm saying that's an acceptable excuse." He gathers a deep breath. "I know I scared you, and I'm completely sorry."

We're sitting around a conference room table at the law offices of Handegraff and Reed. Chad's lawyer clears his throat and fixes his lawyerly gaze on me. "Will that apology suffice?"

"Wait, Hank." Chad looks from his lawyer back to me. "I know part of your mother's agreement to not press charges has to do with my apology to you. But I want you to know I'm truly sorry. This isn't just about getting off legally. I know I was wrong. You have every right to toss me in jail."

Hank clears his throat again. *Loudly.*

"It's okay," Chad says to the guy who is this close to a stroke.

"Don't worry about it, Hank," Aaron says, clapping the attorney on the shoulder. "You'll get paid either way."

Hank glowers.

Silence filters through the room and everyone's eyes are on me.

"Okay, look." I know that doesn't sound like the beginning of a speech that needs to end with "I forgive," but I'm still holding a little bit of a grudge. Sympathetic or not. "My mom's house is going to need a lot of work to get it ready to sell, thanks to your little tirade. How do I know you won't get smashed some night and do it again?"

He blinks, as though he is mortified that I would ask such a thing.

"I mean," I continue, since he just doesn't seem to get it, "have you been drinking long? Is it a problem? Are there alcoholic tendencies? I think this deserves answers that go beyond a simple apology."

He opens his mouth, and I cut him off again. "Don't get me wrong. I do believe you're sorry. I don't think you'd be inclined to take a bat to a house in your right mind.

It's your anesthetized brain swimming in alcohol that I worry about for next time. What steps are you willing to take to reassure us this won't happen again?"

"Now, listen," Hank begins. "I don't think there's any cause to assume this will happen again. My client has complied with Mrs. Bland's wishes." Okay, not the issue at the moment, but hearing my mom called "Mrs. Bland" leaves me a little cold.

Aaron takes my mom's hand and spears — and I do mean spears — Chad with a look. "I think Laini has a very good point. I've seen similar behavior from you in the past. And don't even try to deny it."

"That was three years ago, Dad!"

Aaron nods. "Yes, but you were drunk and violent and destroyed your wife's car."

Chad's face goes white, as though he can't believe Aaron brought it up. "I thought she was cheating," he mumbles.

I turn my gaze to Brenda, who looks miserable. She shrugs at me. I suspect she's had her share of heartbreak over this idiot stepbrother of mine. My heart goes out to her.

"Personally," I blurt out, "I wouldn't let you off the hook without anger-management classes and documented AA meetings."

Hank frowns at me. "Are you saying you'll

forgive him if he agrees to those two conditions?"

I shake my head. "No. I've learned that forgiveness is a gift. I bestow that freely. What I'm saying is that if I were my mother, I would insist on those two things along with his apology to me. Otherwise, I'd press charges." I give him a too-sweet smile. "But that's just my opinion, Hank. I can't begin to guess what my mother will do. It's her decision. After all, it was her house he smashed up."

I turn and meet Chad's narrowed gaze head-on. He doesn't look at all happy.

"Now wait a minute. The agreement was that I apologize to you, and your —" He pauses and I want to forget forgiveness and hop across the table. Jerk. "And your mother here wouldn't press charges."

I refuse to answer. I just keep staring at him and give a shrug.

My mom speaks up for the first time. "Chad, you are about to be a father. I know what it's like growing up in the home of an alcoholic."

She does? She never told me.

"Laini's suggestions are good ones."

Chad scowls. "You would think so. You're her mother."

Aaron slaps the table. "Stop interrupting

and listen."

Mom touches Aaron's hand ever-so-slightly and her new husband immediately calms. "Chad," she says, "I've been watching your wife during this exchange. She's humiliated and, if I'm not mistaken, a little fearful."

Brenda's eyes go wide and I have a feeling Mom hit it on the head. Will the little wife have the guts to speak up for herself, though?

"You don't even know my wife," Chad says, keeping his tone even — deliberately even, I'd guess. At least he's smart enough to do that. I don't think it would take much to push my mom into letting him rot in jail for a while.

"That's true, Chad. But I hope to." She gathers a breath and pans the room, including each person in her line of vision — Chad, Hank, Brenda, me, Aaron. "That's why I'm going to do this: Chad, you've got two real problems that need to be controlled before your child is born. Alcoholism and anger."

At this moment, I marvel at my mother. Chad keeps his mouth shut, and surprisingly, his eyes are not reflecting anger. Something else . . . hope, maybe?

"I want you to get help for both of those

things. Anger management and Alcoholics Anonymous, just like my daughter suggested. You agree to those things in writing, and I won't press charges."

When all is said and done, we accomplish a lot in the meeting room of that attorney's office. Poor Hank is slightly bewildered by the whole thing, though. He and Chad both probably thought they would get off easy. Apologize for scaring the life out of me, pay for damages to the house, and voilà, you're off the hook.

Brenda turns to me as we leave the room and squeezes me a lot tighter than one might think possible, as tiny as she is. "Thank you, Laini. Maybe this will all be worth the trouble."

I hug her back. "I pray so, Brenda."

We make it out to the curb and Aaron hails a cab. After we're settled into the back of the car, I turn to Mom. "I can't believe how great you were, Ma!"

"It was your idea. I was waffling on what to do."

Aaron nods. "It was the perfect solution. He's needed this for a long time. I've been too preoccupied with his mother for the last two years to realize how much he's been drinking."

"You can't blame yourself, hon. Chad's a

grown man. This might have been just the nudge he needed. God is using this situation to get him help."

He is? God? I'm just about to get mad since I'm the one who had to go through the ordeal. But Mom's next words effectively diffuse the bomb about to blow up in me.

"Laini is much more capable of handling this sort of thing than I am. You should have seen the way she held up after her father died." Her voice cracks and she reaches over to take my hand. "I fell apart. But not my girl. She finished school, worked hard, and then had the gumption to start over."

Aaron nods, and I swear I even see pride glinting in his eyes. "It takes a lot of strength to stand on your own two feet like you have. Your mom is right to be proud of you."

All right. I can't continue to let her think I'm amazing when I know better. "Listen, Mom, I have to tell you something."

Her silky eyebrows go up just a smidgeon, and she waits for me to continue. So I do. I tell her all about how bad I am at interior design and how I don't even like it all that much.

"But you enjoyed decorating your apartment."

"I know! I've always loved putting things

together, going to antique auctions and finding bargains that might look nice in a house. But my idea of what works and most people's ideas just don't mesh. My grades are horrible."

Her eyes go wide. "Will you get your degree in May?"

I nod. "Technically, I've passed all my classes. A couple of Ds, mostly Cs."

"I've never known you to receive less than a B in a class."

I give her a rueful smile. "Tell me about it."

"But you will pass this semester?"

"The project is going really well. The concept anyway. After the contractors finish knocking down and building up, Jazz and I will start painting and putting together the furniture and pictures and the rest of the actual decorating. Then we'll schedule an open house where the entire design department will come and observe. We took extensive photographs of the place before, and we have to blow them up and display them on easels." It occurs to me that I'm rambling. But I've lived for this woman's approval for as long as I can remember. The thought of confessing failure makes me nervous. "Anyway, I should pass, but I won't be at the top of my class by any means, and most likely I'll work as someone's assistant."

I stop and take a deep breath.

Mom pats my leg. "It'll all work out."

I wait for the rest. For the part about hard work paying off and how I need to find a job where I'll be happy. But it doesn't come.

"Look," Aaron says, "it's starting to rain again."

And just like that my entire gut-wrenching confession is trumped by a chat about the weather.

"Who is that man?"

I look in the direction my mom indicates as the taxi pulls up in front of the house. My heart does a loop-de-loop. It's Mark. Pacing and inspecting the damage. His dad's black Tahoe sits in our driveway. He rushes to me as soon as I step out of the cab. Before I can greet him, he pulls me in for a hug. What would have been welcome two nights ago suddenly makes me uncomfortable.

"Mark, what are you doing here?"

"I had to hear from Liz that your mom's house was vandalized?" He's frowning, and his tone sets my teeth on edge.

"Well, if you had answered your phone Monday night instead of letting your girlfriend answer, you would have heard it from me."

"Mark has a girlfriend?" Mom whispers loudly enough for everyone to hear.

"No, I don't have a girlfriend," he snaps.

"Don't talk to my mother that way!"

Aaron clears his throat. "I think we'd best go inside and leave these two to talk."

Mark looks to Mom. "I'm sorry, Mrs. Sullivan — uh — I'm sorry, I don't know your new last name."

Mom's face softens and she gives his arm a maternal pat. "Mrs. Bland. But you can call me Lydia. And I know you didn't mean to be rude."

Relief crosses his features. "Thank you."

The two of them leave us in the drizzle and walk into the house.

Mark looks down at me. "Kellie lost her apartment." He takes a deep breath. "I felt responsible. All those years we lived together and I paid most of the bills. I just didn't know what to do."

"So you let her move in with you?"

"Just until she finds a more reasonably priced apartment." He rakes his fingers through his hair.

"She doesn't have family?"

"She doesn't really speak to them."

"Well, maybe she should and she'd have

someplace to go other than your apartment."

"I'm sorry. I should have told you. I was going to tell you yesterday. You've never called me at four in the morning before." He attempts a boyish grin, but I'm not buying it. It's not cute. This is a crazy situation. I can't be part of it.

"Mark, you're a great guy and I like you a lot."

He groans and his face clouds. "Don't break up with me."

"I can't break up with you. There's no commitment between us anyway. But there obviously was with Kellie, and I can't deal with that kind of baggage. Not when you're still carrying it around."

I know I sound selfish and harsh.

"What about when she finds her own place?"

I shrug. "Maybe. If you can cut her loose for good, I won't be put in a position where I'm jealous or suspicious."

He nods. "I understand." His eyes are glistening, and I'm aware of tears lurking below the surface. I don't want to bring attention to it, so I turn my head.

I'm trying to figure out how to bring this to an end and send Mark on his way when the drizzle suddenly starts to come harder and faster.

"Well, I'd better let you get inside," he says.

I nod but don't ask him to come inside. He's driving his dad's SUV, so I figure he must have come over here from the restaurant. He hesitates for a second. "All right, then. I guess I'll call you soon."

I watch him go. My stomach tightens, but I know I made the right decision.

"Well, Laini-girl," I tell myself, "you're on your own again. What are you going to do with your life?"

23

By the time I return home Wednesday night, I have seven new orders for cinnamon rolls, bread bowls, and stuffed sandwiches. Each order is for more than three dozen of everything, and I'm feeling pretty darn overwhelmed. Nancy isn't too happy either.

"Look, Laini," she says. "No hard feelings, okay? But I think I'll have to start looking for another place. You need to be able to use the kitchen all the time, and I need to be able to make a cup of tea without burning my hand on a pan of bread sitting on top of the stove to cool. I mean, I know I could use the kitchen, but it's always so cluttered up with bread rising, cooking, or cooling that I don't feel like I have a right to it." Nancy sounds more frustrated than I've ever seen her. I wonder briefly if something more than bread is bothering her.

"Are you okay?" I ask.

Her eyes fill with tears. "Tyson called again."

My hackles rise.

"He says he's left her for good and wants to see me."

"You told him to go take a hike, right?" Her silent gaze tells me otherwise. "Oh, Nance. What are you going to do?"

"He's flying in this weekend."

"You didn't tell him no?"

"I wish I had the strength." She flops down onto the sofa and covers her face.

Compelled, I sit next to her and hold her loosely while she sobs. When her body stops shuddering, I grab a couple of tissues from the coffee table and press them into her hands. "Thanks."

"Look, I think you need a few days to get your head together without me in the house bugging you. I'm taking my bread and will stay at my mom's house."

She looks at me, horrified. "I didn't mean to kick you out of your own place!"

"You're not. Mom has two ovens anyway. I'll be able to work faster."

Despite her protests, I definitely see relief in her face. I have a feeling Nancy's going to be getting her own place soon. I don't mind. I figure at almost thirty-one years old, it's time for me to be on my own anyway.

I ask my mother if I can stay at her house to give Nancy some space. Since she and Aaron are renting a little two-bedroom apartment and the house is just sitting there while it's being repaired, she readily agrees.

"I feel better having someone staying there anyway."

So here it is Saturday afternoon, and I've been living peacefully alone in Mom's house for three days. I've been baking practically nonstop. I'm ashamed to say I blew off my class last night. But I would never have finished the orders by this afternoon otherwise.

Using Mom's double oven has helped speed up the process, but there's no way I can keep up this pace. I've finished and delivered the first five orders. Despite the heady feeling from raking in the money, I haven't even cracked a book all week, and there's a test on Monday. I scurry around the kitchen while Jazz reads her notes to me over the phone.

"Laini! Are you listening?"

I'm not, really. Mostly I've been thinking about how the last batch of rolls is in the oven and I'll be able to deliver the last two orders and get back before dark. I'm still a little creeped out when it gets dark. I hate it and I know I have to get over it. But Chad really scared me.

Speaking of Chad, he's been to two AA meetings and has his first anger-management appointment with a psychologist on Monday. Mother says Brenda's face has lost that worried look.

Anyway, back to Jazz, who is reaming me.

"Look, if you don't study, you'll bomb the test Monday and it won't matter how good Nick's looks when we're done. And it's amazing, by the way. They're making real progress."

"Oh, you've been over there?"

"Of course! I can't stay away. The guys are getting sick of me." Her laughter twinkles through the phone line. "I'm dying to start decorating, aren't you?"

No. Not really. Mostly I just want to get it over with.

"Listen, Jazz, that reminds me." I slip the rolls into the oven and grab my purse from the counter. "I have the number of a lady looking for someone to redo her husband's office."

"You mean Joe's drunk aunt?"

Oh, yeah. Of course I told her about it. I wanted her input. "That's the one. Anyway, I've decided not to even attempt anything on my own for a while. Not until I get to work side by side with someone. Do you want to call her?"

"Sure, thanks!"

An hour later I'm feeling pretty good about myself as I load up the boxes and calculate how much money I'll be making. I've made enough just in the last week to pay my rent for three months. I'm really rethinking Joe's suggestion of starting a catering business instead of pursuing design.

I wanted to have time to shower off the smell of bread dough and cinnamon, but it's already after three and I have several stops to make. Aaron loaned me his car so I could make the deliveries. There's no way I could carry five boxes of baked goods on the train.

I load up and make my deliveries. Then on a whim I decide to stop by Nick's to get a look at the place. I don't know what kind of strings Joe pulled, but the contractors are there on a Saturday. A holiday weekend at that, with Easter tomorrow.

I thought I'd have to just peek through the window, but the door is open and I walk inside. The chalky dust nearly chokes me and I notice the guys are wearing masks. I guess I know why. No one even seems to notice me as I walk through. The door is open leading to the part of the coffee shop we're turning into an old Italy–style outside café. I walk through the door and, to my surprise, the awning has already been set in place. I can't help but smile. It looks exactly like the proposal we submitted.

The other door is open and I'm dying to see how things look on the other side. I walk slowly across the dirt. No stone path yet, but it will come. I stand at the door and peer in, catching my breath when I spy Joe across the room. I'm about to call out when a man walks up to him and I swear there's a handoff of . . . something . . . from Joe to the guy. I can't imagine what it might be. Unless . . . Money? Drugs? I turn around to get out of there before he notices me, when he does just that.

He flashes me his trademark heart-stopping grin. Okay, I just have to pretend I didn't see that "deal." Whatever it was.

And I have to pull myself together fast, because he's making a beeline across the room to me. I send him a tentative smile.

"I've missed that smile."

Illegal activity (on his part) aside, I realize how much I've missed him too. The image of Cindy throwing herself at him has been more than my brain can handle. I'm sure they're dating, but I don't have the guts to ask Nancy.

He jerks his head toward the rest of the building. "You want a tour?"

"You bet." I'm not sure how to take the look he's giving me.

"It's good to see you." He puts his arm on my shoulder. Something in that simple gesture sends warmth through me. It's all I can do not to lean into him.

"You smell like bread," he says softly.

Heat bursts to my cheeks. "I'm sorry. I didn't have time to shower before I made my deliveries."

His hand slides down my arm and clasps my fingers. "Don't apologize. It's sexy." He winks. "You know the way to a man's heart is through his stomach."

Oh, Joe. Don't do this to me unless you mean it. Darn him. He doesn't even give me a chance to recover or respond. Instead, he leads me through the other side of the coffee shop. My mind can barely focus on what he's saying. I can barely catch my breath and, to be honest, I have no idea if it's the dust in the air, or if it's Joe.

"Nance tells me you've been staying at your mom's house."

I nod. "Yeah, she doesn't like the idea of it standing empty with the workers there fixing the damage Chad did."

He frowns. "What sort of damage?"

"Nancy didn't tell you about my new stepbrother's tirade?"

I tell him the story. His eyes become stormy and his jaw clenches. "What did Mark do about it?"

"Well, that's not really his jurisdiction."

He gives me a look that clearly says I might be a little stupid at the moment. "I mean as a boyfriend. Not a cop."

"Well, since he's *not* my boyfriend, he didn't do anything. Besides, he only found out on Wednesday."

"And this happened Monday night?"

"Yes. Don't ask. It's a long story." If only Joe knew that the warmth of his fingers laced through mine is making me wish we were walking in a garden with butterflies fluttering by. I smile at the ridiculous thought.

"You're smiling again," Joe says.

I cover my tracks fast. "I'm glad to see this place shaping up. It's almost done."

He sends me a curious frown. "You really aren't excited about being a designer. Why not just bake for a living?"

"Yeah, right." I laugh and nudge him.

"Honey, I'm serious. Between me and the family, we could keep you in enough business to make a good living. You could even buy your mom's house."

I start to get caught up in the pipe dream, but the way he said "the family," combined with the memory of the handoff I witnessed a few minutes ago, sort of sours things for me.

"Thanks anyway, Joe. I think I'd better stick with the plan."

He shakes his head. "Okay. But if you change your mind, all you have to do is say the word and we'll get you set up real good."

Now, is that not a mafia way to talk or what? What am I supposed to think?

24

Before I go back to my mom's, I run home to grab a pair of shoes I need for Easter Sunday service the next morning. "Nancy?" I call when I walk in.

First I hear nothing. Then I hear scuffling. Fear grips me. Nancy would have answered me. What if the robber came back? I tiptoe back toward the door, reaching for my cell phone as I go. Just as I get to the door, I hear Nancy's voice.

"Laini. Wait."

Slowly I turn and there's Nancy, her face washed in guilt. She's wearing a satin robe. Behind her is . . . a man. I stare at them in disbelief. I mean, in all the years I've lived in this apartment, no one has ever violated the "man" rule. And this is a clear violation.

"Men aren't allowed to sleep over," I mumble, for lack of anything more intelligent to say.

"I know, Laini. I'm sorry." She takes his

hand. "I honestly didn't mean for this to happen."

The guy isn't wearing a shirt. His lips are twisted in a sardonic smile — which I admit works when Rhett Butler does it to Scarlett, but I'm definitely *not* charmed. He steps forward and offers me his hand. I hesitate.

"Tyson," he says. "You must be the absentee roommate."

Does he think he's funny? My eyes go wide as I leave his hand out there empty, alone. And I don't care. "Tyson?"

"Yeah," she says. Her eyes are pleading, and I can tell she doesn't want me to bring up the fact that I know he's married and is cheating. It's so frustrating to watch an ignorant woman. What's the point of her moving all the way to Manhattan to get away from this guy if all she's going to do is fall back into his arms?

"I just came home to get a pair of shoes for *church* in the morning." I can't believe I just emphasized *church* like that. But this behavior throws me for a loop. I'm not a prude. But I do have my standards. And that was before I started going to church. Before I really started trying to live the way the Bible says Christians should live. And here Nancy is, a Christian by her own words, and she's sleeping with this guy.

I just don't get it.

"I'll go with you to help you find them," Nancy says quickly.

She practically pushes me down the hall and into my room, where she closes the door after us. "I know it! I know I'm an idiot and this is wrong." Her eyes are filled with tears. "I love him."

"I don't know what you want me to say, Nancy. This is wrong. Even if he weren't married and weren't cheating. I thought you felt the same way I do about sleeping around."

"I'm not sleeping around. I love Tyson." She swallows. "I know this is wrong, okay? I don't need judgment from you."

"Judgment? You think calling sin a sin is judging?" I scowl. "You're a big girl. Choose your own commandments to break. But I don't need this kind of stuff going on in my apartment." My heart suddenly softens. "Plus, you don't want a man who doesn't love you."

"He does, though! He's leaving his wife and plans to move here."

Is she kidding me? "Come on. You believe that?"

"I have to," she whispers.

"Then believe him. But don't expect me to condone your actions."

Anger flashes in her brown eyes. "It's so easy for you to stand there and judge me. You have two fabulous men panting over you, and you don't have to do a thing."

"Ha! What planet are you on? I only *wish* I had two fabulous men panting after me."

Her eyes narrow, and her lips curl into a sneer. I've never seen this side of Nancy before. "Little Miss Innocent. Mark wants you so bad he can't stand it. And Joe . . . Don't even get me started on that doofus."

Okay, Joe is *not* a doofus. Nancy barrels ahead without giving me the opportunity to defend myself or Joe.

"Joe won't even look at anyone else since you stepped into the picture. It's Laini this, and Laini that. And 'Oh, this is the lightest, fluffiest roll I've ever had. If she wore this smell as a perfume, I wouldn't be able to keep my hands off her. I'd have to marry her.' He makes me sick and so do you." She spews her venom, but I can't be angry. Not when she's telling me that Joe cares about me. I sort of smile at the thought.

"What?" she says, and her eyes go wide. "You mean you really didn't know? Holy moly. I don't believe it." She shakes her head. "You're a dope, Laini Sullivan."

"Joe's a doofus and I'm a dope, huh?" I grab my shoes from the closet floor and head to the door. "Sounds like we're a good pair."

She follows me down the hall. "I'm sorry, Laini. I didn't mean to insult you. Can we talk about this?"

I turn and face her. "Yes, I'll be back in a few days and we need to talk about what you plan to do. If you're going to move out, then start looking. If you are staying, the rules have to be clearly established again. I have a reputation in this building, and I don't plan to have people speculating about me because of you."

Tyson is standing in the doorway between the kitchen and living room, looking all casual, still shirtless. Still wearing that amused grin.

"Get him out of my apartment."

"I will."

"I want your word you're not going to snuggle back into bed with him after I leave."

Nancy lets out a breath. "Fine. You have my word."

"I had it when you moved in here too. Remember? You agreed that you wouldn't bring men into the apartment."

Her face flushes red. She remembers.

I'm shaking by the time I and my shoes make it to the sidewalk.

During the drive back home, I think about what she said about Joe. "If she wore this smell as a perfume, I wouldn't be able to keep my hands off her."

And tonight he mentioned how sexy I smelled. Joe is either a very weird guy with a dough fetish, or he truly is interested in me.

Oh, sure. Just my luck. He finally shows some real interest. A mobster with a thing for chubby girls that smell like bread. There is something very wrong with my life.

I'm still ticked off at Nancy when the phone rings later. I am in the middle of cleaning the pans I used today. I hate leaving dirty dishes, but since I was running late, there was nothing else I could do. Now my only consolation in all this mess is the thought of seven different paychecks. When I deposit them, I'll actually have some savings. Of course my aunt has to be paid back for loaning me the money for design school, but that isn't until I actually graduate.

When Nancy shows up on caller ID, I'm tempted to blow her off. It's all I can do to be civil.

"Laini, before you say anything," she says, her voice awash with tears, "I just want you to know I sent him away."

"I appreciate that, Nancy," I say quietly.

"He left me."

"Wasn't that the point?"

"He left me for good."

What am I supposed to say? I'm sorry? I can't bring myself to say that. Because I'm not.

"You were right, Laini. I confronted him again and he finally admitted that he'll never leave her." She takes a shuddering breath. "He yelled at me for bringing it up again."

"I'm sorry he yelled at you, Nancy." I know her heart is broken. But I can't help being glad this happened. "I'm in a similar situation with Mark."

She gasps. "Mark's married?"

"No, but he might as well be. The girl he lived with for all those years just lost her apartment, and he feels so responsible that he moved her and her little boy in with him until she finds an apartment she can afford."

"Did he break up with you?"

"First of all, he can't break up with me because I was never his girlfriend, but no, he wants us both. He wants her for her son, I think, and he wants me for . . . who knows what?"

"Your cinnamon rolls?"

I giggle. "No. Joe's the one who thinks

dough is sexy. I'm just a rcbound girl for Mark."

"I doubt that. You underestimate yourself."

"Well, whatever his interest in me, I told him I'm not seeing him anymore."

"Good for you." I have to smile at her cheering me on this way. This from the girl who . . . Well, no point rehashing that.

"What did he say?"

"Oh, he said he wants to call me when he gets Kellie into her own apartment." I give a mirthless laugh. "When *he* gets her into an apartment. I ask you, does that sound like a guy who's ready to turn loose of a former love?"

"Maybe not. But I don't think he's going to give up on you very easily."

"He doesn't have much of a choice. I'm not planning to give him a second chance."

"Okay, listen. I really called for two reasons. One, to let you know that Tyson is gone for good. And I've been talking to one of my friends. Janine Reynolds. She's looking for someone to bring into her design business to sort of train. You could work with her and get paid to learn as you go."

"Did you tell her about my grades?"

"Yes. And do you know what she said?"

"What?"

"She said, 'Girl, I flunked out of my entire first semester and barely made it through the rest of them. You tell that friend of yours to come see me. Sounds like we're a perfect match.' "

As I hang up the phone with Nancy, a new sense of hope springs up inside me. I'm thinking maybe, just maybe, I can do this after all. I glance around my mom's kitchen and I wonder . . . could I buy this place after all? Determination yanks at me. I can't let it go without at least trying. How do I convince anyone that I'm a good risk? I feel like Scarlett O'Hara trying to find that three hundred dollars to pay the taxes on Tara. Maybe if I make a dress from Mom's gold drapes and take the loan officer at the bank a pan of cinnamon rolls . . .

Tuesday morning dawns beautifully. A gorgeous sun peeks through white puffy clouds, and for once, there's not even one little chance of rain in the forecast. Not for at least four days. And that puts a smile on my face.

That is, until I drive Aaron's car to the bank, walk inside, and sit across from Mr. Brady, the loan officer. He deadpans a look at me as though I don't already know there's zero chance of my getting a loan.

But after visiting with my new boss yesterday, I realize I can afford a house note if I'm very careful and supplement my income with baking. I mean, I obviously can't take as many jobs as I do now, but I can make enough for a house payment. And that's what I have to convince him of.

"I know you don't have a lot to go on as far as my credit history is concerned. But as you can see, I'm never late on my credit card payment."

"Miss Sullivan," he says, taking a look first at my credit report and then at me. He takes off his reading glasses. "You have a Sears card and a Visa that is almost at its limit."

Well, I mean, in my defense, a $5,500 limit isn't really fair. If the company had offered me, say, a $15,000 limit, I wouldn't be nearly as close to maxing out. "Yes, but I always pay on time and usually over my minimum payment." I mean, shouldn't that buy me some points even if it's only a few dollars each month? "Plus, I mean, I know I don't exactly have a steady job at this moment, but I have Janine's affidavit that she is hiring me upon graduation in May, and I have a supplemental income as well, which I've had for several months."

A condescending nod from him follows

my speech. "I applaud that. It shows you will eventually be a wonderful candidate for a house loan. Just as your parents were. However, at this time, there simply isn't enough of a credit history to qualify you for a mortgage."

The glasses go back on as he breathes a heavy sigh. That simple action raises my hopes more than I care to admit. I can tell he'd like to help. I mean, it's not his fault. "I'm sorry to see you lose your parents' house," he says, real regret tingeing his voice. "Your dad was a friend of mine." A kind smile curves his lips upward. "But without a current job, a credit history, or a cosigner, there's not a lot I can do for you. However, if you do come up with someone willing to cosign the loan, that might make a difference, provided you are able to make an acceptable down payment."

I've never felt such defeat as I leave the bank. I don't know why — even before I walked into Mr. Brady's office, I knew a loan was out of the question. Mainly I wanted to know my options. I thought maybe a few thousand dollars for a down payment. But sheesh. I'd have to single-handedly line up the stars and achieve world peace before they'd consider me a candidate for their filthy lucre.

How does anyone get ahead in this world if no one will give you a chance?

25

March is a creeping kind of month that never seems to end. Everyone looks forward to April and the promise of spring. But as far as I'm concerned, except for the name and expectation, April is no different from March. Weather patterns are pretty much the same: rainy, fifty or sixty degrees (which makes for cold rain), and not at all the pastel spring everyone pants for during January and February. So why the hype? Why the deceit?

I'm so relieved to wake up on May first. Hopefully April showers are behind me and May flowers are about to bloom.

Mom's house is finally repaired and will go on the market this week. I've been living here since her wedding so that I can make use of the double ovens, and I have to say, I'm not ready to let it go.

I didn't bother telling anyone about my visit to Mr. Brady at the bank. No sense making Mom and Aaron feel bad. If only Mom and Aaron could hang on for a year. Give me time to establish some credit, build up some time on the job. But again, no sense making them feel bad. I mean, they have no choice about selling the house. They're paying rent for a two-bedroom apartment while both of them own a home. Aaron's has been getting some great bites from prospective buyers, though, so they think that one will sell very soon.

One good thing about this past month is that part of Chad's recovery program involves making amends. He's been a real trouper, helping Mom and Aaron do chores around Aaron's house and this one too. It's given us all a chance to get to know one another. And when Chad's not being a butthead, he's an okay guy.

But speaking of buttheads, I'm listening to one, and it's all I can do to keep from socking the perky real estate agent, who is doing a quick look-see through the house. A plump woman wearing a yellow jacket and sensible but noisy shoes. Her voice is a little too loud and her smile a little too wide. Maybe she needs counseling to deal with her self-esteem issues.

A four-hundred-dollar Sony digital camera hangs around her neck, and every so often I hear her say something like, "Oh my goodness. That has to go up on the Web site." Flash.

Mom is accompanying the woman through the house while I sulk in the kitchen and stuff smoky Swiss cheese and turkey into pockets of dough.

The agent practically squeals when she reaches the kitchen. "Double ovens, stainless-steel refrigerator." She makes some scribbles and gets out the camera. "May I?"

"Yeah," I mumble. "I'll get out of your way."

"Oh, no. Stay there. This is perfect. A kitchen lover's delight. You make a perfect picture of the happy little housewife."

"I'm not married."

"That's okay. We're not selling you, are we?" She giggles like she just made the cutest joke.

I feel the blood drain from my face as her flash nearly blinds me. "Just keep working," she urges.

I'm so stunned and revolted by this scene that I don't have the guts to rip that camera out of her hands and blow it up in the microwave.

"Your mother tells me you're staying in the house until it sells?"

"That's right." My defenses go up because

I figure she's going to start telling me to keep it clean, don't leave underwear lying around, flush the toilet, take out the garbage, keep the yard nice, etc.

Instead, her too-bright grin widens even farther. Any second she's going to lose her eyes behind those cheeks that have risen to crazy heights on her face.

"That's perfect. You bake for a living?"

"Well, to supplement my income while I finish design school."

Her gaze sweeps over my mismatched outfit. I scowl. "Interior design."

She nods in understanding. "Well, if we coordinate the times I show the house with your baking, we should be able to get this place sold in no time."

"You mean you want me out of here when you show it?"

"No, no, no, sweetheart. You stand there doing exactly what you're doing, and this house will practically sell itself — well, with a little help from me, of course."

"I'm not sure what you're trying to say." I glance at Mom and silently congratulate her for picking a real winner of an agent here.

"Honey," the agent says, "the smell of baking combined with this fabulous kitchen is going to sell your mother's house in no time. You stay in here using these appliances, and every woman with a smidge of domestic tendencies is going to beg her husband to buy this house. The smartest thing you did was move in here." Her face clouds a little. "Only, you might want to wipe down the counters before we show it. We can't have a mess, can we?"

"Well, don't you think a woman would realize that baking involves a little mess?"

"Oh, I'm sure, but we don't need to advertise that part of it, do we?"

It's at this point that I think my mom realizes I'm still holding a knife because she steps forward. "Well, if that's all you need, I'm late for a meeting and my daughter needs to get back to work."

The woman looks anything but ready to leave, but she nods in agreement just the same. "Of course." Mom escorts her to the door, and I breathe a sigh of relief.

When Mom returns, she gives me a sympathetic smile. "I know this is hard for you, honey. And you do not have to be a circus monkey for that woman. The house will sell in God's timing and not a second before. No matter how much the real estate agent tries to manipulate things."

"I don't mind helping out and keeping the kitchen smelling yummy." I smile.

"Do you have time to come to the church

for the prayer meeting?"

"Prayer meeting?"

"It's the National Day of Prayer. Pastor Moore set up that prayer and praise service. You mentioned you might like to attend."

"Oh, yeah." A surge of regret sweeps me, but there's nothing I can do about it. "I have sandwiches in the oven, not to mention finals to study for. I'm sorry. How about if I pray here while you're there?"

Mom hugs me. "All right. You do that." She glances at the clock on the wall. "I have to go. Aaron's waiting."

One thing I have to admit: My mother has done a 180 since she started seeing Aaron. She's active and happy and really facing her twilight years with optimism.

I'm starting to wonder if my best days are truly ahead of me like Pastor Moore says. But I can't help being concerned sometimes when he mentions it. I mean, are the good days to come only a little ways ahead of me, or *way* out there? That's the part that isn't exactly comforting. If my best days are coming *tomorrow,* I can wait. But if we're talking *retirement,* that's going to be tougher to swallow.

Right now, though, I turn my attention to more immediate issues. The table is cluttered with textbooks, notebooks, and handouts from this semester's class. I'm so overwhelmed. Reading back over the notes from September and October, I'm at a complete loss. I know for sure I wasn't absent from any of those classes. So why is it that all the information I'm staring at seems like rocket science?

Jazz has started working on Bev's house and is too busy to study with me. Also, I'm a little bitter about that whole deal. Turns out, Janine will give me a twenty-five percent bonus for every job I bring into the shop. And I just turned that one over to someone else. That really stinks. I mean, I'm glad for Jazz, but who are we kidding? Between the two of us, who is going to have the most trouble making ends meet in this profession? I'll give you a hint. It's not Jazz.

By the time the clock on the wall bongs seven o'clock, I've baked four dozen stuffed sandwiches and six dozen cinnamon rolls. Even a few bread bowls, though they don't sell as well in warmer weather and people are already starting to look forward to summer.

I call two of my customers, Uncle Tony and Uncle Sam, and put them off until first thing tomorrow because I simply don't have time to make deliveries today. They both offer to send a boy to pick up their order, so I agree. Reluctantly. Like I want the mob to know where I live. But then, according to the annoying realtor, this place is going to sell fast so I won't be living here long anyway.

The doorbell rings barely after seven. I pad barefoot to the living room and yank open the door.

My stomach drops. "Joe," I whisper.

He grins. "Hope you don't mind. Uncle Tony asked me to pick up the stuff for his shop. I'll just take Uncle Sam's while I'm here too. If you want."

"Uh, sure." I'm still trying to recover. I know for sure I look horrible. No makeup. Hair pulled up into a ponytail. And even with valiant effort I know darn well that curls are springing out everywhere.

"Can I come in?"

"Oh. I'm sorry. I just can't seem to get it together today."

I unlock the screen door and move aside as he enters. "What's that?" I ask as I realize he's carrying food.

"Uncle Tony sent you some dinner. He said you sounded tired."

Tears spring to my eyes as my stomach rumbles at the aroma. It's not often someone who loves food the way I do forgets to eat. But Tony struck the nail on the head.

The thought of walking into the kitchen and fixing anything else is so overwhelming, I just haven't eaten. Even picking up the phone to order takeout seems like too much. I try to hide my tears while he follows me to the kitchen. But I'm so exhausted, I'm on the verge of a total meltdown.

"Just put that on the counter," I choke out.

"Hey," he says, setting down the Styrofoam containers. He touches my shoulder and turns me toward him. "You okay?"

My shoulders slump in complete defeat. I look up at him, unable to say a word.

Tenderness washes over his face, and he draws me into his arms. I cling to him and cry out my exhaustion and disappointment.

"Come on," he says.

"Where?"

"You need to get out of here for a few minutes. It's a pretty night. Come for a walk with me."

"I should keep studying."

He shakes his head. "Fifteen minutes to clear your head. Then you come back and eat and I'll take off. By eight o'clock you can be clearheaded, full, and ready to study all night if you need to. Plus, I'll have everything delivered, so that's off your plate.

Please? I'm worried about you."

The concern in his tone squeezes my heart. I nod. "You're right. I have to get out of here before I go crazy."

I grab a sweater, and we step out into a cool spring night. The air smells of freshly mowed lawn, and the insects are happily chirping to one another.

"I've missed you, Laini," Joe says. "I'll be glad when the shop opens again and you get back to coming in. You still plannin' on baking for me?"

The memory of the handoff between Joe and some guy shoots through my mind. I guess I've been avoiding him. Jazz and I have been doing design work for the last week. "I'm not sure I can handle it, Joe." It's an honest statement. "I'm swamped. And as soon as I pass this final and get my degree, I'll be working sixty-plus hours a week for Janine."

A scowl mars his features. "You don't have time for me anymore?"

"I just don't know."

He stops and turns me to face him. "Look, what did I do? If it's about that night I saw Cindy, don't worry. That was all Nancy's idea. I haven't asked her out. And nothing happened on the cab ride home."

"Don't assume I was jealous." I glare.

"Besides, I don't dump my friends because of who they date. So I basically don't care if you were dating Cindy or not. Or Nancy. Or whoever."

"Then why the brush-off? I've been calling for a month."

It's true. He has. "I call you back, don't I?"

"Yeah, barely. Just long enough to tell me you're too busy to talk."

I wish I could explain to him that I don't date mobsters. I know what goes on in that life. I've watched enough of *The Godfather* and *The Sopranos* to have a pretty good education on the lifestyle. The thought of Joe creeping around at night with guns and clubs, knocking off anyone who owes Frank money, makes me quiver inside.

"You cold?" Joe asks.

"No." I start walking again. "I just think we come from different backgrounds. You're a good friend to bring me dinner and be my delivery guy tonight. But . . ."

"You think I did that just to be a good friend? Laini, you just don't get it."

A car honks and breaks up the conversation. I look up to find Liz's smiling face poking out of a car alongside the curb. "Laini! I thought that was you!" Her gaze sweeps over Joe, then returns to me as I walk toward the car.

"How are you?" I ask. The baby is sleeping in the backseat and my heart nearly melts when I see her. "She's even more beautiful than ever."

Liz beams. "Thanks! Her uncle Mark thinks so too."

Maybe Liz just doesn't get it that I stopped seeing Mark the second I found out Kellie moved in with him. Besides, I thought she was pro Mark and Kellie being together. "Liz, this is Joe Pantalone. He runs the coffee shop a couple blocks from my house."

"Oh, the one you're renovating?"

"Yeah."

She looks at Joe. "Nice to get a free designer, huh?"

Joe stiffens, clearly picking up on her animosity. I want to tell her to be careful. She doesn't know who she's insulting.

Joe's jaw twitches. "If you say so. But you have me at a disadvantage. You are?"

"This is Liz," I pipe in.

"Laini dates my brother, Mark."

Joe turns to me. "The cop?"

"That's right. My brother is a police officer."

Joe doesn't even bother to look at her. His gaze pierces me and I nod. It would be tacky to mention that we're no longer dating right in front of Liz, so I decide not to bother.

"Well, I've gotta go," Liz says. "I'll tell Mark I saw you."

And with a last scathing look at Joe, she's off, disappearing as quickly as she appeared.

Instead of continuing our walk, Joe predictably turns back the direction we came. "I guess I'd better get the boxes delivered before closing. Uncle Tony needs the cinnamon rolls for the morning crowd."

We say very little as we walk the few blocks back to the house. I feel I need to say *something* before he leaves. I help him carry boxes to the delivery van he's driving from Tony's. "Tell Tony I slipped in a few rolls he might want to use for his deli sandwiches. They're better than the ones he buys in bulk."

"You going to start making them for him?"

"No. But he could find someone else in the city to do it. I'm not the only person in Manhattan who knows how to bake bread."

I follow him out to the van for the last time. "Look, I'm sorry about Liz. That was awkward."

He walks around the van and stares at me over the hood. "You don't have to explain. Just be careful about that guy."

Isn't that the pot calling the kettle black?

"Don't worry. I'm not going to get hurt. Trust me — I can take care of myself." I'm about to tell him I'm not seeing Mark anymore when he sneers.

"I'm not talking about some girlie heartbreak. I'm saying, he's not everything he seems."

"That's funny, Joe." I jerk my chin. "Because he says the same thing about you."

26

Somehow, I'm not surprised the next day when I have four calls from Mark in my voice mail. I've left the phone off all day while I study. My knees are shaking when I walk out of my class. I can't say with any degree of certainty that I passed the written portion of the test.

The rest of the final occurs tomorrow night at the reception to show off Nick's new look. Jazz and I just have a couple of final touches left — greenery, a picture here and there that we couldn't hang until the paint on the walls dried. . . . But Jazz will attend to that tomorrow.

I'm catering the affair with pigs in a blanket (my homemade croissants, of course, as the blankets), stuffed sandwiches, and my very own lemon-blueberry bundt cake.

I look forward to tomorrow more than I can say. Baking will help me relax before the big event. My professor will be there, along with Janine, my new boss, and Nick's family, including Joe's uncles, whom I've been baking for. It's a pretty big deal for the family.

The family.

I hate the way that sounds. I still keep hoping that some miracle will occur and I'll discover that Joe has no dealings with the mob and I can date him after all. All indications lately point to the fact that he's interested in me as more than a friend. I guess I grew on him.

Our situation brings new meaning to the phrase "too little, too late."

I'm dog tired as I land in my seat on the train from Manhattan to Long Island. I'm sick of trains back and forth to Mom's. I guess I'll be relieved when the house sells and I'm back at my apartment. Although Nancy doesn't really like the baking I do. And she hasn't found a place yet. We'll have the same problem that we had before I starting cooking at my mom's. But I won't be doing as much. That should help until she finds an apartment. She's been looking, but it's not that easy to find a decent place in just a few days. And I'm not about to toss her out on the street for breaking one rule. Even if it was the mother of all rule breakage as far as I'm concerned. She feels bad enough as it is, and after all she *did* get me the job with Janine.

I never thought I'd be happy living alone. Losing Tabby and then Dancy was like surviving death upon death. It was hard. Depressing. But somehow, being alone in the house where I grew up isn't so bad. I'm happy there. And I'd give almost anything for the chance to buy the house.

I get to stay two more weeks before I receive my degree and start my job. And I plan to make the most of every day.

I'd happily put up with the commute if the house were mine, but why spend an extra hour and a half a day getting to and from work when I don't have to? Besides, time to integrate back into apartment life. The inevitable condition of my life for the foreseeable future.

I fight to stay awake during the cab ride from the station to my mom's. It's only nine o'clock but I think the stress of the past few months has finally caught up with me. I must have dozed off because I awaken to a gruff voice.

"Hey, lady. Wake up. My cab ain't a hotel."

"Sorry," I mumble. I slip him his fare and head toward the porch. A shadowy figure rises from the steps and I gasp.

"Don't be scared. It's me — Mark."

"Mark! You could have called. You scared me to death."

"I did call," he says dryly. "Lots of times. I even left messages."

Okay, he has a point there. "Well, you never mentioned showing up at my door in the dark."

"You win that one." He wraps his arms around me and gives me a hug. I have to admit it feels good. But I pull back before it can go any further.

"Why aren't you at work?"

"I took a little vacation time this week. If it makes you feel any better, I go back to work tomorrow."

I hesitate after unlocking the door. Should I or shouldn't I invite him in? The image of Kellie and Kyle and Mark, the happy little family, slides across my mind, making my decision for me.

"Well, it was nice seeing you again, Mark. Good night."

"Laini, wait." He steps forward quickly. "The reason I took those days off," he says, "was because I packed Kellie and Kyle and moved them back to her folks' in Missouri." He towers above me and is so close, the scent of Polo cologne fills my senses. My stomach flips.

"She's gone?"

"Yes." He takes my hand and holds it against his chest. "I told you as soon as I could find them a place without risking Kyle's well-being I would. Well, her parents asked her to come home. So she and Kyle are safe and sound back home in Springfield, Missouri. And I'm begging you to give me a second chance."

I look into those blue eyes, and all the reasons I became so attracted to him in the first place suddenly come rushing back as a little thing like moving his ex-lover into his house for a month and a half fades into oblivion.

"Come inside and let's talk about it over coffee."

His face splits into a wide smile. A relieved smile. I feel sort of special that he wants me back so badly. He stands behind me and buries his face in my neck as I unlock the door. It feels so good, I am not responsible for my next action. I turn in his arms and lift my face to his. Before his face can lower, though, I have second thoughts and turn my head. My eyes focus over his shoulder. Joe's image flashes through my mind. Wait! That's not just through my mind. I really do see Joe. *Joe!* My heart beats a rapid cadence. What's he doing here? Apparently

Mark doesn't notice I've had a change of heart, because he's still going in for the kiss — but Joe has me hypnotized. I'd rather be anywhere but in this situation.

"Laini?" Mark's impassioned tone reaches my ear. Joe doesn't speak; he turns and walks away. I'm not even sure how he got here. But I know I can't just let him leave.

I pull back from Mark, causing him to lose his footing a little. He stumbles forward, right at me. Pushing him back, I leave him to recover his composure as I sidestep and run down the steps. "Joe! Wait."

I run down the sidewalk, but Joe doesn't even bother to stop. And I know darn well he hears me. Just because he doesn't like Mark is no reason to be a jerk.

"Hey!" I grab his arm and finally he whips around to face me.

Anger flashes in his eyes. "What?"

"Well, you came over. Why?" And then I see he's carrying a bouquet of flowers. Not roses, but the kind of mix you get at the grocery store for $11.99. My heart skips. "Are those for me?"

"They were."

"But not now?"

He scowls. "No."

My jaw drops. "Why?"

"You know why."

"Laini!" Mark calls from the porch.

Joe gives me a highbrowed, knowing look, turns, and saunters away.

Anger shoots through me and I stomp after him. "Give them to me."

He glares. "No. They're mine."

"You're being unreasonable and pig-headed."

A short laugh bursts from him as he looks over my shoulder. "Speaking of pig."

I gasp. "Joe!"

"Not all cops are pigs, but that one is."

"Give me the flowers."

He shakes his head stubbornly.

Stomping my feet, I plant my hands on my hips. "Those flowers are mine and I want them."

"They're yours, huh? Did you buy them?"

I dive into my pocket and pull out a twenty. "Here!"

"What are you doing?"

"I'm taking my flowers." Horror of horrors, my eyes well up, and I can feel my lip trembling. "I-I want them. Why are you being so mean?"

"Put away your money," he says, his voice gentle and low. "They're yours. I bought them to congratulate you on being finished with school. You were pretty stressed last night."

I take the flowers. "That was sweet."

"Well, I'm a sweet guy."

I can't help but smile. "Thanks, Joe."

"Laini?" I hear Mark's footsteps on the sidewalk.

"Why didn't you take my advice about him?"

I shrug. "I tend to make up my own mind. Besides, you're wrong. Mark's a good guy." I lean in and lower my voice. "Definitely not a *pig.*"

"Okay. But don't say I didn't warn you."

"Duly noted."

"May I go now that I've given you the flowers?"

I smile. "You may."

"See you tomorrow night at the reception."

"Okay."

"You did a good job, you know. The place looks great."

I nod. "It was mostly Jazz and Nancy. But then, you already know that."

"Well, no one can cook the way you do." He gives me a wink. "I'm going to go before the cop arrests me."

I watch him go as Mark walks up. "What's he doing here with flowers? Did you start dating while we were taking our break?"

"No. He's just a friend. He doesn't think

of me that way."

"His loss." He laces his fingers with mine. "Let's go back to the house and take up where we left off."

"Mark, there's something I want to know about Kellie."

"Honey, I told you everything you need to know. She's gone and that's it. You don't have to worry about her and Kyle anymore."

Something about his statement doesn't sit right with me. Something I can't put my finger on. Something I need to discuss with Dancy and Tabby. And I plan to tomorrow night. But until I get some clarity, I have no intention of taking up where I left off with Mark.

When we get to the porch, I turn to him. "I'm sorry. I've had a crazy week, and I'm ready to turn in. You understand, don't you?"

"Oh, come on." His voice is cajoling, and a little boy grin tips his lips. "You're going to hurt my feelings. Is this because of Joe?"

"I told you I'm not seeing him."

He bends and kisses my forehead. "All right. You do look a little tired. I'm sorry for pressuring you. How about Sunday for brunch?"

"I have church Sunday morning. You could go with me."

"I like to sleep in on Sunday."

"Okay." But it matters to me that he would rather sleep. I mean, not long ago I would rather have done anything than attend services. Now, I can't imagine starting my week any other way.

"How about lunch after church?"

"Okay, we could go to your dad's restaurant."

"Sounds good. Pop'll be thrilled."

He moves in for a kiss. At the first touch of his lips on mine, I'm surprised to realize I don't have the same reaction as earlier. I don't know why. Maybe just getting out of his reach, seeing Joe, and thinking about Kellie and Kyle has changed something for me.

I allow a fast kiss, but when he moves in to take it deeper, I put my hand on his chest and move back.

"Is it because he brought you flowers and I didn't?"

"Hey." I grin. "I'm not that easy."

"Okay. You're right. I'll call you tomorrow."

"Good night, then." I stay on the porch and watch as he saunters toward his dad's car. When he drives away, I'm relieved to see him go.

■ ■ ■ ■

The next night I walk into Nick's and my heart rushes with the excitement I've been feeling all day long, only amplified. The place is lit up with old green (or gray, depending on whom you believe) sconces on the walls. The new decor absolutely transforms the coffee shop into a wonderful Italian-style café.

Across the room, I spot Nick. Wonderful Nick with all that heart buried beneath his gruff exterior. I beeline over to him, even though he's in conversation with a couple of the "uncles." They stop, midconversation, as soon as I arrive. My suspicions perk, but I'm in the mood to let it go.

"Nick! It's so great to see you. I didn't know you'd be here."

He gathers me into a bear hug and practically pulls me off my feet. "Just got in today. I hate airports. But I couldn't miss your big night."

"I'm so glad."

"How's our gorgeous girl tonight?" Uncle Tony reaches out for me, and I step into a big, bold embrace that nearly squeezes the blood from my upper body. "The food ain't stickin' around, doll. I think you should have made more."

"Well, it's supposed to be a reception" — I give him a cheeky grin and nod toward his rounded plate — "not a buffet."

"Can't help it." The portly Italian returns my grin, without the grace to blush.

It's nice to be appreciated, at any rate. "Did you get any of the pigs in a blanket?" Joe sent one of the workers earlier to pick up the food for tonight so I wouldn't have to cart food while I was trying to get ready for my big reveal. "I thought you might want to offer them through lunch." I have to stop thinking along these lines. I'm an interior designer now.

" 'Ey! I was goin' to bring that up," Sam says, pulling me away from Tony into his own warm embrace. It's hard for me to believe either of these guys could possibly be involved in mob activity. They're sweet and cuddly. Gruff, like Nick, but not so anyone would really be threatened by it.

Nick is grinning like he just won the lottery. "You done real good, girly. Didn't she, Pop?"

"Good. Like home." The patriarch of the Pantalone family smiles at me and nods, gesturing around the room. I know he doesn't speak English well enough to express how he's feeling, but I see it in his eyes and it moves me. On impulse, I step close, rise on my toes, and press a kiss to his weathered cheek. "I'm happy you like it, sir."

I feel a stinging slap on my backside and gasp. Turning, I face the fury of Nana. "You must not kiss my husband."

"Oh, Mrs. Pantalone. Please. I would never. I'm so sorry."

"Ma, Laini wasn't trying nothin'." Nick speaks up on my behalf. "She was only being polite."

"Polite is handshake." She glares at me and loops her arm through her husband's, pulling him away from our little group.

"You making a move on my grandpa?" I didn't even notice Joe, but there he is, breathtakingly good-looking. He looks better than Dean Martin, Jerry Lewis, and Frank Sinatra (and the rest of the Rat Pack) all rolled into one. "You look very put together this evening," he says, eyeing me up and down. "I can see why Nana's worried."

"If God truly was merciful, He'd just let the faux stone floors open up and swallow me."

He laughs and so do the uncles. Then, as though on cue, they sober up and silence ensues. The men are staring at Joe, clearly waiting for him to speak.

I frown, looking from one to the other. "Is everything all right, guys?"

Joe clears his throat. "The uncles would like to make you an offer."

One I can't refuse? But I don't say it since it didn't go over very well last time I quipped about Joe's family being mafia.

He seems to read my face, and maybe I do sort of grin, because he sends me a "Don't even go there" scowl. "Look, you guys," he says. "She's not going to listen to me. One of you can talk to her. I'm going to mingle." And he stalks off.

I stare after him. "Sheesh." Rolling my eyes, I give my attention back to the uncles. "You were saying?"

"You know he only gets mad 'cause he likes you so much," Uncle Sam says.

"If he liked me any more, I'd probably be black and blue."

"No. He'd never lay a finger on a woman. Joe ain't that kind. He's a good boy."

I grin at the three brothers. "I know. I was kidding. So what's this offer he was talking about? You're not trying to arrange a marriage between me and Joe, are you? Because that kind of thing doesn't go over real big in the U.S." I'm feeling heady with the excitement of the evening, and that's the only excuse I have for winking at this group. "This might look like the old country, but it's really just the ambience."

"Arranged marriage, 'ey?" Nick chuckles. "Not a bad idea. But we have something else in mind."

"Just as well, because Joe gets on my nerves. I'd probably knock him in the head with a skillet inside of a week. Then who would run this place for Nick?"

"You got that right, young lady. I need that nephew of mine. So don't hurt him."

I grin at Nick, then pan the three faces. "Well, gentlemen," I say. "I'm all ears. What can I do for you?"

Tony looks me in the eye and suddenly everyone is serious. "My breakfast and lunch crowds are up thirty percent since you started sending sandwiches and rolls. And it's the same with these guys," he says, jerking his thumb at his brothers.

Pleasure shoots through me. "I'm so happy for you!" I still haven't had the guts to tell them I'm cutting back once I start working for Janine.

"You should be happy for yourself," Nick says. "We want to set you up in business. Get you a little shop of your own and provide the dough to get you started."

"By dough you mean . . ." Does he mean

ingredients or . . .

"Money," Uncle Sam spits out. "You find a place, and we'll front you the cost of getting started. You can't keep working out of a house. You don't have enough ovens for the orders we're going to have and all the new business you'll get when you're in a better facility. Plus, now we're going to want these croissants with weenies inside."

"Pigs in a blanket," Uncle Tony corrects. "Sam's right. You let us help you, and mark my words, you'll be a prosperous young lady in no time. Believe me, I recognize talent when I taste it." He grins at his own cheesy joke.

Excitement bubbles up inside me at the very thought. "Are you guys serious? You know I can't get a loan. I tried for a house a month ago and they said I don't have enough of a credit history or enough job experience — with the new job — and it's been over a year since I worked for Ace Accounting." Although I don't know who's more qualified than someone who worked for eight years as a successful accountant.

"I know, honey," Nick says. "We want to spot you the money. You'll get fifty percent of the business until we're paid off; then it's all yours."

"And that would be in writing?"

The guys burst into laughter.

"Listen to her," Tony says. "Already playing hardball. You bet it would be in writing, doll. Anything you want in writing, we'll sign. No one has that special touch like you. The place would be a gold mine. And don't worry. You'd charge us just like anyone else. Our cut comes out of the bottom line."

"Well, it sounds good. I'll have to think about it and pray about it some."

"You do that," Uncle Sam says. "I go to Mass every couple of months, myself."

Uncle Tony gives him an affectionate little backhand. "A guy like you oughtta go more than once every couple a months."

"Looks like Joe wants you," Nick says.

I catch my breath. "H-how do you know?"

"Because he's waving for you to go over there by that iron rail. By the steps there."

My face burns. "Oh. Okay, I'll get back to you guys as soon as I've had time to process this."

And just like that, I turn to find Joe grinning at me. Instinctively, I know he was rescuing me from his uncles. He knows all about their plans for me, so when I reach him, it's only natural when he leans forward and asks, "So, what do you think?"

I shake my head, still reeling with all the possibilities. I press my palm to my stomach and try to breathe. "I think your uncles might have just made me an offer I can't refuse."

27

The evening progresses nicely. By nine o'clock, an hour after the beginning of the reception, all the guests have arrived, including Janine, who is amazed by the entire place, especially since we have 11 × 14 glossy posters displaying Nick's before the renovation.

"I just can't believe what you've done," she practically squeals. "I definitely made the right decision in hiring you. Now when do you get the results of your final so you can start going out on calls?"

"I'm not sure." I would love to bask in the glow of all this praise (who wouldn't?), but I know I'm not the one who should be receiving the credit. Really, all I did was suggest the floor. "You know, Janine, Nancy and Jazz were the two who really put this together." I mention my suggestion of a faux stone floor. "But that's really all I came up with. The first proposal blew up like a nuke.

Just ask Joe if you don't believe me."

Janine waves away my concerns. "Listen, honey, I have more work than I can keep up with. You'll learn, so don't you worry. I'm giving you a chance because I see myself in you. When I first started, I had to lie to get a job. But before long, I caught on, and so will you."

I wish I could believe her. But I'm just not so sure. The offer from Joe's uncles seems like such a godsend.

Jazz walks up to us, carrying a plate of food and grinning big. "We're a hit!"

"We sure are." I motion to Janine. "Have you two met? This is my new boss, Janine."

Jazz holds out a hand. "Nice to meet you. You made a great choice hiring Laini, here."

"Actually," I say, because I'm sick of the lie, "Jazz is the real genius behind all of this. She recently redecorated an office for a lady mourning the loss of her husband, and she got three more jobs from it."

Jazz grins with pleasure as I sing her praises. Janine's eyes get wide and I'm sure she's thinking about the commission she'd make if Jazz joined her and gave her the seventy-five percent of the three jobs she's landed.

"I think the two of you should talk." As I stand there watching them, I realize that of the three of us, one of these things is not like the others. And I'm the odd man out. I don't know if I'll take the uncles up on their offer or not, but their confidence in me makes me realize I can work hard and make a living from my apartment. Cooking. Baking. I love it — that's what I want to do. I'd love to tell Janine now, but she and Jazz are deep in conversation.

As I'm trying to figure out a graceful escape, my eyes land on my two best friends in the world. Tabby and Dancy are sitting together across the room. Tabby is devouring the food on her rounded plate. They grin and wave at me when they spy me watching them. It seems like ages since I've seen the two of them, and I realize that I'm aching for girl talk. I mean, who else am I going to tell about Mark and Kellie or this new offer from the uncles?

I turn to Janine and Jazz. "Will you two excuse me?" I grab a bottle of water and a couple of pigs in a blanket and head that way.

"This place is amazing!" Tabby exults as soon as I slide into a cushiony olive green booth. "I'm so proud of you, Laini."

Her eyes water with emotion, and I figure any second she'll be crying with joy. Tabby is a wreck since her hormones have risen to healthy levels for her baby. But she makes no apology and we wouldn't want her to. Our time is surely coming. Surely.

"Thanks." I grin and dip my pig in a blanket in a blob of ketchup.

Dancy is unusually quiet, and she keeps looking down at the table. Suddenly I realize what she's looking at. Her hands are resting on the table just waiting for someone to notice the glittering diamond on her ring finger.

I gasp. "Dancy! You did *not* go and get engaged without telling us!"

Tabby grabs her hand. "Oh, my goodness. Look at that rock. When did this happen and why haven't you told us?"

A look of pure joy flashes across Dancy's face. "Jack just asked me Thursday night, but I didn't want to say anything while Laini was studying for finals. Besides, I didn't want to steal her thunder for tonight."

"Oh, Dancy, that's fabulous! And so much better than passing a final or this reception or getting a new job offer." I'm so jealous I don't even know what to say.

"Wait a minute. Do you know you passed?" Dancy asked.

"Well, no. But I hope so."

"What about getting a new job offer?" Tabby asks. "Do you mean besides Janine?"

"Look who's keeping all the secrets," Dancy grouses. "All I did was go hide an engagement. Spill it, or am I going to have to put you through Chinese water torture to get you to open up?"

"All right. I need your input anyway. It's actually more than a job offer. And it's not Janine."

Dancy grasps my wrist with her left hand, and the light reflecting off the diamond on her finger practically blinds me. "Spill it, Laini."

"Okay, here's the thing." I tell them about "the family" making me the offer.

Tabby's eyes go wide. "Oh, wow. That sounds like a great opportunity."

Dancy nods. "I've always said you should cook for a living."

"So have I," Tabby pipes in. "Don't let Dancy take all the credit."

"I'm thinking about it. But I also decided that even if I don't take the uncles up on their offer, I'm not going to do interior design."

"Bravo!" Tabby and Dancy applaud.

"Take the uncles up on the offer," Tabby says. "It's a great idea!"

"Wait," Dancy says. "It's a great idea *if* you can be sure they're not selling drugs to little kids for the front money. I'm still not convinced at least some of the family isn't connected, if you know what I mean."

"Well, I don't think they'd hurt kids."

"Why? Because they seem so nice?" Dancy scowls. "Listen, most bad guys are really fun to hang around until you try to date one of their family members or run a little short of the rent money or something like that."

"Well, they're the ones pushing Joe at me. So I don't think that's going to be a problem. And as far as the rent goes, well, if they hurt me I won't be around to bake their rolls, will I?"

"I can't believe you're being so flip about this," Dancy says, shaking her head.

Tabby knocks on the table to get our attention. "What do you mean they're pushing Joe at you?"

I glance her way for a second. "They like me even if I am Irish and not Italian." Now back to Dancy. "I can't believe you're being so judgmental. You know Nick. He'd never hurt anyone."

"No. But have you ever met Frank?" She glances around. "Joe's dad is scary."

"I know. I've met him." I wonder where he is tonight. Joe hasn't mentioned his absence, but it's strange, considering his own son is transforming Nick's into a force to be reckoned with.

Tabby gives us a frown. “How come the two of you have met him and I haven’t?”

“Just lucky, I guess,” I say, not quite ready to move on. “Look, I’ll make the right decision based on facts and prayer, not assumptions.”

A scowl mars Dancy’s face, and for some reason when she pushes her hair out of her face with her left hand, I see red. I think she’s rubbing it in that she’s engaged and I’m not.

I can’t believe she’s being so petty about my actually getting a great opportunity, when she has everything she wants. A beautiful condo with a view of Central Park, a book deal with a major publisher, and now marriage to a gorgeous Brit who clearly adores her. Is it any wonder I want to knock her down just one little peg? “Besides, you write for a company that publishes erotica. What difference does it make?”

Dancy opens her mouth, then closes it. “If you don’t see the difference between publishing sexy books and selling drugs to eight-year-olds, then no one will be able to convince you. Do whatever you want to do.” She waves me away, which sets my teeth on edge.

“Okay,” Tabby says. “You two, stop fighting. We should be celebrating. Dancy is getting married, and Laini has transformed Nick's into an Italian villa. It's wonderful. Let tomorrow take care of tomorrow."

Dancy waves her away and points over my shoulder. "Hey, Laini. Isn't that your cop coming in the door?"

My stomach loops as I turn. "Yeah." Mark's in uniform — is he here on duty? There couldn't have been complaints about the noise coming from Nick's. The club down the street is crazy noisy every night, especially on Saturdays like tonight.

Mark and his partner are looking around the room. Mark's thumbs are locked through his belt. He looks like he means business.

"I'd better go see what's going on."

Dancy slides from the booth. "I'm going too."

"You're not leaving me here." Tabby holds out her hand to Dancy. "Give a pregnant lady a boost, will you?"

"Go ahead and go, Laini," Dancy says. "We'll meet you over there."

Joe beats me to the door, but barely. I hear him ask, "Officers, what can we do for you?"

Mark steps forward. "Joe Pantalone?"

Joe sneers. "You know who I am."

"You're under arrest for bribing a city official."

"What are you talking about, Hall?"

Mark whips out his cuffs. "Your father is already at the station, and we have a confession from the official the two of you bribed to get the permits for this place. It'll go a lot easier for you if you come peacefully."

"I'll come peacefully because I know this will be resolved quickly. I had nothing to do with bribing anyone."

I can only watch dumbfounded and heartsick as Joe allows Mark to turn him around and put the cuffs on him. Joe is standing face-to-face with me when the click of the cuffs practically resonates off the walls.

I want to reach out to him. To tell him I know it's not true. But there's nothing I can say. Because the truth is, all my doubts are coming back.

"Let's go," Mark says. He looks at me and scowls. "Maybe you'll believe me next time."

"Laini." Joe's eyes bore into mine, the dark depths revealing emotions I can't even wrap my spinning head around.

"Joe," I whisper, silently begging him to be innocent.

His gaze sweeps over me like a caress. "Believe in me."

■ ■ ■ ■

Predictably, the reception breaks up after that. The good news is that my professor pretty much assures me that I did indeed pass his class. He tells me, without "telling" me, that I have nothing to worry about in terms of getting that degree. I don't have the guts to tell him I've decided not to pursue the profession after all.

Nancy and I walk back to our apartment, and I have to admit I'm still broken by the image of Joe being taken away in handcuffs. I fall onto the sofa, glad to be out of my three-inch patent leathers. Nancy brings two steaming mugs of chamomile tea into the living room and hands one of them to me.

I'm on the verge of tears, and there's no disguising it when I speak. "Wasn't that crazy?"

"Don't believe it." Nancy's tone is a mixture of anger and disbelief. "I mean it, Laini. I've known that guy my whole life. Joe didn't do a thing and Mark knows it. He's just trying to make Joe look bad so you'll stay with him. I bet he set up this whole thing. That's probably a phony confession."

"I hardly think I'm enough of a catch that

Mark would risk his career to frame a man just to get him out of the way."

But Nancy is livid. She's not even listening. "You know what makes me sick? I'm sick of prejudices against Italian families. Why is it that all the mob families in the movies and TV are Italian? I'll tell you. Prejudice. That's why."

I never thought of it that way before, but it's a point to consider.

"What about the so-called confession? And don't say Mark framed Frank and Joe. That's ludicrous."

Nancy gives a snort. "Then he probably beat it out of the city hall guy. Mark's a jerk. Living with one woman and trying to go out with you. Why don't you think he might be capable of framing Joe?"

True, that doesn't speak well for his moral character, does it? But still . . . and besides . . . "He sent Kellie and Kyle to live with her parents in Missouri."

"What do you mean, he *sent* her?"

I shrug, because I've been thinking about that too. "Kellie couldn't find a place she could afford around here, so her parents asked her to go back to her hometown."

Nancy grunts out a mirthless laugh. "More likely Mark forced her out. How could a guy just get tired of a woman who has given five years of her life to him? I mean, the least he could have done was marry her."

"I know. He came to my mom's house last night and wants to see me again."

She gives a cynical nod. "Now that he's sent the other woman away."

"Technically, I think I'm the other woman." I take a breath. "But yeah, that's about it."

The buzzer goes off and I run to the door. *Please let it be Joe; please let it be . . .*

"Laini?"

It's Mark.

"If you buzz that guy in, I'll punch you," Nancy says.

Ignoring her, I press the button. "Stay there, Mark, I'll be right down."

"I'm going to take a bath," Nancy grouses. "You're crazy to even talk to him after what he did to Joe."

Barefoot, I descend the stairs, step outside, and lean against the door.

Folding my arms across my chest, I give him an even look that I hope will show him how angry I am. "What happened with Joe?"

"Can't we go inside?"

"Nancy would stab you with a knife. And she'd probably kill me too."

A scowl twists his features. How come I

never realized before how cold his blue eyes are? "I hope you believe me about that guy."

I shake my head. "As a matter of fact, I don't."

His jaw drops. "What?"

"If anyone bribed a city official to get the permits, it wasn't Joe."

"You don't want to believe it, that's all."

"You know, Mark" — I give him a pointed look and decide to get this out once and for all — "I always try to believe the best of my friends. Just like I tried to give you the benefit of the doubt when you told me about Kellie and Kyle."

"Friends? I'd say your relationship with Joe is a little more than that." He sneers.

"You mean like yours with Kellie?"

An unapologetic shrug lifts those massive shoulders. "She was there. I needed someone and she did too."

"She still does."

"I want you." Again, an unapologetic shrug.

Does this guy have any heart at all?

"Don't call me anymore, Mark."

"What do you mean? You said when Kellie was gone . . ."

"I didn't say we'd be together. I said we'd see. And we did. I don't think we fit."

"But you fit with Joe?"

"Joe has never been anything but a friend, but if he asks, I'll date him."

Mark expels a frustrated breath. He lifts his arms and drops them back to his sides. "This is what I get for trying to protect you from that family." He shakes his head at me. "Just don't say I didn't warn you."

"I guarantee you I will never say that."

"Fine. And remember, you're the one who gave up what we have between us."

I can't even respond. I look at this man I apparently don't know at all.

"I'm out of here," he says. "Oh, by the way, we released your boyfriend for lack of evidence. Charges were dropped."

Spinning on his heel, he shoots off down the sidewalk like he's being chased by a rabid dog.

And I sort of wish he were. The creep. Joe was right. He *is* a pig.

When Mark is out of sight, I turn to go back inside. The door won't budge and I realize I'm not getting in without help. How could I be so stupid? I ran down without my keys or my purse. Everything is inside.

I buzz for Nancy. And buzz. And buzz again. Come on, Nance! After five minutes, I suddenly remember my roomie saying she was going to take a bath. Nancy's an iPod girl and takes long, steamy baths. There's no chance I'm going to get back inside that apartment for at least thirty more minutes.

A raindrop hits me. And another. And another. Great. Can tonight get any worse?

28

I'm not sure how long I stand in the rain before I realize what Mark's last words were. Joe was released. So, he's probably home. What am I doing standing in the rain when I could be at Joe's in five minutes if I run?

In a flash, I find my steps leading me away from my apartment. Moments later, I'm standing, soaked, in front of Nick's. Of course the coffee shop (if it can really even be called that anymore) is closed. As a matter of fact, it's not even set to reopen until Monday.

I walk around the side of the building and take a deep breath at the bottom of the steps leading up to Joe's apartment. Slowly, I start to climb, barely paying any attention to the rain trailing down my face.

I hesitate only a second before knocking on the door. The lights are off, and after a few more knocks, I realize he hasn't made it home yet. But I'm not going to be deterred. Lowering myself to the top step, I'm determined to dig in and wait it out. I just wonder how long he'll be, because it's so cold out here my teeth are chattering.

I hug my wet body trying to get warm. But a cold rain at midnight won't allow for warmth no matter how tightly I wrap my arms around myself. I'm glad when I start shivering. Everyone knows shivering is the body's way of warming itself. But after five minutes of shivering, I draw the conclusion that there's something wrong with my warming mechanism.

Suddenly a shadowy figure at the bottom of the steps gives me a start. "Joe?" My teeth are chattering like crazy.

He climbs the steps. "Laini? How long have you been here?"

"I-I d-d-don't know."

He wraps an arm around me while he unlocks the door.

"Wh-what hap-happened?"

"First things first." He brings me into his bedroom, where he rifles through his dresser drawers and finally pulls out a pair of sweats and a sweatshirt. "Go into the bathroom, get out of those wet things, and put these on."

I know I should be grateful. But the first

thing that crosses my mind is *What if the sweats are too small?*

I guess I stand there staring at him for too long because he frowns. "Laini, do it, before I undress you myself. And believe me, watching you shiver in a wet, clingy dress is tempting enough as it is. Don't push me."

He isn't even almost joking, like I would think if he said those words any other time. I guess the humiliation of being arrested in front of friends and family, being questioned at the police station, and then coming home in the rain to find a girl on your doorstep isn't exactly the best way to draw on one's humor.

I snatch the clothes from his hand and practically run into the bathroom.

"Good choice," he calls after me. "For your sake."

When I return, he's changed into a similar outfit and is in the kitchen. "You like tea, don't you?"

I nod, my heart thrilling that he even remembers from that night at my mom's. He fills a kettle with water and sets it on the stove. We fall silent as he turns. There's nothing to do but wait for the water to boil. He stares at me, his eyes clouded with defeat.

"Are you okay?" I ask softly. "Mark said

the charges were dropped."

The gentleness leaves his eyes, and anger flashes through every nerve ending. I swear if he could, he'd throw flames with those eyes. "Your boyfriend is the one that finagled all of this."

"You mean Mark framed you and your dad?"

He scowls. "No. My dad is guilty. He'll probably get probation and a fat fine. And it serves him right."

"I'm sorry, Joe."

"Don't be. I told you I prefer to do everything by the book. My dad took matters into his own hands, and now he'll pay for not listening to reason in the first place. I never wanted special treatment or quick paperwork. But he has a God complex and thinks he has to make things happen." He does air quotes around "make things happen."

"Okay, I'm not taking up for Mark, but if your dad is guilty, how can you blame Mark for orchestrating all of this?"

"He got suspicious and went digging when the permits to renovate came through so quickly. The guys he questioned all say he kept mentioning my name. Like he was leading them to finger me. When they pointed to my dad, he wouldn't believe that

I had nothing to do with it and convinced a judge to issue a warrant."

"I'm truly sorry, Joe."

"I tried to tell you that guy wasn't what he pretended to be. But you wouldn't believe me."

I draw a deep breath. "You know what? I just had this same conversation with Mark an hour ago about you, and I'm tired of it. You act like it's my fault you got arrested."

"That's what I'm trying to tell you. Your *boyfriend* thinks I have a thing for you. Otherwise, none of this would have happened. The idiot wanted me out of the way by any means possible."

"Oh, he's an idiot, all right. Not just for thinking you'd have a thing for me, but for thinking I'd ever have a thing for you."

The teakettle whistles as I whip around and head for the door.

"Where are you going?"

"Home!"

As I step out into the rain, I hear him rattling around trying to move the kettle and turn off the stove.

I'm so humiliated, so angry, I rush down the stairs, still barefoot, and take off toward my apartment.

"Laini, wait. Let me at least walk you home."

"Forget it."

"You know I'm not letting you go by yourself." His tone is rife with annoyance, which provokes me even more.

I whip around and face him. "I don't see why not. I'm nothing to you. You even said so."

"When? When did I say so?" He massages the back of his neck and stares at me like I've lost my mind.

"You said Mark is an idiot for thinking you have a *thing* for me."

"Mark *is* an idiot, but that's not why, Laini." He walks slowly toward me. "He's just an idiot. For a lot of reasons. The fact is, my feelings for you are probably the only thing he was right about."

Exasperated, I stare up at him in the dim glow of the streetlights. Rain is soaking us both, but I, for one, couldn't care less. "You mean you do like me?"

"*Like* you?" His lips twist. "What, are we in junior high?"

I choose not to take that wrong. Instead, I nod. "I feel like I am when I get around you."

Stepping closer still, he reaches up and pushes my kinked, soaked hair from my face. "I love your curls."

"I spent two hours straightening them

today. It wasn't supposed to rain."

"A waste of time."

I nod.

"Your hair's never looked lovelier." He fingers a curl, caressing it. "*You've* never looked lovelier."

He moves in and I lift eager lips. Is it possible that I ever kissed anyone besides this man? At the first warm touch of his mouth on mine, I'm his. Heart and soul. He has no choice. If he didn't mean it, he never should have kissed me. Because I'll never belong to anyone but this man. When he lifts his head I stare into his eyes.

"Don't kiss me like that if you don't love me, Joe Pantalone. Because I'll never be happy being kissed by anyone else. I'll be an old maid and live alone in my apartment with ten cats. And one day they'll find me dead, surrounded by my starving pets. Then you'll be sorry. You jerk."

Joe laughs and yanks me against him. "You're crazy, you know that? I love you, *bello* woman."

"Did you call me beautiful?"

"You know you are. I haven't been able to keep my eyes off you since the day Uncle Nick introduced us last fall." He presses a kiss to my forehead. "Haven't you noticed?"

"You said we were just friends."

"No. *You* said we were just friends. I agreed so you wouldn't think I'm a chump."

"I have to know something."

"What's that, *Belle?*"

I smile. I can definitely get used to being called beautiful in Italian. Actually, *beautiful* in any language will do. But right now I have to find out the truth before I can move forward with this man. "Are you a mobster?"

He gives me an incredulous frown that sucks the romance right out of the atmosphere. "Are you still thinking about that? After everything I told you? After I was sent home and the charges were dismissed?"

"Well, what about that handoff at Nick's that day?"

"What are you talking about, woman?" he roars.

I refuse to be intimidated by his outburst. This is a time for honesty. "I saw you give something to one of the workers, on the sly. It looked like drugs."

"For crying out loud. Have you ever seen an actual drug exchange?"

"Of course not. What do you take me for?"

"Well, how did you come to that conclusion when you've never seen one?" He closes his eyes for a second, fighting to calm his emotions. "Listen, if you're talking about

Robert, he was running low on money and I spotted him enough to pay his rent. He paid me back two weeks later. Satisfied? If you don't believe me, we can go see him."

Relief slides through me like the rain sliding down my body. I throw my arms around him. "Okay. I believe you."

"I can't promise anything about the uncles, though, except for Uncle Nick. He's on the up-and-up for sure. But the other guys — well, there's no telling."

"And your dad?"

He shrugs. "Let's just say he's got connections. That's all I know and all I want to know. Can you love a guy whose father has connections? I promise I'll never be involved in anything illegal."

"I already do love a guy whose father has connections, Joe."

"I don't have a ring yet, but . . ."

In the rain, Joe gets down on one knee and takes my hand. "Will you marry me?"

"Are you sure? It's pretty quick."

"I've been waiting all my life for you. I don't need any more time to decide. But if you do . . ." He starts to get up.

I plant my palm on his shoulder, forcing him back down. "Stay there, buddy. You can't get up until I give you an answer."

"Hurry up, then, will you? I'm in a

puddle."

"All right, fine. Big baby." I kneel down in front of him until we're face-to-face. "Fair is fair." I take his wonderful face in my hands and look into his eyes. "I promise I'll never make you regret waiting all of your life for me to come along."

Leaning forward, I press my mouth to his. My hands leave his face and I wrap my arms around his neck. He pulls me close.

"You haven't said yes yet."

"Yes," I say against his mouth. Our breaths mingling, lips together, we seal our promise of forever.

Epilogue

"Get car!" Nana shrieks. "Baby coming!" She pats my fat cheeks and smiles. "You be fine. Just fine."

Turning to Uncle Nick, she shrieks again. "Go-go-go! Baby coming."

Back to me. She pats my cheeks, harder this time. It feels like a slap, but I'm going to have to give her the benefit of the doubt. "You be fine. You be fine. I have *many* babies. Very easy. You will have many, also."

That's what she thinks. Pain squeezes my back and radiates to my stomach. My water broke fifteen minutes ago, and I swear if these clowns don't get me in a vehicle soon, I'm taking the delivery truck.

Nana hated me for the first two years of my marriage to Joe. But as soon as we announced my pregnancy, I was suddenly the Madonna, a woman to be honored and revered. I think she secretly prays the baby will not have red hair, though.

"Has anyone called Joe?" I ask.

Uncle Nick offers me his hand and pulls me to my feet with a grunt. "Tony called him. Joe's meeting us at the hospital. You relax and trust Uncle Nick."

We're like something out of a ridiculous movie by the time I reach the hospital. I waddle painfully through the door. Four male senior citizens — Tony, Sam, Nick, and the baby's grandpop, Frank — try to hold me up, two on each side. Nana's bringing up the rear. The old woman has her hands pressed against my back, pushing me forward as though I can't walk on my own. "Go-go-go," she says to the nurse at the counter.

"How far apart are the pains?" the nurse asks, bored.

"A few minutes. My water broke."

She stands up and wheels a chair around. "Sit down. I'll have someone from labor and delivery down here in a jif."

"I don't need a wheelchair. I can walk."

"Not if your water broke. Sit down and be a good girl. I've had enough unruly patients tonight." She gives me a you-don't-want-to-mess-with-me look.

I zip it and settle back to wait.

I don't know why everyone is so freaked out. I know from experience that it takes a full day for first babies to be born, and I haven't been in labor more than two hours, at the most. I've been through two births with Tabby and one just last month with Dancy, so I know what I'm dealing with here. But try to calm down a whole family of type A Italians. Seriously, just try it sometime. Everything is such a big hoopla with this bunch.

"Laini!" Joe rushes through the door just as the nurse from labor and delivery arrives. "How are you doing?"

"I'm fine." Except that my heart is about to blow up for loving him so much. "Who's minding the store?"

"I closed."

"Joe! We had orders."

"Well, what was I supposed to do? I couldn't stay there, and, well, I didn't think about having one of the employees run things today. I'm sorry."

No one ever proved anything illegal against the uncles other than Frank and his bribery of the city official, but Joe and I decided not to risk it by accepting their offer to "set us up in business." We did, however, accept a collective wedding gift of my mom's house.

I kept up the baking in our house for a year and we saved every dime possible until we could get a business loan. Now we own a house and a shop of our own on Long Island, and we work hard to make ends meet. But the mortgages are all ours. Every dime we pay on them is one step closer to the life we want for each other and our children.

"Okay, ow. I think they're getting closer together."

" 'Ey, nurse," Uncle Tony says, "where's the drugs for the girl? She's hurtin'."

"As soon as we have her all set up in bed and assess her situation, we'll see if her doctor wants to prescribe something for pain."

"Laini! Wait up!"

Wait up? What the heck?

Tabby and Dancy rush up, one on each side of my wheelchair.

"Breathe," Dancy says. "You can do this. Remember our techniques."

"Forget all that, Laini," Tabby says. "Ask for drugs. It's the only way."

I'm getting seriously miserable here. And the urge to push is nearly overwhelming. "Um. Nurse. I want to push."

"Now, honey. You have a ways to go before you need to worry about that. You just sit there while I get your IV ready. If the pain gets bad, just try to remember your breathing techniques."

"No, I mean it." The pain is nearly unbearable, and I feel like I'm having one long contraction. "This is serious."

Joe steps forward. "Maybe you could get her into a bed and check her before you do the IV."

I'm in way too much pain to care that Joe's manipulating the fifty-year-old woman with his sex appeal. I'd let him do a striptease if it'd get me drugs.

"All right, everyone out except the husband."

She slips me a gown. "Put this on and slide into bed. I'll be back in a second."

The "second" turns out to be about fifteen minutes. She hurries in, apologizing profusely. "It must be a full moon or something because we are absolutely filling up with women in labor. You about ready?"

I'm in no mood to chat. And poor Joe barely has any feeling left in his hands from the way I've been gripping them with each pain. She slides on a pair of gloves. "All right, let's see where you are and then we'll get your IV in and call the doctor."

Five seconds later, she stares at me, wide-eyed. "Whatever you do, honey, don't push. St-stay here."

She opens the door and hollers. "Get Dr. Rife in here now."

"That's not my doctor."

"Trust me. You don't have time to wait."

Two hours later, I'm lying all cleaned up and in very little pain, holding my perfect little boy. Who looks exactly like Joe — only with wild shocks of red hair. With one look at her great-grandson, even Nana doesn't seem to mind that he's half Irish.

My mother arrives just as I'm about to nod off. She kisses Joe before coming to my bedside. "Oh, honey. I'm so sorry I wasn't here."

"It's okay, Ma. Come meet your grandson."

"A little redhead." She nods and smiles.

"Tell her what we named him," Joe nudges.

"Grandma, say hello to Sean Patrick Pantalone." After my dad, of course.

Mom's eyes water even as she laughs. "Your father would be honored."

Later, Joe and I sit quietly together looking at our baby sleeping peacefully in his little bassinet next to my bed.

"He's something, isn't he?" Joe asks.

"Yeah."

The door flies open. I gasp and reach for my son as the uncles file in like they're the fairies in *Sleeping Beauty.* My room is fragrant from the flowers filling every bit of possible space.

"We want to see the boy."

"Well, pipe down," Joe growls. "He's asleep."

The boy. Good grief.

"Would you look at that?" Nick says. "Ain't he something?"

Uncle Tony rubs the tip of his finger over Sean's red hair. "Looks just like me."

Uncle Sam chortles. "I don't see how. Ma and Pop adopted you from an orphanage."

"Ha! Someone left you on the doorstep."

Joe steps up. "Okay, fellas. Laini needs her rest."

Uncle Tony nods. "Yeah, we know. But can we at least kiss her good-bye?"

"Make it quick."

Each uncle smiles and presses a kiss to my cheek. Uncle Tony runs his hand over my head. "I knew you was somethin' special first time I ever saw you." He kisses me again, on the forehead.

"I love you, Uncle Tony." My eyes are misty. I love them all, but this one squeezes my heart. I pray for him every day. Like I do all of them, but Tony — I guess I pray a little extra for him.

Joe and I watch them leave, each turning to wave good-bye before they close the door.

Affection surges through me as Uncle

Tony turns one more time and waves at me through the window. I give a contented sigh. "Our baby is blessed to have family like that. He'll always know he's loved."

"Those crazy guys? They're never going to leave us alone now that we have a baby."

"They never leave us alone anyway." I take my husband's hand and give it a kiss. "But it's okay, Joe. You know why?"

"If you say it, I'm going to . . ."

I grin. I can't help myself. "That's amore."

AUTHOR'S NOTE

Dear Readers,

Wow, I can't believe we've come to the last book in the Drama Queens series. A lot happened in my life during the writing of this series. Life-and-death stuff, spiritual growth, tears and laughter. Changing seasons, literally and figuratively. But through it all, this series was such a blessing to write, and I grew as a writer during the process.

I learned a lot from Laini Sullivan. She is so much like me in so many ways. I have big dreams. Dreams of some things I'm really good at and some things I'm not. During my lifetime I've dreamed of being a writer, a singer, an artist, a fireman, a cop, a soldier in the army, a teacher, a doctor, and a lawyer — and these were all things I dreamed of doing as an adult. But not every idea is a God idea. For me, the trick was finding the thing that God had already placed in my hand — writing — and doing my best to make it better and use it for His glory. That's sort of what Laini had to do with cooking. She loved it, but she couldn't quite believe she could use that particular gift as a career.

God has planted desires and goals in each of us. Plans that He would like us to fulfill. Sometimes we struggle so hard with finding that path. . . . But all we really have to do is search for the thing we're the best at and then ask Him to give us a plan to use that talent for His purposes. Then we can enjoy our labor as we work to make a living.

If there's one big thing I'm grateful for, it's that God showed me I could be a writer. An elusive dream that no one thought made sense. But it made sense to me and to God. And the rest is history.

So don't stop short of the goal. Keep searching until you know you're positioned where God wants you. Daniel 11:32 states, "The people that do know their God shall be strong, and do exploits." It takes strength to step out of the status quo and follow a dream. But those who do are able to walk into God's plan, His purpose, His best for them.

Thanks to everyone who read and loved the Drama Queens. You bless me in more ways than I can say.

God bless you and keep you.

Sincerely,
Tracey Bateman

READING GROUP GUIDE

1. Laini is sort of a jack-of-all-trades, master of none. She has a lot of different interests and isn't quite sure what she should do with her life. Why do you think she is so unsure of herself?

2. Have you ever had a passion for one thing but an aptitude for something else? Laini is a fabulous cook, but she seems to see it as nothing more than a hobby. Why doesn't she consider it a viable option for a career?

3. Dancy and Tabby encourage Laini to go for the interior design school even though it's obvious she isn't that great at it. Are they wrong to encourage her? Would she have listened if they hadn't supported her?

4. Laini feels deeply responsible for her mother and wants her to move on, but then resents it when her mom does just that. What do you think about that? How much

is Laini's mother at fault for the way Laini feels?

5. Laini resents when Tabby tells her, "Your time will come." It seems patronizing and makes Laini feel put down as a single woman. As married women, do you walk on eggshells around your single friends so as not to offend them? And if you're single, how can you convey to your married friends that you don't need them to constantly try to reassure you about singleness and marriage?

6. Laini is lonely and ready to get married. She's pretty and smart and not at all closed off. Why do you think it took so long for her to find the right guy?

7. Mark initially appears to be everything Laini's looking for. Why do you think it takes so long for her to get the picture that he isn't the one?

8. Joe's family is morally iffy at best, and Laini has hesitations about him because of that. Is it fair to look at a person's family and judge the potential for a relationship based on that?

9. Laini's relationship with God grows as she returns to church and begins to fellowship each week. How important is it to a Christian's spiritual growth to hook into a body of believers?

10. After years of looking for Mr. Right, what is it about Joe that convinces Laini he's the man for her?

ABOUT THE AUTHOR

Tracey Bateman lives in Missouri with her husband and four children. She has been a member of American Christian Fiction Writers since the early days of its inception and served as vice president and president of the organization. Her hobbies include reading, watching the Lifetime Movie Network, hanging out with family, helping out in her church, and listening to music.

The employees of Thorndike Press hope you have enjoyed this Large Print book. All our Thorndike, Wheeler, and Kennebec Large Print titles are designed for easy reading, and all our books are made to last. Other Thorndike Press Large Print books are available at your library, through selected bookstores, or directly from us.

For information about titles, please call:
(800) 223-1244

or visit our Web site at:
http://gale.cengage.com/thorndike

To share your comments, please write:
Publisher
Thorndike Press
295 Kennedy Memorial Drive
Waterville, ME 04901